Airplane Games

A Turbulent Love Story
Cat Wynn

Book Cover by Cover Apothecary, www.coverapothecary.com

Editing by Deborah Nemeth

First   edition   of   2023

To anyone who's a little bit polarizing

Content Warning

Airplane Games deals with topics some readers may find difficult, including death of a parent (off page/in the past), car crash (off page/in the past), panic disorder, depression, and recreational drug use.

Chapter 1

Parker Donne hiked his bag over his shoulder and climbed the tall stairs to board the private jet. He would be red-eyeing back to the States on his client's dime, and he hoped to get a good sleep while in flight. He didn't have time for jet lag. He had to pick out a couch for his empty living room when he returned home to Chicago. A good goddamn couch.

He sighed big when he trudged to the back of the jet to the sleeping quarters. He'd been on private planes before, of varying levels of luxury. This one was the fanciest he'd ever seen. There were not one but two large beds at the end of the space with privacy walls and doors to close off the areas.

"Can I get you a drink, Mr. Donne? Champagne perhaps?" A platinum blonde flight attendant who probably was a high-end model in her spare time appeared with a tray of already poured flutes, but Parker shook his head.

"Not tonight, thanks."

The attendant smiled, a little too warmly at him. "Anything else? Anything at all?" Her eyes roved up and down Parker's body from torso to shoes and suddenly Parker got the feeling that he was being watched very closely indeed.

But he was *not* in the fucking mood.

It wasn't that he wasn't flattered. Or that he hadn't participated in his fair share of hookups. Hell, he'd made the mile-high club. He fucked a girl in an actual airplane bathroom before, her leg bent around his waist, his hand cupping her ass, her back pushed against a wall (overrated and he'd found it disgusting because of the bathroom. It'd been her idea). But he was thirty-seven now, and the days of pretending to revel in useless hookups were well behind him.

"You're still young, dude. You act like a fucking geriatric, Jesus Christ." That's what his best friend Pamela had said to him as she gently bounced the newborn strapped to her chest, unloading groceries out of her minivan.

"You're one to talk. Look at what you're driving these days," Parker had lightly ribbed. Pamela had been a high-end traveling auto mechanic like Parker once. They'd even been in business together. But now she was a stay-at-home mom. Secretly, he was jealous. Also, he really wasn't one to talk. He didn't even own a car.

Pamela and her wife had given birth to their precious baby three months prior. Parker had been anointed godfather. Not that he believed in god. Not that Pamela or Rebecca did either for that matter.

"But you're rich. And we wouldn't want Avery with anyone else. Well, except us," Pamela had said. "And frankly, I'm worried you're gonna die alone, so there's that…"

Well, she certainly had a point there.

Parker yanked off his shirt and jeans and stabbed his legs into a pair of flannel pants. Then he changed his socks out to the nice cashmere ones provided on the plane. He was ready to sleep like the dead.

"Oh. My. Fucking. God. Who do these wild-looking Pumas belong to? Are you kidding me right now?"

Parker sat straight up in his bed, when the privacy divider ranked open loudly. He squinted at the light breaking through into his quiet, dark cocoon. "Excuse me?" *Who the hell was this?*

He'd been told he'd be the only passenger on this plane, but it was clear that there had been a mix-up because in front of him appeared the curvy silhouette of what he could only imagine was a beautiful bag lady. She had a lot of bags on her shoulders, which she let drop to the ground.

"Miss. Miss." The flight attendant rushed to the end of the plane. "Your sleeping quarters are to the left. Your left, miss. Not my left. See?" The flight attendant turned to Parker. "I'm so sorry, sir. We didn't mean to disturb your sleep."

Now *both* women were staring at him and his bare chest. He wasn't a prude so it wasn't like he was going to cover up or something. Instead, he ran his hand over the stubble on his jaw, shaking his head. "No problem."

"Nice shoes, dude," the curvy woman said to him, her gaze scrutinizing.

"Nice rack" is what he would've said if he was a total fucking creep which he wasn't, but so many of the men around him were. Sometimes their voices echoed in his head. He could see her clearly now after his eyes adjusted and he could tell she was...well. Attractive.

Very attractive.

More attractive than was necessary for him to deal with at the moment.

But now wasn't the time.

The flight attendant disappeared to the front of the plane, but the woman stood there, assessing him, one hand on the generous curve of her hip, elbow jutted out. His eye followed the line from hip to waist to breast to shoulder to neck all the way to the little ski-jump nose in the middle of her face where she smirked at him. Damn.

"You need something?" he asked, his voice was rough from having not spoken more than twenty words all day. He sounded on the verge of sexual, which he certainly wasn't going for.

She tilted her head, fiddling with the tied black belt at her waist. She was in some kind of all black ensemble, her jet-black hair tied in a shiny but severe ponytail. Even in the dim lighting he could see that her lips were bright red. "Well, I didn't know I'd have company on this flight. Lucky day. We should get a drink. What do you like? Lemme guess. Macallan 12? Or are you more a beer guy? Cheap beer. Old

Style. Tell me I'm right because I know I'm right and because I love to hear it. Go on."

"I'm trying to sleep."

She scoffed at that. "Sleep is overrated. It's for old people and babies. How old are you anyway?"

"Old enough."

"I'd guess thirty-seven. Maybe thirty-eight."

Jesus, is she some kind of psychic?

Parker merely grunted, turned on his side and yanked the blanket over his shoulder. But the woman actually stepped into his compartment and perched at the end of the bed.

"Holy shit, I guessed it on the nose, didn't I? Damn, I'm good. What's your name? Mine's Elliot. Don't call me Ellie, that's obnoxious."

"I won't call you anything. Sleeping."

"Next question. Zodiac sign. I know you won't answer so I'm gonna make an educated guess and if I get it right you have to have a drink with me, deal? Deal."

Parker remained in his sleeping position. Did this woman's indecency know no bounds? He peeked a glance at her through the crack of space between his arm and body and saw that she was tapping away at her phone now too. He wondered who she was typing to. A boyfriend maybe?

Wait, he didn't care if she had a boyfriend.

"I'm gonna guess you're a…" She looked up and tapped at her nose thoughtfully as she spoke. "A Virgo." She awaited confirmation.

With a sigh, Parker sat up in bed, aware that her eyes were again on his naked chest. "Jokes on you. I don't know my zodiac sign."

Her eyebrows shot up at that. "Oh, how quaint. Well, when's your birthday?"

"I'm not telling you that."

"Sure you are. We made a bet. If I guess your sign, you'll have a drink with me. Wait, *two* drinks actually. Three would be the most fair, but I'm a simple gal. You owe me from when I got the other thing right from before."

Tenacious, wasn't she. Parker leaned forward intending to intimidate, but Elliot leaned forward too, as if he were about to tell her a secret.

"Were you born in September?" she whispered.

For some reason, this caught him off guard. "How'd you know that?"

She clapped her hands together. "Ah-ha! Baby, you got big Virgo energy written all over you."

He rubbed his sternum, soothing the sudden burst of adrenaline. Her enthusiasm was infectious but annoying. More than Parker was used to in his fancy garages around grunting men. But she wasn't making him nervous.

No, worse. She was making him excited.

"This is a fun game, isn't it? You wanna play more, don't you?" This time she kicked her legs up on the bed, splayed out like a pinup model. She really could've been a pinup model.

He raised an eyebrow in response so he didn't have to say yes. He wanted plausible deniability. Didn't want her to notice how his dick had started to jump with interest, which was rare for him nowadays. Of course, if she did notice, that was her fault and not his. He hadn't invited her into his bed. She'd done that on her own.

"Okay, what would you like me to guess about you next?" She gazed up at him under a thick fringe of black eye lashes. Blue. Her eyes were a light sea blue. He stored it away in his memory bank although he wasn't sure why. He would definitely never see this woman ever, ever again.

He leaned back against the wall, crossing his arms. "If you guess my full government name, I'll have a drink with you. One. One drink. If you can't, then you have to give me something of yours."

"Oh, the big, serious brooding man speaks. Très radical. Tell me your terms, Mr. Serious, and I'll tell you if I like them."

"If you get it wrong, you have to give me your phone."

A shocked scoff escaped her lips. "What? My phone? That's ridiculous. It's, like, the most precious item in my entire life. It holds everything about me. Why should I take a silly bet like that?"

Parker shrugged. "Bye then." He resisted the upwards tug of the side of his mouth—he wanted to smile at her but if he did that, it'd be all over for both of them. He'd have her face down on the mattress, filled to the brim with his dick, chanting his full government name like it was the Lord's Prayer.

But Elliot's face changed after only a moment. She glanced at the phone and then gave him a sly smile. "Actually, I'll take this bet. But you have to give *me* something bigger than a drink. Fair's fair in a betting game."

Another upwards tug threatened Parker's mouth so he cleared his throat, rearranging his weight on the bed. "Speak on it."

"You have to give me your number."

Bold. He liked it. His dick was working even harder for attention now, which was starting to amuse him a bit. But this Elliot was trouble and he could tell. She had it written all over her. Parker had had his share of trouble-women and he really wasn't snooping around for more. Although he seemed to attract them like mosquitos. He rubbed the stubble on his chin. "Now, why would I want to do a thing like that?"

"So I can call you up and fuck the hell out of you."

He shook his head with a slight smile on his face. She was trouble all right. And he was about to play. "Fine. I agree to your terms."

She got up on her knees, then sat back. "Figured you might. You're not made of steel under there." She cocked her head, trying to get a peek around Parker's body. In return, he whipped the blanket off his lap so she could get an eyeful of his rapidly growing dick. He wouldn't normally be so bold, but she'd said she wanted to fuck him, so all was fair in fucking and private airplanes.

Her eyebrows went up. "Guess you are made of steel." Then she smiled. "Okay, time for the fun." She closed her eyes and brought her hands in a prayer position at her breast. "I'm envisioning your name in my mind's eye. Catching letters—oops! There goes a P and an A and an R, K, R...ooooooooohhh..."

Perhaps the flight attendant had used his first name? But she hadn't. But maybe she had?

Elliot cracked an eye open. "First name Parker. Am I right?"

"I didn't say first name. I said whole name."

"True true true true true. All right, let me get my psychic connections back open. Okay, what's the rest of Mr. Serious Parker's name? Let's see...I'm getting...weirdly, I'm getting metaphysical English poet. I'm getting Church of England. I'm getting sixteenth century chic. Fascinating, right?"

Parker's heart rate sped up. "What in the hell?"

Elliot smirked, then closed her eyes again. "Ah-ha, that's it. Parker Donne. Tell me I'm right. I just love to hear it so much."

Parker grimaced. Then nodded towards her hand. "Give up the phone. You got it wrong."

Elliot clutched the phone to her chest. "What do you mean I got it wrong?"

"I said full government name. And you only guessed two thirds of it, which leads me to believe you heard one of those flight attendants earlier. Or asked them. But you laid down the terms of the bet, not me." He held out his hand. "Give it over."

Elliot's frown quickly turned to a smile. "Oh I don't think so, Mr. Parker *Lance-Loves-Laurie* Donne. I don't think so.

The smirk on Parker's face dropped. "How the hell did you know that?"

Elliot tossed her head side to side. "Psychic powers." Then she reached into her pocket and tossed something onto his lap. "Plus, I stole your wallet. You shouldn't leave your pants on the floor. Now. You owe me some digits. Are Lance and Laurie your parents?"

He did actually want to give her digits. More than one kind. He was a mechanic after all, good with his hands. But also he didn't. He wasn't interested in hookups and wild energy, the kind Elliot was giving off like exhaust from a souped up muffler.

But a bet was a bet.

"Impressive. Fine, hand over your phone. Promise I won't steal it. Bet's a bet. And yeah, they're my parents. Were my parents. They're dead now."

Elliot presented her phone to Parker. "Don't give me sad details, Mr. Serious. You won't get sympathy from me."

His gaze trailed up to her as he typed on her phone. "Fair enough."

He handed her phone back, and she nibbled on her lower lip, distracted. Good sense told him to stay far, far away.

"But I do like you," she said. "I like airplane games, if you know what I mean."

He chuckled. "Like that scam from the eighties? The pyramid scheme?"

"No, not like that." She laughed, but then held his gaze, as if she were examining a million different things about him at once. "I mean that the rules are different when you're flying. A whole different playing field."

Heat rose from his torso. He was one second from changing his mind and snatching her up, dragging her beneath the blankets.

But then she stood, dusting off the lap of her black jumpsuit. "Changed my mind. Think I'm gonna drink alone tonight. Ciao."

Chapter 2

"Hey, you fucker."

An expensive-looking handbag dropped onto the tabletop, a raven-haired woman in a bright red sweater behind it. Then with a rattle, a plate topped with mini sugar donuts landed next.

"You gave me a fake number, but it's actually okay because I wasn't going to call you anyway."

Parker slowly sipped from the draught of light beer in front of him to quell the tug at the corner of his lip. How'd this Elliot woman find him here? Not that he'd been thinking about her. He'd forgotten all about her in fact. The raven-haired, curvy pinup lookalike he'd jerked off to in the shower immediately after their encounter was someone else entirely. And now, days later, he hadn't thought about her at all. Really.

"How'd you know the number was a fake if you didn't call it?"

Elliot slid her shapely thighs—not that he noticed—into the seat across from his, unwrapped her scarf and placed it next to her on the leather cushion. "If you must know, I was deleting your contact when something strange caught my eye."

Parker raised his brow. Curious.

"Because it's that carpet installation company's jingle. *Eight-hundred five-five-five, one-two-three-four...*" she sang.

"*Rentmiiiireess...*" Parker joined in, singing the last line, chuckling a bit to himself. That was a catchy tune. Then he scratched his chin. "So you're from Chicago? They only run that commercial in Chicago."

She gave him a glare. "Oh, I'm not from anywhere. I appear and then disappear, if you're lucky. Hey, while I'm here get me a dirty martini, will you?"

"The drinks are free here. Get yourself one."

"It's the thought that counts. You owe me after scamming me out of your number. Now that I know the kind of guy I'm dealing with, I won't be so trusting next time. Plus, I just put all this stuff down." She gestured to her bags and then shoved a sugar donut into her mouth.

"It's ten a.m."

"You're drinking!" she exclaimed, mouth full, chewing.

"A beer. Beer is like water."

"Oh." She leaned in close, swallowing hard, her voice quiet. "Do you have a problem? Is that, like, *your thing*? You don't wear a ring so I know you aren't married." She *tsked-tsked-tsked* with her tongue. "But a guy like you? Single on the market? Must be a bloodbath when you go out."

He paused, his eyes giving her the once-over. Then he abruptly got to his feet. "I'll go get you that drink."

"Yeah, you go do that, Mr. Serious. And when you come back, bring a little conversation with you too, eh? I'm like a camel looking for water in the desert. I've been traveling since Monday and I could use a fucking friend."

"Ssshhh," someone shushed behind Elliot.

"Shhh, yourself. I don't come to the business class lounge to get shhhed by some fuckwit suit with a goatee. Get fucked."

Despite himself, Parker smiled. Not a big, real smile. But a smile enough. Quickly, he cleared his throat, returning his mouth to its usual glaring, stiff line.

Elliot clapped her hands together. "Well, hop to on the drink, mon frère."

When Parker returned with the dirty martini ("Extra dirty actually!" she'd yelled from her seat), his heart was racing. Heartbeat was something Parker knew about. He had an unusually slow one. The doctor would always comment on it when he went in for checkups. "If your heart goes any slower, you'll be catatonic, ha-ha-ha." He clapped Parker on the back. "Just kidding. Look at this physique. You have an exceptionally efficient heart. But let's keep an eye on things just in case."

Something about this Elliot woman made his heart speed up, and that made him curious enough to let her hang around him at the international business class lounge at the

Amsterdam airport. After all, what were the odds he would see her *again* again?

She took a big gulp. "So, I'm coming here by way of Dublin and heading back to the States tonight, thank god, but you know what I think about Dublin?"

"What's that?"

"Everything is grey and ugly except for the grass, which is bright and green and everyone's wearing a hooded sweatshirt and looks miserable, which is an energy I can really vibe with. You feel?"

"So, did you like it or not?"

"Eh." She kicked her feet up onto the leather seat cushion and slugged back her entire martini, the tender muscles of her neck working as she downed the liquid. "You watching me, Mr. Serious? Thinking about how much I can take down my throat?"

A lesser man might've balked at her statements, and usually he was not caught off guard, but in this moment he was briefly rendered speechless. "What the hell is wrong with you?" He shook his head, but this time he smiled. And to his own disbelief, his smile broke into a chuckle.

She wiped her mouth with the back of her hand, with a doubtful look on her face. "What?" But then she paused, breaking out into laughter too, shaking her head, until they were both laughing together. "Dude. If I had the answer to that question, I wouldn't be sitting with you at this fucking airport right now. I'd be living in a billionaire's fucking mansion on Mars."

Just as he was about to ask more questions about that particular subject her phone rang. She held up her index finger. "One sec, Mr. S. I'll be right back. Watch my stuff? Hey, babe, I miss you. Will you be in Lincoln Park tomorrow? Not my scene, but we can hit up Wieners Circle. Bring Henry! I need all the support I can get, I've been in a hell of a dry spell." She flipped her shiny hair over her shoulder and winked at Parker as she walked away, chatting to whomever *babe* was on the phone. "You won't believe who I ran into at the airport…"

She was in a dry spell.

Hmm.

"Oh another drink, you trying to get lucky with me?" Elliot sat back down and sipped the dirty martini Parker had replaced in her absence.

"I don't need to get girls drunk to get lucky."

She lifted her eyebrows and gave a quick incline of her head. "No, I don't suppose you do. That's why I'm glad we're friends, Mr. Serious."

"Have you forgotten my actual name?"

Suddenly, a weird feeling washed over him that he didn't think he'd ever felt before. Suddenly, he *really, really* cared whether or not the woman sitting in front of him actually remembered his name. How could she forget after all they'd gone through in that plane together? *Did Parker really mean that little to her?* He ran his hand through his hair at the uncomfortable thought. What was going on with him? He must be tired from all the travel. Too much work. He needed a vacation.

But Elliot was immersed in her phone now, typing away. "Hmm?" She paused before looking up at him again.

"You have a boyfriend? Is that who you keep messaging?"

Elliot smiled, then passed her phone over the table. "Boyfriend? What do I look like to you, a Christian?"

Goddammit, she broke another smile out of him. Was he going soft?

She tapped on the screen on her phone drawing his attention downwards.

There it was, a brightly colored, aesthetic and beautifully curated Instagram page. *Elliot Sheer, Photographer for Your Next Destination Wedding.*

"So, you're a photographer?"

"No, I'm a carpet installer. Just kidding, you got it right the first time. Yes, that's me, Elliot Sheer, wedding photographer to Instagram celebrities and generalized rich people extraordinaire. Getting hitched anytime soon? I'm for hire." Her eyes twinkled as she glanced up at him.

He couldn't quite figure her out. Last week on that private jet she'd practically offered to fuck him. Now she was recommending herself to photograph his wedding. A wedding he most certainly wasn't having. Not because he didn't want to get married—he did—but because with his job, he didn't have the time or the space for meeting women. The right kind, at least.

A pointed shoe kicked him beneath the table.

"What the hell was that for?"

Elliot smiled, gave a little shrug. "Dunno. Sometimes I purposely hurt the people I like."

His brows drew together, and absently he stole a sugar donut off her plate. "You like me? Not sure I can tell. You give a lot of mixed messages." He hadn't had a donut in at least a decade. What was he doing?

He returned the donut to her plate, looking for his napkin to wipe off the sugar when a brightly manicured hand reached out and grabbed his wrist, stopping the motion in midair.

She lifted his hand to her mouth, drawing in his finger so that her tongue was circling the sugar on the tip. She pulled it out with a pop. Then she sat back, a mischievous look on her face. "I do like you. I like you a lot."

His finger cooled in the air between them, and slowly he brought it back to his lap, discreetly wiping it off with a napkin. What she did was sexy, but still…germs.

Even so. He had to admit. He might like her too. Or maybe he didn't, but he was, if nothing else, keen to know more, which was unusual for him.

He nodded at her phone. "Give me your number, Elliot Sheer Photographer to Instagram influencers and rich people. For real this time."

Elliot regarded him under those dark, thick lashes of hers. "Nah. You're looking a little too serious for me, Mr. Serious. But I'll tell you what. I'll do you one better. I'll meet you in that bathroom over there in five minutes." She pointed to the single family bathroom twenty feet down the lounge.

Parker's gaze flickered towards it. His dick was hardening by the second. And Elliot. She was…well, she was something.

But, and it pained him to even think it, he couldn't have sex with Elliot in an airport bathroom, not even a fancy international business class lounge bathroom. It simply wasn't what he was looking for anymore. A fuck with a stranger he'd never see again? Too lonely. He wanted to know her. Really know who she was.

But not everything came up aces all the time.

Parker downed the rest of his beer, the glass landing with a dramatic clank against the table. He collected his leather valise and stood from his booth. "It was nice to see you again,   Elliot."

Chapter 3

The bad thing about flying commercial was that there was always a chance one could miss their flight due to the usual rigmarole of airport navigation.

Parker didn't usually run late when he knew he was on a deadline, but this time was different. This time it was Avery's four-month anniversary party, and Parker had godfather duties to attend to. For one thing, he'd personally baked the cake and piped the frosting. Pamela, Rebecca, and Avery's father had all schlepped over to Parker's condo in Streeterville to celebrate. Normally, they wouldn't have such events at Parker's, but he happened to have to best view of the city, way up high on the fifty-fourth floor, and they planned to walk Avery around Navy Pier afterwards. Years ago, Parker had left Wicker Park for his current place which was nicer, bigger and in a ritzier part of town just south of the Gold Coast. Maybe the move would manifest the familial life he wanted. That was the idea, at least.

Also, a while back his twin sister had signed Parker up for pastry baking classes. Classes Parker missed due to his rigorous schedule, and ever since then, he'd been salty enough to learn how to do it on his own.

Besides, it was the least he could do for Avery. The kid would barely get to know Parker at the rate Parker traveled.

"You know, most people would dream to have your life, maybe you should stop complaining." Pamela shoved a paper plate of a plastic wrap-covered cake slice into Parker's chest, which he waved away as he gathered his coat and luggage. He considered catching the Red Line and then transferring to the Blue Line out to O'Hare, but when in a rush, a cab was the reasonable option, even if he avoided taking them when he could.

"Who, like you? You did have my life. Gave it up." And she'd been a better mechanic than him, which was saying something because Parker was one of the best in the world.

Pamela shrugged. "Yeah, well. I married rich."

"Maybe I should try that."

"You already are rich. You've been doing this shit for so long, just retire already."

"And then what? Retire for whom? I'm not even forty. I singlehandedly run a niche industry." The kind of business Parker had created wasn't just for anyone. He was only for hire via referral and only to people with the rarest and most expensive vehicles. There weren't a lot of people like him. It all started after Parker had crashed and burned out of a very short-lived career as a racecar driver. Even he could see the irony of racing cars when his parents had died in a car crash. Pamela had worked with him for a few years before she got out of the business. It's how they became friends.

Pamela shook her head, rolling her eyes. Then she leaned in and gave Parker a hug. And then Parker leaned down and gave baby Avery a kiss on the cheek and he gave Rebecca one too.

Rebecca was the first woman Parker ever of approved of for Pamela. Not that Pamela gave a rat's ass about Parker's opinion. Still, he knew they were good for each other.

But now he was running late, and he hated that. A thing like this would've never happened at the beginning of his career—that's part of how he built such a stellar reputation, his professionalism.

But with power came leniency. The more Parker came into demand, the more he required of his clients and not vice versa. *The man with the magic hands.* And the more they had to put up with to get him.

Parker dug into his pocket to check the gate on his boarding ticket. Opposite end of the airport, a real pain in the ass at O'Hare, which wasn't small. He analyzed the situation. It was a busy travel day and the moving walkway was a shit-show, people leaning against the railing, their carry-ons blocking the path.

It was faster for him to walk, his stride was relatively huge.

He began at a fast clip, the familiar sound of rolling behind him. He only glanced back once when he could've sworn he heard someone calling to him. But no, couldn't be. Until he heard it again.

"What the hell…" Parker muttered to himself, and as he was turning around, a body slammed into him.

WHAM!

"Jesus, dude, you really know how to make a girl run for a good time."

Parker's jaw slackened. No.

But *no.*

It couldn't be.

"Well, I'll be damned. Third time's a charm, Elliot." He moved to the side of the airport aisle as travelers bustled by, a particularly large man shoulder-checking Elliot, sending her off-balance.

He also took the opportunity to check her out. Because, and he had to stop himself from biting down on his own knuckle, *motherfucker* she was one exceptionally beautiful woman.

And she was huffing and puffing, leaned over her spinner, a huge bag slung over her shoulder. No wonder she was so out of breath, she was lugging around forty-five pounds at least.

Camera equipment. Parker realized. Because she was a photographer. Probably had some expensive hardware in there that she didn't want getting into the wrong hands. For a moment, he admired her standing in front of him.

She was an artist. He'd followed her on Instagram from his fake account, and she did good work. Really good work. He understood why she'd gotten where she had in life so far. Not that her social media accounts belied anything personal about her. It was all curated work content.

Plus she worked with all kinds of equipment, just like him.

And now, in three dimensions, her cleavage was heaving like a tank engine right in front of him. She really did have an amazing rack, one of the best he'd ever admired. This time she had on a pair of fitted black pants with a low-cut black wraparound top and matching black ballet flats.

"For someone who turned down my proposition, you sure do like staring at my tits."

Parker's eyes shuttered closed. "I'm sorry."

Elliot straightened up, pushing her hair from her face. "No apologies. But don't think I don't notice when people do that. Because I do. I notice things."

Parker nodded. "Duly noted."

"Attention passengers: Now boarding Zone One to Cody, Wyoming. Attention passengers we are now boarding Zone One to Cody, Wyoming."

He could barely make out the announcement but his phone had dinged to let him know it was boarding time too and he snapped back to reality. He had to get all the way to the end of the walkway to board, and with a first class ticket, he always boarded first. He hated getting on late. Hated the

28

hustle. He hated being late in general, except, again, if it meant spending more time with his godchild Avery.

He pointed towards his gate. "That would be me." And without further ado, he turned to leave.

"Excuse me, it's incredibly rude to walk away from someone in the middle of a conversation." Elliot was following. But due to their height disparity, she was having to jog to keep up, which wasn't easy with her heavy bag and spinner.

"Sorry, but airplanes wait for no man," Parker called over his shoulder. "Except the pilot."

They were coming up on a moving walkway and Parker watched long enough for Elliot to do the math on catching up with him by taking the platform.

"I wouldn't recommend that if I were you," he called to her. He was gaining lots of ground by walking beside the platform, avoiding the stragglers in the way.

"Don't tell me what to do! And pilots can be other genders too, you know." Elliot dodged and ducked people, flattening herself against the side railing to let a particularly tall man and woman pass by her before scurrying along. For a brief moment she was lockstep with Parker.

She held her hands out like a wingspan. "Caught you!" But then her bag strap shifted down her arm, nearly sending her off-balance, and Parker passed her by. "Ah, fuck."

Despite himself, Parker chuckled, his unimpeded stride almost nearing his terminal.

And that's when Parker made the mistake of looking back again. Because that's when Parker saw the future: a pair of adults with several kids holding armfuls of candy, milkshakes, and snacks talking amongst themselves further along the moving platform.

Elliot wasn't watching, her head was turned as she watched Parker, running as best she could on her tippy toes when …

Parker couldn't watch. He closed his eyes.

She ran straight into them, candy and milkshakes everywhere.

"Mom, my gummy bears!" One kid yelled. Another started crying.

But Parker had already passed the walkway and was approaching the seating area at his gate rapidly.

He wanted to look back.

Wanted to snatch up Elliot, save her from the moving platform gangs. But she could only save herself. That was life.

Still, as Parker boarded, he couldn't deny the strange, guilty feeling he had in his belly.

Running into Elliot a third time wasn't merely a coincidence. At this point, it was more than chance. It was a curse.

Or was it fate?

He settled into his second row window seat on the plane, accepting sparkling water from the flight attendant. And as he picked up his phone to turn on airplane mode, he heard something he'd never heard before.

A message notification from his fake Instagram account. Quickly, he tapped to open the app and read the message.

He was surprised (or...possibly *relieved*) to see an avatar of Elliot in his inbox. But not from her work account, not from the one she'd shown him at the airport lounge. A different, private account.

He opened the message.

"Caught   you,   motherfucker."

Chapter 4

It was a bad night to leave Chicago. Of course as far as Parker was concerned, almost every night was a bad night to leave Chicago, but this night was a particularly bad night, especially because he was due in Charleston, South Carolina in less than four hours.

As he sat in his plane seat, he absently flipped through his fake Instagram account that he mostly used to keep up with Pamela and Rebecca and their private posts of Avery and some other car and work-related activities.

But as he'd done many times since their last encounter, his fingers made their way to Elliot's private account. At one point he'd put a rubber band on his wrist and snapped it every time he wandered over to snoop among her digital footprint. But that backfired because he liked the bite of the snap too much.

He housed a dark streak, apparently. Must be Elliot's fault. She brought something out of him.

Her private Instagram had provided Parker with a wealth of information about her, although he had no idea how she'd managed to find his fake account as there was nothing posted to it except for three accidental duplicate pictures of the cake Parker baked for Avery's four-month anniversary (it was much improved from Avery's three-month anniversary cake).

He hadn't even bothered deleting them. Seemed on brand for her, though. She was crafty. Or smart. Or something.

And hot.

And her private account was positively brimming with almost naked pictures of Elliot. It irked Parker a little, not because he didn't think she should be posting those pictures—that was her obvious prerogative, but that he, in return, couldn't post pictures of a similar ilk on his own account. Since the one he was using was a fake, and his other account was for professional purposes only. And making a new account so he could thirst trap seemed a little too obvious. Elliot would flay him alive. She'd smell out his desperation and exploit him for everything he was worth.

Still, it was a shame because when he wasn't traveling, and when he wasn't with friends, Parker was working out. And he was well aware of the type of body he had and the attention it got him. *Six foot four and cut like a sharpened knife*, one date had described him. He might dress in an unassuming albeit expensive way, thanks to Rebecca, but all the better for women to notice him.

"You're a tease." Rebecca had told him as she helped him pick out the fabric for a bespoke grey suit. "You're all look no touch."

Although that wasn't entirely true. Parker had slept with many women in the last two decades. He just hadn't done so *recently*.

Parker wondered what Elliot thought of men in suits. She'd certainly never seen him in one, which was fine, he almost never wore them. She didn't even know what his profession was. How good he was with his hands...

And mouth for that matter.

No, it wasn't the nearly naked pictures that bothered Parker. It was all the stories Elliot posted of herself out on dates, or what looked like dates. And sometimes they weren't even her stories, they were reposted stories from other people who had caught her making out in the corner booth of a restaurant or hanging on the arm of someone on the sidewalk after a concert.

To say he felt pangs of jealousy was the understatement of the century.

Which was silly, because he didn't even know Elliot.

And worse yet, what he did know about her, he knew was *all* wrong for him. He was ready to settle down. He wanted serious. He wanted feelings. He wanted for real. Not that he had the time or space for serious/feelings/for real.

As far as he could tell from Elliot's Instagram it wasn't even clear if she had her own apartment. And her Instagram bio simply stated "good time not a long time."

Ominous if you asked Parker. She couldn't be more than a few years younger than him after all. Not all that young anymore.

Another message popped up on his screen.

Heard you were coming to town. Wanna talk?

Parker grimaced, shifting uncomfortably against his tightened plane seatbelt. Cameron Joy, Charleston socialite and Parker's ex-girlfriend. If he could even call her that. She happened to be married to an extremely wealthy attorney who practiced in an office overlooking the Charleston Harbor.

Who also happened to be Parker's client.

Risky business right there. Of course, that was one of the reasons he'd ended things with Cameron. It'd been painful but ultimately easy in the sense that Parker knew it didn't serve him. Yet she'd still managed to break his damned heart into about eighteen thousand tiny little shards.

The hard question was asking himself why he started up with her in the first place. And to Parker, it hadn't been worth it. He knew better than to get involved with a married woman anyway. They were lucky they hadn't been caught.

Not that Cameron's husband gave a rat's ass what she did.

But Parker did. And Parker found out he wasn't the only man Cameron was cheating on her husband with.

Not that he could blame her. He'd gone into it with eyes wide open and she had been up-front. Cameron and her husband had *an arrangement* and Parker could be a part of that arrangement for as long as he could follow the rules of arrangement.

No dates while Mr. Joy was in town.

No late night phone calls unless Cameron was out of the house.

No sex in the master bedroom.

Parker was disgusted with himself. But like a rat to a coke-dispensing straw, he kept going back for more, pushing that lever. Cameron had an easy charm about her, as if nothing in the world had ever gotten her down. And she'd treated Parker like an object. An object she wanted to keep for herself.

Why had that appealed to him so much? At first at least. Until he'd found out that objects were collected by the handful, and so were Cameron's boyfriends.

"Would you like a drink, sir?" The flight attendant asked.

"Scotch on the rocks."

Normally, he wouldn't drink on a plane. But a message from Cameron called for a stiff one. He picked up his phone to message her back.

Won't have time.

Better to keep things short and sweet. Better not to give her an inch. And oh boy, could she ever take an inch. The flight attendant handed Parker a tiny napkin and a low ball filled with scotch.

"Thank you." He tossed the whole thing down in one, straining his throat to swallow.

Another message appeared on his phone.

C: Sure you will. I checked your schedule. I have access to all of Charles' itineraries. I know when you land, I know when you work, and I know when you leave. So unless you're seeing some other woman on the Southeast Coast, I won't take no for an answer.

Parker rubbed at his brow in frustration. He wasn't a pushover. Or maybe he had turned into one. Best not to answer.

Until another message arrived.

Charles is leaving at 2. I made us reservations at Stakes for 8. C'mon, Park. For me. Just this once.

He better not tell Pamela and Rebecca about this. They'd kill him.

Parker sliced the edge off his dry aged sixteen-ounce ribeye. He could make a better steak at home in his sous vide, but the occasion never really called for it.

Across from him, Cameron sipped her glass of pinot noir. She wore a bright pink wrap dress and nude heels. As per usual this time of year, the weather was balmy and hot in Charleston.

"You look well." Cameron crossed and uncrossed her legs, the skirt of her dress riding up, relaxing and then riding up again. It caught Parker's eye. Her legs were tan, taut from all those hours with her personal Pilates instructor.

One of the other men Cameron either had been or currently was seeing.

"As do you." In his frustration, Parker's knife squealed across the plate. He breathed in for a moment, then set his fork and knife down. "How about we forgo the small talk for tonight. What do you want from me?"

Cameron set down her glass. "Obviously, I want you back Parker."

"Well, obviously that's not going to happen."

She tossed her shining blond hair over her shoulder. "I think about you all the time. It's interfering with my everyday life. I can't eat, I can't sleep, I can't—" She leaned in. "Look, I ended things with Mark. I can't even go to Pilates."

"So? What about Chris and Jonathan and…and…"

"All of them. They're all done."

Parker lifted a brow. "And Charles."

"You know I can't leave Charles," Cameron hissed. "I wouldn't have enough to survive on from the prenup. I'd be destitute."

"I have money, Cam. I told you."

She reached forward, smoothing his hair with her hand. "Don't be silly, Park. What is it you want from me? I'll give it to you, as long as you'll take me back."

He ducked his head away. "I want a real relationship. One where we hold hands and walk through a park together."

Cameron scoffed. "Sometimes I don't know what to make of you."

"You asked. I answered."

Cameron squeezed her eyes shut and let out a big exhale. "How about I blow you in the bathroom?"

"Ah, fuck, oh shit…" Parker's hands were braced against either side of the wide, private stall, pants around his ankles with his dick balls-deep down Cameron's throat. She was on her knees, hands digging into either side of his thighs.

She was aggressive with the sucking, almost too much so. Parker grimaced, breathing deep so that the sensations couldn't overwhelm him.

She popped off his dick, ducking her head lower, the heat of her breath bathing his balls. She began to lick and suck each one as she jerked him off, her hand slippery from her own saliva.

Parker's head spun from the blood rushing from his brain and heading south, but she wanted him to come. This was how she liked to operate. She liked control.

"Not so hard…please…" he breathed, and she looked up at him with a grin and wrapped her mouth around the head of his dick and then bobbed lower and lower until she met the lower end of his shaft. Although he was uncomfortable, he could still acknowledge that she really was a multitalented woman.

He swallowed thickly. "Okay, I'm close," he panted.

"*Good*," she hummed around him. Then she used the final move on him, what he liked to think of as her finisher.

She grasped hard onto his shaft with her free hand and then eased up to the head of his cock swirling her tongue up and down, up and down on the sensitive head as she jerked him off.

He felt the pressure rising inside of him, muscles tensing and tightening in his stomach and neck, near minutes away from shooting one hell of a load when an unfamiliar sound rang out from his pocket.

Cameron only slowed for a second, but then continued sucking and stroking as usual. But when the sound went off again, Parker realized what it was: an Instagram notification. He never got those. Ever.

Elliot.

"Stop, stop stopstopstop." Parker eased his dick away from Cameron's eager mouth and pulled up his pants in a hurry.

"Parker?" Cameron's voice was alarmed, and she got up from her knees and wiped her mouth with her hand.

But Parker wasn't listening, he was zipping back up, wincing as he tucked his cock away, and quickly tapping his phone to get to the message. His heart pounded as he saw it.

One message from Elliot Sheer. The second message he'd ever received on a personal social media account before.

"Parker, what the hell is going on?" Cameron's voice gained strength.

You aren't watching my stories tonight. You don't like me anymore, Mr. Serious?

Parker fell back against the stall wall, chest heaving.

So, Elliot had been watching Parker watch her. Well, how about them apples. He glanced up from his phone with the realization that Cameron was literally inches in front of him in a crammed bathroom stall in a restaurant in downtown Charleston. "Sorry, sorry," Parker murmured. But what the hell was he doing anyway? Sure, his rock-hard dick ached like a motherfucker, but Cameron? She was a dead end. An enthusiastic blow-job-giving dead end.

And it wasn't fair to him.

"I gotta go." Parker shoved his phone back into his pocket. "Sorry, Cam. This was a mistake."

Cameron crossed her arms and stuttered out of the way as Parker opened the cramped stall door. "You've got to be fucking kidding."

He stepped outside the door and then, awkwardly leaned into hug her. "Thank you…though. For…for the blow job. You're very good at that. Although I think you have many other talents too." He leaned in and kissed her on the cheek.

As he exited the bathroom he heard her yell from the stall, "Fuck you, dickhead!"

He paid the bill on his way out and caught a cab back to his hotel, his phone burning a hole in his pocket.

She would never admit it, but she cared.

Elliot Sheer fucking cared.

Chapter 5

Baggage claim was one of the worst, most mundane-type experiences any kind of human being could ever go through. At least that's what Parker believed. He only wanted to get to his hotel, jerk off to the semi-naked picture Elliot had posted to her Instagram friends-only story hours before, fall asleep in his clothes, fix his client's Bugatti Veyron Super Sport (he'd charged a flat fee of a hundred grand), catch the train out of LA, and get back on a flight to Chicago.

He was a simple man with simple desires.

But even a simple man with simple desires would have his patience tested when stranded at the LAX baggage claim carousel for fifty-seven minutes. Airport purgatory. Where miserable spirits went to wait around endlessly for their miserable earthly belongings.

Parker didn't have an assistant to run tasks like collecting his bags because he didn't like managing people. Despite running his own business, he didn't live to fulfill some kind of entrepreneurial spirit. He'd rather do the tasks himself than send someone else on errands he was perfectly capable of.

He was never going to win at grind culture. But he didn't have to grind much anyway. He didn't have to do nearly as much as everyone else to gain respect in his field or elsewhere. He was aware. He wasn't trying to rub it in, but it didn't make him hate his job any less.

Wait, did he hate his job now? Hmm. That was a new thought. Maybe he did. Or maybe he needed a change.

These were the kinds of self-aware thoughts baggage claim could albatross onto a man's shoulders.

Parker's gaze followed the baggage carousel in a hypnotic circle until something strange caught his eye. He narrowed in on the large spinner suitcase with an ironed-on emblem on top.

E.T.

He chuckled to himself at the little grey alien, reminding him of Elliot. *Elliot.* Well, when wasn't he thinking of her lately? It was almost like she was stalking him but stalking his mind and not his physical space. Just knowing she was alive somewhere in the world up to no good got his dick a little bit hard.

And that's when his gaze shifted slightly to the right and he saw her. Elliot Sheer, in the goddamn flesh. She was wearing a pair of black jeans with an oversized black sweater hanging off her shoulders. Her hair was tied up in a bun but little pieces were wispy around her face, like maybe she'd slept like that. She was staring at her phone, hip cocked, shoulders lopsided with the weight of her heavy bag. She didn't see her suitcase whirling by.

And Parker was sure it was hers.

And in that moment, Parker had a choice to make. He could either stand back and passively observe Elliot. Watch her snap to attention, gather her suitcase and exit right out of the airport, remaining nothing more than a series of lewd, sexy videos and pictures in his phone.

Or.

Or he could go get her. Stoking the flames of whatever gas fire he was dead set on igniting between the two of them. Glutton for punishment, was he? It wouldn't be the first time.

He ran his hand through his hair in frustration, but then snatched the E.T. suitcase along with his own and rolled up next to her.

Parker stood silently as she tapped away, hyperfixated on the screen in her hand. He rocked on his heels a little, hands behind his back.

At first it was kind of funny, but as minutes passed, his mind wandered too far. Maybe she was talking to another man. Maybe they were dating. Maybe she liked him more than Parker. Maybe she called him Mr. Goodtime instead of Mr. Serious.

Parker loudly cleared his throat.

Elliot's gaze fluttered upwards, then she let out a little huff of air, shaking her head. "Fucking A, Mr. Serious in the flesh. Well, I know you must be stalking me now. Do you watch me while I sleep?"

On the outside, he wasn't even smiling, but on the inside adrenaline was popping off in his stomach like fireworks. "I don't even watch your Instagram stories."

He hadn't in the last few hours at least.

He rolled the suitcase in front of her. She eyed it. "What if this wasn't mine? What if this belonged to some little kid and you stole it from them?"

"Then I'd tell you to run for it because a gift's a gift and I don't take returns."

She narrowed her eyes. "You're different than I thought you'd be. Different and the same." She pivoted on her heel, hiking up the heavy bag around her shoulders that always seemed to be weighing her down, and dragged the E.T. suitcase.

Parker strolled easily behind her. "Where you heading?"

She stopped briefly. "Wouldn't you like to know?"

He smirked. He loved this back and forth they had, even if it seemed like at any moment it could blow up in his face. "Thought we were friends."

Her wheels bumped over the metal railing on the exit. "Only a freak would think you and me were friends." Then she raised her eyebrows. "That actually checks out since you are a freak. A hot freak. A serious freak. But a freak nonetheless. It's too bad I don't like you anymore."

Resist the smile, Parker. Resist it. "Is that right?"

They stepped onto the sidewalk, the air crisp and slightly chilled. "You left me to the wolves on that moving walkway. I'm still pissed about that."

"I warned you. That was all your choice."

She glanced at him, rolling her eyes before undoing the knot of hair at the top of her head, letting it fall down in a shiny black curtain around her shoulders. He breathed in deep. Jasmine and something else. He would remember that. "And all so you could be the first person to board the plane. You could've waited, oh I don't know, like thirty more seconds to politely end the conversation. Which would've been the most normal and sane thing to do. Again, you are a fucking freak. I bet you fuck like a champ though."

He pursed his lips together, refusing to take her bait. "You're not interested in polite."

She glared. "Don't tell me what I'm interested in. This is why you don't have any friends." She dug into her bag, searching out her phone again.

Parker look confused. "What? Pamela's my friend."

She paused, looking up with a face filled with disgust. *"Pamela?"*

He nodded. "And Rebecca too."

"Pamela and Rebecca? Who *the fuck* are they?"

"They're my friends. You said I don't have any friends, but you're wrong. I named two."

"Well, Mr. Serious. I'm so glad you have two, count them one-two friends because *we* are no longer friends starting right now. And frankly, I don't ever want to see you again. Here, can you hold this, I gotta get my camera out." She pushed the roller handle into his chest, which he didn't grab. There was no need as they were both standing right in front of it.

"What are you photographing?"

"You."

"I thought you never wanted to see me again?"

"Only in person. That's your eternal punishment. For having friends who aren't me."

"I'm not allowed to have friends who aren't you? A little controlling, don't you think?"

Then without warning she leaned in close to him, her lips at his ear, breath tickling his skin. "And I'm going to block you on Instagram." He nearly flinched when her fingers slid to the fly of his jeans, fingertips creeping over the waistband against the trail of hair that led straight down to his dick. His ab muscles tightened. Her voice went low and husky. "No more jerking off to those pictures I send you."

His eyes followed the trail of her fingertips as they moved from his waistband all the way up the flat plane of his stomach to the center of his chest. His heart pounded as they stood there together under the harsh fluorescent lights of the airport pickup strip.

Then, as if nothing had happened, she turned around, rummaging into her bag to grab her camera.

"Oh, motherfucker. No, this *cannot* be happening. Fuck, fuck, fuck, I am so fucking screwed." Elliot's hair draped over her shoulder as she leaned over her bag. She straightened, camera in hand, lens now attached. "It's the card slot. I'm terrible at fixing these things."

Parker put out his hand. "Here, let me see it."

But Elliot cradled the camera close to her chest. "Are you kidding? This is a professional camera, it costs a fortune. I'm not gonna let some lay person fiddle around with it."

Parker crossed his arms over his chest. "I'm a mechanic."

The look on Elliot's face was one of shock. She stabbed her index finger into his abs. "You? You're a *mechanic.* Wow, there goes my theory that you pose for the romance novels. My second theory was MI6. Not FBI. Way too hot for that. But like, still some kind of square, you know? Huh. I had you pegged for rich. Guess not."

"Hand it over."

"You don't even have any tools. This requires detailed work."

He bent his outstretched hand in a come hither. She stared for a second and then sighed. "Fine, but if you make it worse I murder you and steal all your earthly belongings as well as your identity and possibly mortal soul."

He chuckled, hand wrapping around the camera. "Deal." With his other hand he leaned forward and unzipped the front pocket of his luggage, and then inside that the travel tool kit he kept with him. With a small flourish he whipped out his pink Swiss Army Knife. His twin sister Jen had given it to him as a gift for their eighteenth birthday. The birthday they both had days before their parents died. He brought it with him everywhere that he could.

Using only the smallest screwdriver and a small attached magnifying glass and the bright light from above, Parker tampered with the hinge of the card slot until—

"Holy shit, you fixed it."

He flipped the tools on his knife and returned it to his pocket. Then he handed over the camera. "You might want to keep a screwdriver with you. It's an easy fix. I can show you."

Elliot looked at him, eyes filled with what could only be described as wonder. "This is the single hottest thing anyone's ever done for me." She slapped her palm against his sternum. "Ever."

He couldn't help it. He smiled. A real smile. The one he knew was a sure nail in the coffin every time. "Are we friends again?"

She tilted her head at him as if she were watching a very interesting documentary. "You know what's unfair, Mr. Serious?"

"Really starting to wonder if you don't actually know my name."

"It's not fair that you can watch *me* but I can't watch you. I've looked and you don't have anything posted on the internet. Best I could find was an estimate of your age and the fact that you once lived in Plainfield, Illinois. Boring, by the way. And I guessed your age right too. You're older than me. That means you'll die first."

She was rambling, and even for Elliot it was weird. "Are you okay?"

"Why don't you ever respond to any of those videos I send you?"

"I thought you were sending them to everyone."

She shook her head. "I only want you to think that."

Parker scratched the side of his face when something occurred to him. "You wanna watch me too, don't you?"

She stroked the strap of her camera, staring out into the distance. A slight buzzing noise came from her pocket, jolting her out of it. Quickly she removed her phone. "My ride's here." She grabbed the handle of her suitcase. "You know, it's funny. Every time we see each other I'm convinced it'll be the last."

Then she lifted her camera and *snap.*

Chapter 6

Parker's new Instagram account had gone *slightly* viral. He hadn't meant for it to, it just sort of happened. Rebecca helped him take a few pictures and then the next thing he knew he had 35,275 followers and counting.

"*You*, Parker Donne, an Instagram influencer?" Pamela asked, cutting into the swordfish Parker had prepared for Pamela and Rebecca's small dinner party. Seared swordfish with tomato-saffron coulis. He'd seen Ina make it on the Food Network. It was the first Friday he'd been home in weeks. "Talk about shock of the century."

"But at the same time totally not shocking at all." Rebecca leaned back against the dining room chair as Avery cuddled against her. "I mean, look at the fucking guy."

Rebecca had been partially to blame, or credit depending on one's view, for Parker's popularity.

Because it wasn't the posed car pictures and Bean sculptures that skyrocketed Parker into mini-fame. Nor was it the shirtless photos of him jogging down Lake Shore Drive, nor was it the casual but also posed street pictures of Parker against artfully mural-ed and graffiti-ed walls.

No, it was so much worse than all that. Parker's tiny-virality was all because of one tagged post from Rebecca that caught the eye of the owner of a popular feminist meme account that thought it was absolutely swoon-worthy that muscular, tall mechanic-to-the-rich Parker Donne was piping frosting on a cake for a baby's birthday party.

Rebecca was already popular on social media as well as a fashion designer, which only padded the views of Parker in the first place.

But who knew a man frosting a cake could be such a big deal?

Plus, the baby-holding. After the cake piping, Parker and Avery were featured on his main account (where baby Avery's face was covered with a smiling emoji). Every comment went berserk. *Daddy* is what they called him.

He looks like a stern daddy.

I'd let him spank me when I'm bad.

I don't know what y'all are talking about. Daddy? How about start with husband because this man is grade A husband material.

"This shit better not go to your head." Pamela pointed a steak knife at him threateningly.

But Parker didn't give two shits about Instagram fame, or social media influencing, or whatever the hell it was called.

He cared about one thing: that Elliot was watching.

And she fucking wasn't.

He thought he had read her right, that this was the game they were playing. But apparently not. It was enough to drive a man to desperation.

"Oh hush, Pamela. Parker doesn't care about the kind of trivial social stuff the rest of us clamor over. Although it has been great for me, the more followers he gets, the more followers I get." Rebecca stood and placed a now sleeping Avery into the stroller. "So, Parker my friend Aimee is interested in meeting you. She lives in Lake View but she does runway in Milan. Very…leggy."

Parker grunted, pouring the end of a bottle of wine into Pamela's empty glass. "That's nice."

Pamela rolled her eyes and sang quietly to herself, "He gonna die alloooone…"

Rebecca plopped back down in her chair, downing the rest of Pamela's wine. "Well, as long as he's not with that Cameron woman."

Parker lowered his eyes to his glass; he was a bad liar and he didn't need any questions in that regard.

Needless to say, Cameron was dutifully watching all Parker's stories. Liking all his posts.

He cleared his throat. "Dessert, anyone? I've got tiramisu."

"Oh, not another cake then, Park? For all your thousands of adoring fans. *Shocking,*" Pamela called after him.

Chapter 7

"I'll give you a hundred bucks to switch seats with me. I've got a single over there in row six."

The familiar voice filled Parker's ears as he removed his tablet from its case, his morning tea and cream balancing on the large divide of his business class plane seat, en route to Singapore.

The man next to him looked confused at the opportunity he'd been offered, but then shrugged his shoulders, took the one hundred dollar bill from the extended hand, and said, "Yeah. Great. Sure." He gathered the items from in front of his seat and moved over to the single window seat behind Parker.

Parker stifled a smile when a beautiful raven-haired pinup girl in a pair of baggy jeans, sweatshirt, and dingy sneakers collapsed next to him on the plane with a dramatic huff.

When he didn't respond, she stretched awkwardly to lean her head to rest on his shoulder, which proved difficult because of the huge divider between them. Then, when she seemed to realize it was too uncomfortable, she sat back up and slapped her hand on the divider, causing Parker's tea to jump, splashing dangerously close to the rim. Parker went to pick up his mug, but she grabbed his hand, took the tea from him and took a sip. "Looks like we can finally have another drink together, Mr. Serious. We have lots to discuss."

⋮

"You've never checked your message requests, what's wrong with you? I thought you were a dude with a dark side, but you know, maybe I misjudged since you wouldn't fuck me in that bathroom at the Schiphol lounge. Your loss of course. Then again, you could always fuck me in the bathroom over there." Elliot pointed a finger up the aisle and then returned to scrolling through Parker's unread DMs. DMs he hadn't even known existed. Apparently there were quite a lot of them.

Parker rubbed the stubble on his chin. He didn't want his face to betray any emotion since Elliot so often loved to *fuck* with him, but his dick was really responding to the idea of screwing her in a bathroom right now. Or anywhere at this point. In fact, he was so fucking hard at the moment, he was surprised he was able to form full-fledged words. Was there any blood left for his brain? He couldn't believe at any juncture in time that he'd ever turned her down. Was he a complete rube? Better to not answer questions like that. So instead he said, "Sex in a public bathroom isn't really my style."

"So you've done it before?"

"Done what?"

"You've had sex in a public bathroom."

He grimaced. "That's a personal question."

"Oh my god, you have. But you wouldn't fuck *me* in the bathroom? I've offered twice now. Have you fucked someone on a plane?"

"I repeat, that's personal."

Elliot's jaw dropped. "Ugh! I'm beyond offended. Most people wouldn't turn down my offer. In fact, I don't think I've ever been turned down in my whole life. But *you*." She pointed a finger at him. "*You*, Mr. Serious. You don't want to fuck me at all, do you? Wow, I don't think I've ever been so heartbroken."

Parker shifted uncomfortably in his seat. Luckily, the enormous erection he was sporting was covered by the blanket provided by the airline. Oh, he wanted to fuck her. He wanted to fuck her badly. But giving her that information would prove deadly. The second he let on, she'd lose interest in a heartbeat.

Elliot turned to face him, the large plane seat allowing her to sit with her legs crisscrossed, her back to the aisle. She held up his tablet. "Who you do want to fuck of all these girls who've sent you messages? This girl with the big tits right here? How about this one? Oh shit, look, she sent you a picture of her cleavage, I bet she'd come running to suck your dick from a last-minute booty call at three a.m. You've got a lot of dirty DMs in this box. A whole lot. And every single one unread, wow. Tell me something, Mr. Serious, when a girl has big tits do you like to come on her tits after she blows you or do you still let her swallow you down like a good little girl?"

Parker had to cover his mouth when he choked on his single malt scotch (He'd agreed to order *one* drink with her, so naturally he was now on his second).

Her face looked so satisfied at his reaction, Parker almost shook his head. She thought she had him now. She thought she'd win this round. Shock him into compliance.

But Elliot would learn that Parker wasn't an opponent to be fucked with.

Once recovered, he knocked the rest of his drink back, pulled out his seat tray and opened his laptop, pretending to attend to more pressing work matters.

Without looking at her, he said, "Guess."

"Hmm." She leaned in close to him. Jasmine again. And something else. "I'd say you like to make a girl choke a little bit while she's sucking you off. But you don't go for it right away. No, you're too polite for that. You'd ease her in. First you'd start gentle, with your hand stroking the back of her head, giving her cheek a gentle swipe."

His gaze crept over to her and Elliot paused to examine his face, which he somehow kept straight despite his wire clenched jaw.

"But then, once she really started getting going, you know, getting sloppy, getting your dick all slippery and wet, hand stroking, gagging and humming around your shaft...then I bet you act like a maniac. Lose control. You fuck her face, hips snapping in and out, have her straight-up gargling cock until she's red all over, mascara running down her cheeks. Because you barely fit...I know it's gigantic, I wasn't born yesterday. I know a man who's packing when I see 'em." She stopped to take a sip of her vodka soda and lime.

Parker briefly wondered if someone could die from too much blood running to their dick.

"Anyway. When it's time for you to pop off, when you're finally ready to bust, after she's been working on your dick for so long she can't even feel her jaw anymore, after neither one of you can stand the buildup any longer, I bet you make her take it all right down her throat. Every last drop. If she's been good, that is. If she's been bad, then you'll spray her tits until you're dripping off her nipples. A little punishment for her subpar work." When she leaned even closer, her voice was almost unrecognizable, sexy and whiny and pouty all at the same time. "Did I guess correctly?"

Parker swallowed hard, then closed his laptop, the equipment making a tepid little click. "I'd say that about sums it up."

Welp. She'd won. What could he say other than Elliot Sheer fucking won this round. He couldn't come back from that. There wasn't a damn thing he could say.

And then she grabbed the hem of her oversized sweatshirt and pulled it over her head, her hair coming halfway loose in the process. Underneath she wore a white wifebeater, the dark peaks of her hardened nipples poking out. No bra. "Which do you think you would do to me? Mouth or tits? Or maybe there's another place entirely where you'd like to blow your load?"

Parker's nostril's flared. He was angry now, somehow because she really was crossing a line. He was so completely pissed off that his voice sounded rough and crude when he spoke. "I'd have to see your tits first."

"Don't tempt me with a good time, Mr. Serious." And she lifted her shirt on one side enough to show him the underswell of one perfect (he knew it was perfect, he just knew) breast.

"Goddammit. Do you or do you not know my name?"

She let the material fall. "Why does it matter so much to you?"

"Because I like to make a woman praise the right god when she comes around my cock."

That wasn't really the truth although it was true.

But he'd gone too far. He'd crossed the line he didn't want to. Now they were in familiar territory. Sex. Fucking. Blow jobs. Cum. Nipples. She was turning the ship dirty. And he wasn't ready. He wanted more from her than this.

But he also wanted *this*.

"I think about you all the time, Parker," she murmured.

Ah-ha. Ah-HA! She knew his name, she did. He knew she did.

"How? How do you think about me?"

"I thought I was being very clear about that."

Jesus Christ. What was he doing? He pushed her wadded-up sweatshirt into her lap. "Put your shirt back on."

"I thought you wanted to examine my tits."

"I've had too much to drink."

"You've barely had two."

"Boundaries. It's called having boundaries, Elliot. Maybe you should get some."

"Okay, fuck *you*. Lighten up. Maybe you'd actually enjoy life a little if you did." She tugged her shirt over her head, shoved her arms in, and yanked the front down over her stomach. "Since you clearly don't value having fun at all. You prefer to judge me instead." She crossed her arms over her chest.

Oh how wrong she was. About judging her. Maybe not about the fun part. He wasn't really looking for fun per se, but still he didn't want to judge her, he just wanted her. All of her, in a whole form, not in the weird snippets she was giving to him.

But he knew that was too much to ask. Too much too soon, and too big. He had to keep reminding himself that he didn't even know her, technically speaking. He didn't even know her favorite restaurant or how she took her coffee in the morning or her favorite dessert (he could make it for her, if she'd let him.) Or if she liked walks in the park.

All he knew about her was that the under curve of her breast was a perfectly formed half circle. And that the scent that wafted from her hair and skin was jasmine. And something else he couldn't identify.

So why couldn't he stop?

He cleared his throat. "Do you play any instruments?"

She scrunched her face. "Eh?"

He awkwardly scratched at his ear. "Like violin, piano...I don't know, harp, bagpipes?"

The skeptical look on her face remained. "What's this, what're you doing?"

"What? I'm trying to get to know you. In the usual way, by asking a question."

"Trying to *get to know me?* Are you one of those work retreat leaders who makes you stand up and participate in *ice breakers*? Always hated that shit."

"So you've worked in an office before?"

"Yeah, I mean after college didn't every—no! No. You're tricking me into divulging real information about myself to you." She tilted her chin back. "Sneaky motherfucker. Who fucking knew, tsk, tsk, tsk."

"Asking someone basic questions about themselves isn't sneaky. It's just…society."

"Oooohh, society. Wow, should I call you Mr. Philosophical now instead of Mr. Serious?"

"I wish you'd call me Parker. I really do."

She quieted at that, hands falling into her lap, fiddling with the frayed cuff of her sweatshirt. "You don't want to do this with me, Parker."

He shook his head but internally he blazed at the sound of his name being seriously spoken by her lips. "What is it I don't want? Why are you so cagey with me?"

Her voice took an edge. Not lighthearted and jokey as it was before. "Oh, you know, just a response born of a lifetime of lessons learned from interactions with men. Especially the ones you *think* are good."

Parker narrowed his gaze. "What do you mean by—"

"Excuse me, sir, ma'am, would you care for dinner? The menus are located in your front compartments." The flight attendant appeared bright eyed with a smile.

Silence fell between them, until Parker picked up a menu. "Yeah, I'll have the salad and the chicken."

"And I'll have the burger. And we'll both have more scotch, make 'em doubles, thanks."

"I didn't want another scotch."

"I don't think you know what you want. Fine. Forget the scotch. I'm getting tired anyway."

His eyebrows knitted together. "Are you—are you mad at me?"

She was somehow quieted now. Dispirited. Not at all like when she pretended to be mad at him before. It deeply unsettled him.

She yawned, stretching her arms above her, the bottom of her shirt riding up on her soft belly. Then, she retreated out of sight as she lowered her seat flat, turning to her side and pulling the airline-provided blanket over her face. "You can eat my burger if you want it. I'll drink your scotch later."

Parker couldn't sleep. He couldn't sleep but Elliot snored softly next to him. Normally he would prioritize health, and rest on an airplane, given how much he had to fly. But this time he'd drunk too much. Now he was staying awake when he should be resting too. And he might have to visit a medical doctor regarding a rock-hard hard-on persisting for longer than four hours.

But worse than all that, he couldn't shake this weird guilty feeling he had.

Like he'd really fucked up with Elliot. Like she was maybe never going to talk to him again.

The thought freaked him out.

Mostly because it was more than a guilty feeling. And he hadn't really *fucked up* with Elliot. He'd drawn a real boundary with her about sex. Namely, no having sex. Not yet. And then he'd tried to actually get to know her as a person, like *people do*, and she'd drawn a real boundary with him. No getting to know her. Maybe not ever. He really didn't know. She had her reasons, though.

He stole a glance at her sleeping form, although he didn't feel good about seeing something so intimate as her sleeping body. Only the top half of her face and messy ponytail stuck out. She was facing him too, mouth slightly open in that unselfconscious way only a sleeping person could do.

"You watching me sleep?" Her voice was heavy and also soft, a slight curve at the corner of her mouth but her eyes still closed.

Parker let out a little puff of a regretful laugh. "More like listening to your snore."

Elliot stretched and lazed up from her repose. She rubbed her eyes, the mechanical gears of the seat whirring as it returned to an upright position. "Are we done fighting, Mr. Serious? Because it would be a real shame if we didn't like each other anymore."

"Would it?"

"Oh yeah." She leaned over and snagged the bag of chips off his tray, snapped them open, and popped one in her mouth. "Mmm. Haven't eaten since yesterday. Late night, early morning, you know how it is."

Parker reached into the bag of chips, taking one for himself. "No, I don't know. I go to bed at eleven every night and wake up at six thirty every morning. On the dot, without an alarm."

"Gross."

As she chewed, he twisted off the cap of a bottle of water and handed it to her. The flight attendant had passed out extras while she was sleeping.

She accepted it, a suspicious look on her face. "What?"

He shrugged with a smile. He shouldn't *trick* her into emotional intimacy with him. Should he? "Nothing. Tell me about your night. Not so that I learn anything important about you but so you can school me on how the other—fun and exciting—half live."

She took a slug from the water and rolled her eyes. Then she set the bottle down and folded her hands in her lap. "I will for a trade."

Parker raised a brow. "Okay." He wasn't one for making bargains, he was a more take-it-or-leave-it kind of guy. He was also willing to pay a high price for something he wanted, when he wanted it, for the convenience of having it then and there rather than wait for a sale or waste time shopping around. But for Elliot? "Sure, why not."

"I tell you about my day."

"Right…"

"And you show me your dick."

Parker breathed in deep. Should've seen it coming.

"Hard dick. None of that flaccid shit."

He rubbed his eyes and glanced around. Nobody would ever see them unless a flight attendant was serving them at that very moment. Although the public display wasn't really his major concern. He was more concerned about how absolutely toxic this kind of trade was. He deserved a woman who wanted to have real conversations. Not just sexually laced banter.

But he couldn't deny that it was also hot. So fucking hot. Just like her.

Argh. Did he love toxicity? Was it the only way he could get off these days? Not for the first time, he had to wonder.

"No touching."

"I would never."

He shrugged. "Go on then. Tell me all about your day, darling."

She scrunched her face, throwing him a look of disgust, but then she smoothed her hair and straightened out. "Well, it started with a flat tire."

"Oh, you have a car. What kind of car do you drive?"

Her gaze cut to him briefly. "A Prius. Anyway, so I got this flat tire on my way to a gig, a local gig and not the destination wedding kind obviously. It was for an influencer who was throwing a huge party and she wanted all these shots of her in this designer dress."

"Who's the designer?"

Elliot gave him a look like he was a total weirdo. "*Anyway*, I ended up being late to the gig, but that wasn't the biggest problem, although that was part of the problem because it sent me down the wrong mental path, you know? And that's part of the reason why I haven't eaten anything. Too much running around. Frazzle-dazzled."

"So what's the biggest problem then?"

"The biggest problem is that I tore that bitch's dress."

"How did that happen?"

She let her head fall back a bit in the seat. "Yeah, okay, so I did it on purpose because she's a bitch. And because she told me to shut up when I directed her into a better pose than the pointless waste of time basic ass influencer bullshit she was trying to do. So fucking sue me, I'm an artist, Parker. A goddamn artist!"

Her voice was steadily rising until the end where she stopped talking, tension high. When she spoke again, her voice had returned to a calm cadence. "That's the problem, though. Their kind loves to sue the help." She sighed. "So, anyway. As I was saying. I got a flat tire, I showed up late, I tore a bitch's dress out of spite, and after my gig I stayed out all night partying and drinking and throwing dollar bills at strippers who were way hotter than me. And don't get jealous but a guy ate my ass on the rooftop of the building at the after-party. He did an okay job."

Parker was immediately jealous. But instead of bursting into flames, he nodded like she'd told him she bought stock in Apple last month.

"And then I got here bright and fresh and early, bribing a man with the cash on me from the night before, so I can have his seat and sit next to quite literally the sexiest man in the universe. That's you, although you're still a serious weirdo. Not having eaten a damn thing in, oh, maybe a full twenty-four hours. I did shower though. Because a girl's gotta smell her elfin floral best if you know what I mean."

He didn't. He had no idea. He wanted to ask more questions. He wanted to squeeze all the details about her life. To fill in the gaps from the Instagram stories and posts and pictures. But she would recoil at that. It was always better to leave someone wanting a little more than taking a little too much.

"You're right. That was light and exciting. Everything you promised it'd be." So, without further ado, he pushed the blanket down past his jean's zipper, his hands undoing the top button, the metallic zip of the zipper the only sound in the silence between them.

"Holy shit," she breathed. "I didn't think you were actually gonna do it, but holy shit you are. Oh my fucking god, I can't breathe." She fanned herself dramatically with the flat of her hand. "I've never wanted to see a dick so bad in my life. Can I take a video? No face, I promise, but Jesus fucking Christ I'm going to masturbate to this about ten thousand times. Now show me how you come. If you show me yours, I'll show you mine."

He merely grunted with a nod as she took out her camera, downward facing. Then he grasped the hard shaft from within the slit of his boxer briefs, letting it spring to life right in front of her very eyes. He ran his thumb over the leaking head.

"Oh, that's the fucking stuff, man. Show me how you stroke that big cock. Damn, I wasn't wrong, that thing is big. How would it even fit in this tight little pussy I've got? And after I've been such a bad, bad girl, I deserve a hard, fast pounding."

She was full-on dirty-talking him with a pouty little whine. Pre-cum leaked from the head of his dick, but he refused to stroke it. "You're filthy, you know that?"

"Just a little bit, Parker. C'mon."

The sound of his name made his dick twitch. He couldn't believe he was even doing this in the first place. (That was a lie he was telling himself, he knew this was exactly the kind of toxic shit he had been caught up in with a woman many times before.)

She knew he liked hearing his name from her mouth so she kept repeating it. "Stroke it, Parker. Just give that big, fat cock one good up and down. I wanna see it, Parker."

Her hand trailed down her stomach to the front of her pants.

"Don't you fucking dare," he growled.

"Then puhle-e-e-e-a-s-e." She bounced on the seat with her whining.

Finally, holding back the grimace deep inside of him, he gave his dick one, long easy stroke.

He hated himself for what he was doing, even though he was willingly doing it. He hated that he was willing to play little sexual games with her to keep her in his life. To keep her interest sparked for a moment longer. This person, a near stranger. He hated himself for it.

And this was exactly who he knew himself to be.

Parker Donne. Some woman's plaything.

Chapter 8

"**S**ir? Excuse me, Mr. Donne? Sir, it's time to wake up."

Through the narrow slats of his tired eyes, Parker blinked the outline of a flight attendant.

He glanced around. He was the last one on the plane. Elliot was gone like a thief in the night. Shit, he'd passed out at some point. He couldn't remember when. The feeling unsettled him.

Reflexively, his hands scooted around his body, checking his shirt and jean pockets. (Why'd he think his wallet would be stolen? No, but it was there in his front pocket.)

He nodded at the flight attendant, undoing his seatbelt. "I must've been tired."

She smiled at him. "This is my last stop if you'd like to grab a drink."

Ah. He smiled back. "Sorry, I've got somewhere to be."

Her lips pursed and she reached above the compartment, letting Parker's carry-on hit the floor with a bump. "Well, then. Have a great night, sir."

Just before he was about to clamber into the aisle, still a little sleep drunk, he noticed a white paper sticking out from Elliot's seat pocket.

Hmm. His instinct told him she'd left it for him. And while a part of him wanted to rebuff her…the other part of him was curious as always. He snagged the paper, folded it and slipped it into his wallet. Then he nodded at the flight attendant on his way out. "Actually, I found a little time in my schedule if you still want that drink."

Elliot wasn't the only one who could play games.

"Can I confess something to you?" Tessa, the flight attendant sipped her champagne, legs crossed, toes tucked beneath her chair, knees pointed towards the large gap in Parker's spread legs. He leaned back, one arm splayed across the top rail, nursing a sparkling water.

Gentle music and chattering hummed around them at the fancy restaurant inside Parker's hotel. He'd met Tessa there when she was done with her shift. She'd changed from her flight attendant uniform into a long-sleeve yellow mini-dress that went well with her wavy brown hair. Large gold earrings dangled from her ears and complemented her warm, golden complexion. She was beautiful by any standards.

Parker raised his brow. "Confess away."

"I thought you had a thing going on with that woman sitting next to you."

He suppressed a surprised cough with his fist. "Ah, that's funny." A slight tinge of panic nipped at his gut at the idea that Tessa, this perfectly nice woman, had seen him whip his dick out on an airplane. He didn't want her to think of him as some kind of perv. Jesus, *was* he some kind of perv? Elliot certainly was, and he *liked* that about her.

"Hmm. Yeah. She looked pretty hungover."

Parker nodded. "You might be right about that."

"Listen. I asked you out because I thought you were handsome. And I'm the kind of person who likes to take action. But after talking to you for a while, I think I actually like your personality, too." Tessa winked playfully.

They'd been discussing a myriad of things during dinner, including Parker's very brief stint as a racecar driver when he was twenty. His career had ended with a literal bang, like so many other things in his life, but he aimed to keep things light. He talked about Avery. His friends. His French pastries. He smiled. "Is that right?"

She nodded and then cleared her throat. "You know what? Screw it. I'm just gonna put it out there because I get some kind of energy from you. I'm good at reading people's energy."

He shifted uncomfortably in his chair. "Put what out there?"

Tessa leaned forward, threading her fingers together on the table surface. "I'm ready to get out of the air, Parker. I can't live this lifestyle forever. I want to settle down. Feet on the grass, white picket fence, two kids, and a Honda. You want that too, don't you? I can tell by the way you talk. It's actually pretty rare for most men."

The things she named were indeed the things he wanted. And yet...What was his plan, anyway? Why had he asked Tessa out in the first place? Surely, his impulse was proactive. If he wanted the life he claimed to want, then he had to find the right woman. *That's* why he was sitting with Tessa right now.

But also, it was reactive. Reactive to whatever mood Elliot put him in.

Tessa swirled her champagne, a coy downward glance at the bubbles. "I don't suppose you'd want my number?"

The question pricked his doubt, but Parker unlocked his phone and set it on the table before her. "Put it in for me."

Once she was done, she looked up at him, lips to her flute. They were a muted pink. He wished they were red. He hated that he wished that. "I don't suppose you wanna go up to your room?" she asked.

He smiled. A fake one. "I'm not looking for a one-night stand."

She smiled back. "Obviously neither am I. But I don't believe there's anything wrong with getting to know someone you're connecting with a little better."

His gaze fell on the phone now resting in the middle of the table. He was trying not to think about Elliot, but she was like a virus: easily spread within his mind and soul, slowly poisoning his good sense. Regardless. He was lonely. And Tessa was good company. She actually talked to him, wanted to get to know him. Actual basic human interaction. Her life goals were aligned with his life goals. Wasn't this what he wanted most? Tessa wasn't going to play an international game of cat and mouse over a phone number.

But even if his feelings were clear, physically, he wasn't ready. Anxiety welled in the pit of his belly at the idea of being physical with someone he barely knew. It wasn't the same with Elliot. He did want that with her, but he also wanted more. Maybe if he *tried it out* with Tessa, his feelings would catch up? She certainly was the more reasonable option for him and what he wanted with his life. He nodded. "All right then. Let me pay the bill."

Tessa rested her hand on his. "I insist on splitting."

"Not happening." Parker stood and walked over to the bar to collect their bill so Tessa couldn't sneakily pay.

He retrieved his wallet and was rifling through to find the right credit card when the white paper fell out that he'd grabbed from Elliot's seat pocket. His heart ticked steadily but heavily in his chest. Slowly, he unfolded the paper.

"You're all set, sir." The person at the counter handed Parker's card back to him. Parker's gaze popped up.

"Thanks." He headed back to the table, a funny feeling in his throat.

Tessa was collecting her coat as he returned. "You're a gentleman. Thanks for dinner. Shall we?"

Parker turned to leave and then pivoted back around, wincing. "Ah, you know, actually. Maybe it'd be better if we didn't."

"Oh?"

"Uh, just. It's all a little fast for me. In fact, I should probably tell you the truth." *Elliot. The paper. His feelings...Elliot...the paper, his feelings!* He cleared his throat. "I can't be physical with someone right away. It takes me a long, long time. It's just a thing I have. I need to get to know the person first, feel a deep connection. I know it's not...it's not *normal*, or conventional. And when I was younger, I did a lot of things I regret just because I thought I was supposed to. So, I hope you can understand what I mean when I say I can't tonight. I'm looking for something serious only. And for me that means going a little bit slow. And also, I wasn't entirely honest before. That woman on the plane. I do know her. But I don't know how to describe our interactions. Strange, to say the least. We're not together, but I'd be lying if I said I didn't have feelings for her."

Tessa tilted her head, eyes narrowed. "Interesting. Is that all?"

Parker pursed his lips together. "Yep, I think that'll do it."

But Tessa's expression remained unmoved. "I'm going to be frank with you."

"Okay."

"I'm a grown woman, Parker. I've seen it all because of my job. I saw that woman you have feelings for. I've seen lots of women like her. And, honestly, I'm not worried. She'll burn you out, take everything, and leave. And then what will you be left with? I want you to know that I'm not that kind of person. I'm serious about the future. About what I need out of life. And that when I find something I want, I'm not afraid of a little competition."

Parker was stunned. "Wow, I…wasn't expecting that."

"I don't have time for pretend. I'm thirty-three years old." Tessa rustled through her purse, then pulled out a clear tube, dabbing sheer pink gloss onto her lips. "So, let's keep in touch. You never know when you might have a change of heart. And something tells me you just might soon enough. I have an intuition for these types of things."

Cold relief spread over his chest. In a way, Tessa had let him off the hook. He didn't have to reject her outright. He struggled to reject women, it's why he'd slept with so many in his youth. Tessa was leaving the door open. He kind of liked that, too. She certainly would be a compatible fit with his life in practically every way. He grabbed her hand and gave it a brief squeeze. "Okay, then. I'll certainly keep that in mind. Let me get you a car."

And then he waited until a car was zipping Tessa to her hotel to pull out the piece of paper again.

The paper with the entire month of Elliot's travel schedule printed onto it.

|

Rebecca stared at Parker suspiciously from their bench at the dog park. Neither of them had dogs, but Pamela was napping with Avery, and Rebecca and Parker decided to take a walk. The dogs' joyful, carefree play soothed Parker's soul.

"You're acting happy. Why are you acting happy? I don't like it and I don't trust it. It's weird on you." Rebecca leaned over to pet a wayward dachshund, its owner rushing up to gather the dog.

"Sorry…" The woman said, tucking her hair behind her ear. Her lashes fluttered as she scooped her dog into her arms. "Oh…hey, don't think I've seen you here before."

"He's my husband," Rebecca snapped, eyebrows raised, a serious look on her face.

The woman blushed, scooting backward. "My bad…"

"Why were you so mean to her? Usually you're trying to fix me up with any beating heart. What was that?"

"*Something* is up with you, and you're not spilling the beans. You can tell me, I won't tell Pamela."

"You will."

"Yeah, yeah, I will, but its better coming from me than you. I know how to finesse words. You barely form sentences."

Parker grunted in agreement. Then he gave Rebecca a cheeky smile. She whacked his arm.

"I'm not telling you anything."

"Then I have to invoke the Friendship Act of 2017."

"Oh come on, don't do this, Rebecca. Come on."

But Rebecca was already scrolling through her phone and pulling up the document that she and Parker had signed together, drunk one night. She spoke loudly over Parker's protests. "The Friendship Act of 2017 clearly states that you Parker Lance Loves Laurie Donne under no circumstances shall keep any secrets be they of major or of little consequence from either of the signed parties below, that's me and Pamela, due to the time—"

"Due to the time I got really drunk and accidentally married that woman in Vegas and had to have you both fly there overnight to help me find her to get it annulled." He finished for her.

Rebecca smiled. "Yes, Parker. That's right. When you *accidentally* married a whole entire woman without telling us and got yourself in a world of trouble! She could've taken off with half your money, and that's just for starters. And that's why we created The Friendship Act of 2017, therefore no transgression shall ever be committed again because Pamela and I have the power to stop your wily ass. Because you're a big softy and I'm not flying to Vegas again."

Parker exhaled. "Fine. You're right. There is a girl. A woman, I mean."

Rebecca held up her index finger as she dug into her purse with her free hand. "Hold on, I'm gonna need to smoke a joint before I hear this story. Thank god I filled all those bottles this week. You wanna hit?" She puffed on the little rolled cigarette and held it out, flipping the fire to her lighter.

Parker shook his head, one palm rubbing against his chest, self-soothing "But don't get mad when I tell you. You asked."

Parker and Rebecca sat back to back on the bench, legs straight. In his lap, Parker stroked a fat Chihuahua that had wandered over while its owner chatted with another dog-park goer.

"You know, Park, normally I'd say you should burn that schedule you got from this woman, but..." Rebecca shook her head. "From what you've told me, kinda seems like she's the type to try to send you a message. And you're into it, which is kinda weird for you considering how you've been lately."

Parker's fingertips massaged the Chihuahua's head and in response the Chihuahua let out a satisfied roo-ing noise. "That's what I'm saying. She wouldn't have left that paper if she didn't want me to find it. I don't think, at least." He thought for a moment. "On the other hand, I don't even have her number. She doesn't even follow me on Instagram. We don't ever talk outside of the times we see each other at the airport or on a plane."

"And you're really telling me you just keep *by chance* running into this woman over and over and over again?"

Parker shrugged. "We both travel for work. And she hasn't admitted it, but I think she's based out of Chicago. See, that's another reason I shouldn't use this schedule to bump into her. She won't even tell me where she lives."

"Hmm. But on the *other* other hand, she sends you videos of herself from her Instagram. And you never respond, so I'm sure that's confusing. Plus, she clearly *likes* you. In some kinda way at least. *And* have you ever considered that somehow *she's* the one orchestrating these meetings? How about that for a conspiracy? How do you run into the same person four times in four different locations? It's madness, I tell you. Pure madness."

Parker nodded. "You might have a point. But on the other other *other* hand—"

"Hold up." Rebecca reached behind her, awkwardly hitting Parker's head with her hand. "I'm gonna stop you there.

Look, normally? Normally I'd tell a guy to fuck off and leave this girl alone. But Parker, I know you. And I know how women act *around* you. And I think if you like her, you might as well go for it. The worst that could happen is she tells you to back off and never speaks to you again, right?"

"Hmm…yeah, I might want to avoid something like that—"

"Precious? Oh my god, I've been looking everywhere for you!" A woman with a braid down her back wearing matching workout gear came jogging up to Parker and Rebecca. And Precious, the dog apparently. She scooped the dog out of Parker's hands and gave him a dirty look until her eyes registered on him fully. "Oh, hi. How are you?"

"Married! He's married!" Rebecca pointed aggressively to her ring.

"*Bitch*," the woman whispered under her breath as she huffed away.

Rebecca and Parker both stood from the bench, dusting off their pants from the dirt that coated everything in the park. "Welp, if past experiences are any proof, I think it's a safe bet that she likes you, Park. Like the rest of the entire straight female population. Mind boggling to me, but I don't make the rules. You might as well fucking go for it." She clapped her hand on his shoulder as they walked away.

Chapter 9

When Parker wasn't trying to run into Elliot, it seemed all he could do was find her. Now that he was on the lookout, she was nowhere to be seen.

He unfolded his legs in a quiet booth in the business class lounge, sipping on a Guinness. His client had actually been ecstatic to learn Parker was bumping him up on the schedule (so he'd be flying out the same time as Elliot.) After all, his Aston Martin DBS wasn't going to drive itself.

He kept checking his phone. Maybe Elliot's schedule was wrong. Although it'd been right so far.

So far Parker had run into her only twice at various airports. It'd taken some finessing on his part, getting his client's schedules moved around to accommodate. But in the end, he knew it'd be worth it.

Because, and here's where things were murky, he was going to *get to know* Elliot Sheer if it killed both of them.

No, not really. If she rejected him, he would politely back off.

But so far she hadn't. At Heathrow, she'd spotted him first, collapsing onto his lap (instant boner) and squeezing his neck so tight he thought a vein might pop. But then she immediately ran off after that, having apparently switched her flight to the one earlier.

That was that for that encounter.

The next time was a little better. He was idling on a moving platform, when a tickling whisper feathered against his ears. "Well as I live and breathe, Mr. Serious. Fancy seeing you here in Atlanta. Don't you love these sculptures? It's almost like you're following me."

He'd smiled at her then. Because she was trying to fuck with him but he just didn't know in what way yet. Had she planted the schedule? Did she already know his schedule as Rebecca had suggested? Or was she just completely unbothered by him regardless? Was he just another person in the roster?

He knew she was still hooking up with other people, or at least she was making a good show of it if she wasn't. The Instagram stories hadn't stopped.

He turned around on the moving platform. "You came up behind me. By definition, you're the one following."

Her eyes traveled upwards for a moment as she considered that, and then she linked her arm in his, leaning against him. "Good point. After all, I am pretty obsessed with you. Hey, will you show me your dick again if I tell you about my day?"

Just then, the moving platform ended. She immediately dropped his arm and began searching for her phone. "Shit, shit, shit," she muttered to herself. When she finally procured it, she held up her hand to wave at Parker and answered. Then she spun around. "Gotta go, Mr. Serious. Ciao."

And now…now she was nowhere to be found. Parker checked his phone one more time. Five minutes before his boarding and it was time to call it. He wouldn't be seeing Elliot tonight.

He didn't want to admit it, but his heart ached at the thought. An aching, painful loneliness crept through him at the thought of not even getting a five-minute interaction with her.

Each time they'd seen each other, no matter how fleeting, had just stoked flames to the fire. He followed every crumb she dropped, and he'd let a goddamn witch eat him too if she led him to a candy house. *Wait, maybe he was getting his metaphors confused.*

His airline app pinged him with a boarding alert. What a disappointment. He trudged himself up, making his way to his gate.

Idly, he picked up his phone as he waited in line, when he noticed he had a message.

Another Instagram message.

His heart raced because he knew, he *knew* it was from her.

He opened it.

Miss me? Flight was canceled ;)

Eventually, time passed and Elliot's schedule was up. Parker no longer had a way to find her. He'd only seen her two measly times total, and what a bust those were.

And now, now he was in a real fucking pickle.

He'd unwisely helped a wealthy businessman in Pennsylvania with a last minute tune up for his collection of one-of-a-kind all-white 911s. It was unwise because everyone warned him not to go to Pennsylvania in the dead of winter.

But he'd been so down about not seeing Elliot that he figured why the fuck not? He might as well sulk in his sad, lonely reality.

"You're not sad and lonely," Pamela had admonished him. "You're impossible and picky and you love *trouble*."

Be that as it may, he'd been waiting in the airport for over two hours now, flights delayed due to inclement weather.

He sprawled out on the hard plastic chair—there weren't any fancy first class lounges at this airport. He should've demanded a private jet, but he always felt guilty about that anyway. Plus, a private jet couldn't help him now either. In the end, nothing could win against Mother Nature. Not even billionaire dollars. He'd always known that.

Through the windows, planes landed and the gate opened, the crowd of people rushing inside. Each one tired and haggard from the flight.

And of course. Of course! That's when he saw her.

He shook his head just to make sure he wasn't hallucinating, but no, of course it was her. Who else would he run into, on a snowy day in Pennsylvania, trapped at an airport, with nowhere to go?

At first he thought it was a curse. But now he was positive it was fate.

Without thinking, he jumped to his feet. "Elliot." He waved his hands. "Hey! Over here."

Elliot's face turned to look at him directly, and butterflies caught air in his belly. Wow, he really did have it bad. He better not see her in Vegas anytime soon or he'd be in trouble.

And that's when he saw something much worse. She was holding hands with *some guy.*

After all the people Parker had inadvertently watched Elliot make out with on her Instagram stories, nothing hurt like seeing Elliot engage in such a tiny intimate gesture.

He wanted to hold her hand.

But all she wanted to hold was his dick.

Irony. Ugh, was he really so mushy inside? Why couldn't he be chill? Why couldn't he be fine with that? Why couldn't he find another woman? Tessa. Right? She was such an obvious choice. She'd been texting him.

"Holy shit." He couldn't hear her, but Elliot's mouth formed the words. Unlike the few other times they'd run into each other, Elliot looked genuinely shocked to see him. She leaned up and said something into the guy's ear. The guy was rumpled looking, lanky and tall, dark eyes and a beat up leather jacket. He inclined his head at Elliot's whisper. But then she dropped his hand.

Parker looked sheepish now, standing with his waving hand in the air. He gave one more impotent wave, then shoved his hands in his pockets. He regretted his actions, but she was already on her way over without the dude.

"How did you know I'd be here?" She looked confused. As if all the other times hadn't been confusing as well. And she was dressed like she'd just left a party, a fitted black one-shoulder dress. Except she was wearing sneakers with it. Her black eyeliner was smeared, but her hair, glossy and shiny, still hung like a curtain down her back.

Parker raked his hand through his hair. "I didn't. Who're you with?"

Elliot furrowed her brow for a moment, tossed a look over her shoulder. "That's Bruno. Don't worry about it."

"It looks like you're together."

"So? Appearances are just that."

He rolled his eyes. "Fuck. Whatever, Elliot." He turned and gathered his bag, hiking up the handle. He wasn't going to fucking even try right now. What he really needed to do was find a goddamn hotel room to stay the night in because he knew he wasn't going to get out of Pennsylvania anytime soon. "Goodbye."

"Wait, where you going?"

"Nowhere. There isn't anywhere to go. We're fucking stranded."

The hotel room that Parker was just barely able to book was connected to the airport, smelled like cigarettes and potpourri, and its windows didn't open. He had paid $500 a night for the goddamn honor of not sleeping on the airport floor.

He collapsed onto the scratchy duvet, toeing off his shoes and kicking off his pants. Yanking off his shirt. Then he just lay there spread out and tired. What a fucking terrible day.

Like a reflex, he grabbed his phone, his head lolling to the side to view the screen. *Don't look at Elliot's shit, you unrelenting asshole.*

He dropped his phone again, shaking his head.

Then he took a breath to collect himself and endeavored *not* to think about the fact that she'd held another man's hand right in front of him. He picked up his phone again. There was a text from Tessa.

Thinking about you.

She had been texting him since their initial meeting. Friendly mostly. But right now, after seeing Elliot, his insides burned raw and sore. He began typing.

Parker: Maybe we should meet up sometime.

He waited.

Tessa: Tell me your schedule, and I can work something out.

Then another text appeared, a picture. A selfie of Tessa, bright as the morning day. She was in her flight attendant uniform, an empty plane behind her.

Tessa was the right kind of woman for Parker. She was so up front. Friendly, even. And she was normal. Capable of talking. Giving and receiving normal human feedback.

And she was perfectly beautiful, which didn't hurt matters. Nor did it hurt that she was willing to wait for him physically and otherwise.

So maybe he would try to make it work. Maybe he really would.

He picked up his phone, prepared to tell her that, when once again, another message appeared.

Elliot: What's your room number, Mr. Serious?

His eyes narrowed at the Instagram message. It went to his burner account, the only one they'd ever messaged on.

He clicked off the screen, picked up his phone and tapped Tessa's number.

It rang once, twice.

Then another message.

Elliot: Oh come on, are you mad at me?

This message went to his other account. The one he'd wanted Elliot to watch. So she *did* know about it. A weird gentle relief rushed over his body. She had been watching him watch her, but she was also watching him in secret.

He shouldn't like it.

But he was fucked up.

The phone rang a third and fourth time.

Knock, knock, knock. Someone was at his door.

Parker sat straight up on the bed.

"Hey, you. I had a feeling you'd want to see me." Tessa's voice.

A knock on the door again.

He stood, walked to the door and opened it, phone pressed to his ear, body clad in nothing but boxer briefs.

Elliot leaned against his door frame, one shapely leg hitched over another, the single strap of her dress slouching lazily from her shoulder, her head tilted. This time she was barefoot. Lips bright red.

"Parker, hello?" Tessa's voice was a tinny distant echo far away.

"I —" Parker gulped. "I gotta call you back…" He let the hand with his phone fall from his face.

Elliot straightened her posture, slipping her thumb beneath her strap to push it back up her shoulder.

In the next moment, she was on him.

Her hands threaded in the hair at the back of his neck, her breasts pushed against his bare chest, her lips pressed to his in a fierce kiss.

His eyes went wide in shock and then shuttered closed, his arms frozen at his side. They shared an inhale, and her fingers curled, fisting at his hair, pulling tightly as she pushed him into the room, kicking the door shut behind her.

And just as quickly as it began, he broke away, breath labored, dick hard without much cover. He snatched his jeans up from the ground, stabbed his legs inside, not bothering to zip up, and rested at the end of the bed, legs wide, leaning on his elbows. "How'd you find my room?"

"I told the front desk guy you were my boyfriend, and I lost my key and that I was too empty-headed to remember where my room was. Easy." She hovered like a shadow before him.

"What about the guy?"

She twirled a strand of shiny black hair around her finger. Her nails were painted a jet black as well. "Bruno? Why do you care?"

"You were holding his hand."

She tilted her head to the other side. "But I came here to see you. Tonight." Then she slowly eased herself onto the small space at the end of the bed to his right, twisted on her hip to look at his profile.

His throat tightened at her nearness. "Lemongrass."

The back of her fingernails glided up his bare inner forearm. "Huh?"

"You always smell like jasmine and something else. It's lemongrass. Or cigarettes. But I think that's the smell of the room."

"You really pay attention to details."

He turned his head. She was staring at the muscles in his arm, index finger tracing a vein upwards, then middle finger tracing downwards.

"Because when I look at you, I see you. I use all of my senses. Pay attention when it matters."

Her hand stilled. "Like the way I smell? That matters to you?"

He took his arm away from her touch, rubbing the back of his neck. "I hate to break it to you, but you might matter to me."

She stared at him for only a second before she leaned in closer. "Fuck me, then. What are you waiting for?"

Even though he was resisting, he let his fingers caress the smooth skin of her cheek all the way down to the hollow of her neck before flicking his hand away. "If that's all you want from me, you should leave."

She frowned. "It's not fair what you're doing."

"How so?"

"We're supposed to flirt. Hook up. Mess around. It's only normal. You're making me feel guilty for having perfectly normal desires. And it's especially not fair because, well, look at you. You know I've been building my social media as a professional photographer for years now and all you have to do is post some picture of yourself with a pastry bag and a hint of biceps and it's like *boom*, success. And you don't even want me? Insult to injury, my dude."

"I knew you knew about that account. Why don't you follow me?"

She scoffed. "Why would you possibly need me to follow you along with your many other admirers? Unless you're a narcissist—which I'm not ruling out by the way—I don't see the point."

He rubbed the stubble on his chin. "Huh. I thought we were…doing a thing I guess."

"A thing? What kind of thing?"

"Like…watching each other watch each other."

She inched in closer to him. "Everybody watches everybody watch everyone. It's called…what did you say before? Oh yes, it's called *society*."

He chuckled. "Point taken."

They sat in silence for a full minute. Parker's anxiety wafted and then evaporated with her nearness, even though everything was all wrong. But the way she was sitting with him now was different than on the airplane.

He dared a glance in her direction, but she wasn't looking at him. She was hunched, nibbling on the edge of a jet-black fingernail.

A slip of sadness nudged at his heart, but he couldn't quite place why.

He sighed, pushing back to the headboard, legs drawn out, settling in on some pillows. "C'mere," he said softly.

She glanced over her shoulder at him skeptically. "Why?"

"Because I have room on my chest for you to rest your head. You look tired."

She chuffed at that. "Thanks a lot."

She glanced at her manicure and then back to him, and then finally she sighed, crawling on her knees and curled up into him so that his arm was around her shoulder and her head was on his chest, right over his heart. Which was probably thumping like an excited metronome. Her fingers strayed and she plucked at a few of his chest hairs and he let her, reveling in the bright momentary prick of pain. Reveling in this moment of closeness with her. In this moment of quiet.

She rubbed her nose against his sternum. "You smell like skin."

"Hmm?"

She lifted her chin. "You think I smell like jasmine and lemongrass. To me, you just smell like skin. Like familiar skin. Like skin I've smelled before. Maybe some other lifetime."

His phone buzzed at his side, his gaze only fluttering over for a moment.

"You wanna get that?" she murmured.

His hand came to caress the skin of her arm; she was soft and warm. Absently he let it travel up her shoulder to her hair, dense shredded silk tangled in his fingers. "Nope. Not in this lifetime."

The touching felt oddly forbidden, like she might disappear into a puff of smoke at any moment.

The phone buzzed again. Her fingers stopped their glide across his chest. "Are you sure you don't want to check that?"

"Why does it matter to you?"

"I don't know, it's just that *I* would look to see who was frantically texting me. But that's just me, a person with normal reactions to things."

He chuckled, leaning his head down to nuzzle in her hair, the scent at first overwhelming and then dissipating in his lungs. "You have beautiful hair."

The phone buzzed again.

"Okay. What the fuck." She wiggled from his grip abruptly, reaching over and snatching his phone from the other side. The phone previewed the message. "Tessa? Who is Tessa? Is she your third friend? It's weird that *all* your friends are women. Don't you work with mostly men? What's even up with that?"

Parker gently removed the phone from her hand, changed it to silent and set it down on the nightstand next to the bed. He didn't care if she looked at his phone. Didn't care if she read his messages. Elliot hadn't asked him for anything, had demanded nothing of him, and therefore he had nothing to feel guilty about. Nothing to hide. Well, hypothetically, at least. So, what was that strange quality in her voice?

He cleared his throat. "Tessa is a woman I'm seeing. Or at least, thinking about seeing."

"Shouldn't you lie to me about that?"

He raised an eyebrow. "Why?"

She was looming over him, resting up on her elbow. "Because I'm lying next to you in your bed. Because you just ignored her to lie here with me."

"Kind of like how you were holding hands with some man and then scammed a front desk receptionist to find my room."

Her eyelids fluttered. "Yeah, kind of like that."

He gave a small smirk. "I know you like me. At least, I think you do. Because you've said it before."

Elliot collapsed back down in his arms, flipping over dramatically to bury her head in his chest again. "Like is cheap, baby boy."

His hand found its way back into her hair, but this time digging deeper all the way to the tightened skin of her scalp. When he wasn't working, Parker kept his hands exceptionally clean, exceptionally neat. Even if oil wanted to cling to him forever. He let his fingers curl into her scalp, gently pulling at her hair right at the root, tipping his forehead ever so slightly to breathe her in.

She moaned lightly. "Why are you doing this to me?"

His fingers scraped, curled and released. Scraped, curled and released again, her body slowly starting to wiggle against his hip. "Because I know you like it."

She moaned another release of air. Her fingers had found their way back to his chest hair but were slowly making their descent to the plane of his corded stomach. His muscles flexed at the trailing touch until she made it to his belly button. His hand came to cover hers, to stop it from further following the path of his happy trail.

His hand stilled in her hair, but the heat from her body radiated softly into him. *Remember this moment.* He'd spent so much time up in the air that being grounded, even if against his will, felt freeing. That's what he really wanted. The feeling of heavy feet on the pavement. No more floating in the wind like the smoke from a spent match. Tangle him up in Elliot's hair instead.

"I see that look in your eyes," Elliot's voice was soft.

"What look?"

"I've seen it before from other men. Like you want to catch me in a net. Pin me down with needles to a block of wood, splay me out like a patient on a table. I've had enough of that in the past. Never works out well for any of us."

"I would never want to pin you down." *At least not in that context.*

Because Elliot wasn't some elusive butterfly. She was a full grown woman capable of making her own decisions, although Parker might think some of them were strange, or possibly unfortunate. Like, where did she even live? Suddenly, it occurred to him.

"You don't have an apartment."

Elliot shifted slightly. "Huh?"

"You don't have an apartment, do you? That's why you said you're from everywhere and nowhere."

The smile from her lips pushed against the skin between his arm and chest. "Wow, a regular Sherlock goddamn Holmes, how about that?" Then she sighed. "I got used to traveling. Lots of work-provided Airbnb's and other such rental properties. Sometimes I'll stay in hotels if I'm in a city for long enough. And fine, if you must know, since you seem pretty hell-bent on teasing information out of me, Bruno is one of my best friends. He travels with a band. He lets me stay in his guest room when I'm in Chicago. Plus I have a storage unit there, and if things get really dire I can sleep on the couch I've stored away. Although things don't get dire. Usually."

"I don't understand how anyone can live like that."

"I don't understand how anyone can't. See, you are judgmental! This is exactly why I didn't want to get into it with you Parker. You're too serious for me. I don't even know how to do laundry."

"Laundry is easy."

"It's not for me."

"I can show you how."

"I use a laundry service. Stop trying to fix me. Or worse yet, *teach me*. I'm thirty-two years old and I'm thriving in a profession most people can't even get off the ground. I work for myself. I live a totally fucking baller life. And I'm not looking for *you* or anyone else for that matter to teach me how to do laundry because it's *easy*." Her voice gained an angry edge. "And I shouldn't have to remind you that people have different definitions of *easy* anyway."

Oops. He might've fucked up again.Apparently, he was good at pushing her buttons. He didn't even mean to.

He waited a beat, then said softly, "I use a laundry service too."

She shook her head laughing. "Hypocrite."

101

Her hand was still beneath his on his belly. Feeling like a criminal getting away with breaking the law, he very carefully interlaced his fingers with hers. As if she wouldn't notice.

"I feel like you're doing the opposite of trying to seduce me."

"I don't need to seduce you. I need to get to know you."

"You know my position on that offer."

"And yet you're holding my hand as we speak."

Elliot held up their clasped hands and stared at it for a moment. "What will you give me in return?"

"I'll tell you about my childhood. I used to be a racecar driver, you know."

"Oh, boy." She scoffed. "I'm not trying to be crude, I'm just so goddamn horny when I'm around you. Men like you should be against the law."

He bit back his smile. "Can't we just be here together right now?"

She sighed. "Fine, I suppose this isn't so bad. I guess it's nice to know a thing or two about you."

Hmm. He wasn't expecting that from her. It made him …curious. He cleared his throat. "Then we should wait."

"*Fine.* But it's like you don't realize that I have needs too. I'm a fully grown woman."

Ah. His dick jumped a little at the thought of her needs. For some reason, the framing of her words turned on his light bulb. He *had* been selfish in that regard. He'd only been thinking about them together, not what she might need on her own.

"You can't just put a moratorium on sex stuff because you feel like I owe you emotional currency first. That's kind of fucked up. And if you don't want to have a physical relationship with me, you should just admit it already. Stop sending me mixed messages. Relationships are about give and take."

Interesting. He smiled. "Tell me about this relationship we're in."

She rolled her eyes. "I mean relationship in the sense that any two people together are in a relationship. Like, how I have a relationship with the guy at the security check or the flight attendant who brings my vodka soda or the man who ate my ass on the roof the other day. They're all relationships, just different in nature. You see?"

"And what would you call this relationship? Our relationship."

She wiggled her fingers over his, but he grasped on tight, turning to his side to face her and yanking her hard against his chest. Hard against the erection springing to life.

She was right. She had needs. And Parker was being selfish by not tending to her needs. And look at how hard she had tried. Holding *his* hand now. Talking about her job, her apartment, or lack thereof.

"I would call this a fucking problem." Then she rocked her hips slightly against his, his erection rubbing against the cradle in between her thighs. "Let me do something about this problem…" she whispered.

Before she could make a move, Parker grabbed her other hand in his, then pinned both hands over her head, so that the skirt of her dress was riding up high on her thighs.

"You getting serious with me, Mr. Serious?"

"You said you have needs too. You're right. I'd be remiss to neglect them."

Elliot's chest heaved; even beneath the tight black material, the tips of her nipples were pointed and hard. He longed to put his mouth on them, to twirl one around his tongue like a lollipop. To nip and bite as he rode her hard while grasping onto the padded, soft flesh at her hips.

"Oh my. Happy to see me?"

His dick had fully hardened at the thought of fucking her, and now she was rubbing herself against it. He held back a groan as his hips moved involuntarily. She bit her lip, watching him closely.

"Your body is unbelievable…" She gasped a bit, as she gently rocked up and down. "You make me feel gross in comparison. I hate it."

He growled in her ear. He didn't like to hear her talk about her body negatively, not while it was writhing against him. Not while she was hot with wanting. Not ever. "If you're gross, then I want gross. Then I like gross." He knew his voice must sound crazed right now, but he didn't care. "Your body is perfect. It's a fucking marvel of the universe…"

She giggled, but then her giggle was quickly swallowed up in a moan, her leg now snaking around his hip. Was it just him or were his words slurring. He was going to come in his jeans if he didn't knock it off.

She would want that. She would give a lot to see him come. And then she would lose interest. So he couldn't give her that.

But he could give her something else.

"Keep your arms up above your head," he said, releasing his grip on her hands that he didn't even realize had become so tight. He trailed down her body to the hem of her skirt, pushing his head in between her knees.

"What are you doing—"

But her voice died down when he hiked up the skirt, revealing a skimpy pair of black lace panties beneath. He shoved his face in between her thighs and inhaled. He wanted to breathe her in.

"Oh my fucking god…" He heard her voice above him.

He settled in, hoisting up either of her thighs around his shoulders, feeling the weight and heat of her body hold him to the bed. He hoped she squeezed him to death with her legs, because that's how he wanted to die. But he wasn't going to say that now. Now, he had work to do.

He ran his tongue along the scrap of fabric between her legs all the way from back to front until he knew he would meet the little sensitive bud of her clitoris. Then he suctioned his mouth over it giving a gentle kiss.

"Mmm…Parker, you are one sneaky motherfucker, *ughn, fuck…*"

Before she could stop talking, he had latched his finger around the fabric and yanked it to the side. He was going to taste her now and there was nothing either of them could do about it.

For just a second, he only looked. He pushed her skirt up further so that it was around her waist. Her pussy was a glistening pink slit. Hairless. This didn't surprise him. He didn't mind either way, but it was on brand for her. Not even stubble.

He flicked his tongue out lightly at the top of the slit, against her smooth, slick skin. She rocked into him, trying to work herself against his tongue. He found his hands reaching for her hips, fingertips digging into the flesh there to hold her still as he gently continued to flick his tongue along her.

"You're a fucking jackass," she groaned, trying to fight against his grip, but Parker held steady, enjoying this slow, steady time with her. Enjoying the taste of her. The smell. He was already addicted.

It was gonna be a bad fucking time.

But it was one he signed up for.

"More, just a little more." Her hips wiggled in his vice lock again. "Put your fingers inside me."

His hands squeezed her flesh at that, but he wouldn't listen. Although he could die in this moment, his mouth continued to lightly glide up and down the seam of her pussy, only briefly stopping at the clit feathering it with his tongue, kissing it gently.

"How is this even worse than not touching at all?" Her voice was strained.

Utilitarian. That's what this was. Not the bells and whistles. He had to stop playing and get to work.

With one more long lick up and down, he scooted in deeper so that her legs had to brace around his head. Then his mouth zeroed in on its target: her clit. That's all she'd get from him tonight. One, big long gentle orgasm.

His philosophy: only give enough so that they want a little more afterwards.

He pressed his mouth to the hood of her pussy, letting his tongue fall flat against the top of the slit, waiting only the briefest moment before circling his head over it, so his tongue glided easily. She was so wet by now he had to resist the urge to lap it all up, even when she was dripping down her thighs.

She moaned softly above him, voice breathy. "Parker...Parker, please...harder please..."

But he remained unmoved, continuing in the same rhythmic, slow motion that he started with, tongue flat and soft against her, occasionally lifting off her to glimpse her body. Her back was arched so that her tits were pointed upwards, her hands and arms dutifully above her head. And her head dropped back against the pillow.

He knew she needed more to come the way she wanted to come. But he wouldn't give her that. She would come how he wanted her to come. And she would obey.

This wasn't his first rodeo. And it sure as fuck wouldn't be his last.

Her soft moans turned more acute and high pitched the longer he circled his tongue in the same steady tempo, her thighs quivering and then squeezing, pulsing around him.

Because of this response, he increased the pressure of his tongue *ever* so slightly, with a minute uptick in the rhythm.

"Oh fuck, oh fuck." She responded right away. "Oh fuck Parker, just like that…just like—"

And then, she began fluttering, her whole body. He didn't dare stop doing exactly what he was doing exactly how he was doing it. He was about to ride this orgasm wave out with her.

His dick ached and he resisted the urge to reach down and furiously stroke it, reaching his own climax and coming all over her belly.

A deep noise emanated from her diaphragm, her hips fighting against his hands to buck into his mouth. But he continued with his gentle ministrations until the noise broke from her.

"Mmmgmm, I'm coming, yes, yes, yes, mmmghhmm, oh god Parker, Oh fuck, oh god."

His lips curled into a smile despite himself. He loved this part. Loved when a woman came on his tongue, loved when she bucked against him while he held her down. Loved that she did the thing he wanted her to do.

Her body lurched and tightened one more time, and then with labored breaths she collapsed against the mattress.

"Fuck. Fuck. Fuck. Fuuuuuuck."

Her hand came down, slapping his head, and he realized he was still licking her, trying to wring out more and more of her orgasm. He gave one last lick, and breathed in deep, and then he moved to the headboard again, turned on his side to look at her, wiping his face with the back of his forearm.

He wished he could frame this moment in time. But instead he'd have to settle for fleeting memories.

Her head lolled over to him. Her pale skin was flushed red, her skirt still hiked up all the way to her belly. Her panties yanked to the side. "That was really good."

He smiled. "I know."

She squinted her eyes. "You know? What do you mean you know? That could have all gone south quick, buddy. All women are different."

He reached over and brushed a shining black strand of hair from her face. "Everyone is different. And yet, also the same."

Her voice went soft. "So you use that trick on all the women you go down on?"

"Would you be jealous if I did?" This time, he felt distinctly as if he was winning the conversation, unlike on the plane or generally any time he was talking to her. But he wasn't even sure if it was what he wanted. How could he explain to her, without her freaking the fuck out, that she was different than every woman to him? That he didn't know why, but that he'd grown completely addicted to her very presence. That he thought about her every morning as he drank his tea and dreamt about her every night.

She turned on her side to face him, wiggling her hips and working on the hem of her skirt to yank it down. He put his hand on hers to stop her from covering up. "Leave it," he said. Then he cleared his throat. "Leave it up."

Her gaze darkened for only a moment, which he wanted. Good, give her a little, and let her beg for more later. Then she held her hands up in front of her like a thief. "Whatever you say, boss."

Then she reached out and fingered the waves at Parker's forehead. He was shaggier than usual, having forgone his usual eight-week haircut to change around his entire work schedule on the off chance of running into her. His eyes closed at the small gesture. Then she dropped her hand, bringing it back between them.

"Yeah. I am a little jealous. But let us never speak of it again."

A little smile tugged at his mouth which he held back. He licked his lips, the taste of her still on him. "Deal."

She yawned, the light dim in the room. It was getting late. The frigid outside storm contrasted starkly to the stuffily warm room. But he didn't care that it was stuffy, or smelled like cigarettes, or that the duvet was scratchy.

He pulled her in towards his chest, her body giving and compliant. *He'd licked her into compliance*, and the thought made him hot as an iron.

She snuggled into him, her head pushed against him, his head on top of hers. He buried his nose into her hair, enveloped by the soft fragrance.

"You won't be here when I wake up, will you?" Despite his throbbing erection, his eyes had grown heavy, tired with emotion, tired from all the kinetic energy he'd just expended, tired from the long day of snowy drudgery.

She rubbed her nose against him. "You worry about the wrong things, Mr. Serious."

Chapter 10

Pamela kicked open Parker's front door, a stack of frozen lasagnas in her arms. "Oh, dude. Where's your fucking couch? This is a dire situation, Park. Why didn't you get this together before today? I thought you ordered one from that Crate and Barrel catalog."

Parker took the stack of lasagnas, opened his freezer, and placed them at the bottom. It was empty aside from a bag of ice. He'd been traveling a lot lately. The fridge was empty too aside from a case of Old Style. ("You are a monster," Rebecca hissed at him when she saw it. But Parker liked what Parker liked and he wouldn't be ashamed of it.)

"Yeah, the couch came, and I had to send it back."

The door swung shut with a crack. "Why? Was it damaged?"

He opened the case of Old Style, pulled out two bottles, and twisted off the caps. He handed one to Pamela, who made a face but accepted it anyway, sitting on a chair next to his island counter.

Parker leaned over the island across from her. "It didn't *feel* right."

Pamela rolled her eyes. "Your desire for an empty living room is pathological. Jen's gonna hate this. She really is."

"Jen's only staying for a week and I have a very nice guest bedroom. I don't see how the couch matters."

"Does that bed have a headboard?"

"Yeah, I'm not a total monster. Jesus. Haven't you known me long enough?"

Pamela swigged from the bottle. "Some would say too long. It's just very weird to walk into such an empty apartment, especially after all this time. It feels...*haunted.* If you want a family, you have to start living in a place that could actually *sustain* a family. Not this drafty, trendy loft."

"You used to love this place."

Pamela lifted her bottle. "Yeah, and now I drive a minivan."

Parker nodded. "Touché. But it's too late anyway. She's due in an hour. I won't get a couch in that amount of time."

Pamela lifted her bottle. "You won't fix your life in that time either. That reminds me. What's going on with you and that woman?"

"Ah, so Rebecca spilled the beans."

"Obvi."

Parker took a long slug of his beer. "Last time I saw her, she slipped out of my hotel room before I could even say goodbye. I sleep so hard when she's with me, I don't even wake up when she runs away."

Pamela's eyes were suspicious. "I see."

Rattling footsteps came from outside of Parker's condo door.

"And she's early." Pamela smiled.

"Here we go," he muttered.

And within a moment, his door swung wide open, the female version of him standing in the frame.

Jen Donne was a statuesque, beautiful woman—although not as tall as Parker, of course—with long, wavy brown hair. Looks-wise, they could be twins, which made sense because they were.

But personality-wise, they couldn't be more different.

"Guess what, I have news!" Jen marched in, went straight to the fridge. Parker closed the door behind her. She examined the Old Style and then went to the pantry instead, pulled out the bottle of Macallan 12 and took a swig straight from the bottle. "I have the craziest news!"

"I have very nice glassware, you know." Parker got up from his seat and opened the top cabinet in his kitchen where he kept the nice glassware. He snatched the bottle from Jen, threw in a large sphere ice cube, and poured her three fingers.

"Don't be such a stickler." But she accepted the glass from him, took a sip and smiled.

"What's the news?" Parker sat back down next to Pamela, one arm reclined over the top rail.

"Well, I wanted you to be the first to know, which is why I booked my flight as fast as I could. But Parker, Pamela, I'm getting married. Ahhhh!" Jen's eyes excitedly darted back and forth between the two of them.

Parker's jaw dropped. "I—I didn't even know you were seeing anyone."

"Me neither. I mean, I wasn't. Before, that is. It all happened so fast, it's just a huge whirlwind."

Pamela and Parker exchanged a look.

"What! Don't even look at each other like that. This time, it's for real. This time I mean it. And who are you to judge?" Jen punched Parker's arm.

"Hey! That was hard." He laughed.

"You're always picking the wrong women, it's like a curse. You got married in Vegas! *And* had to have it annulled."

Parker's face went blank. "How'd you know about that?" Then he turned to Pamela. "What the fuck, Pam?"

Pamela shrugged, looking guilty. "We didn't know what to do, Park! I had to call Jen just in case we needed reinforcements getting you out of the situation."

Jen could talk her way out of anything. She once convinced a cop who was writing her a ticket to pay for it himself. "That's what the fucker gets for pulling me over in a school zone." She'd later laughed to them.

"I want you to walk me down the aisle, Park." Jen rustled through the handbag on her shoulder. "We don't want a long engagement. Six months tops, but I'm gonna stay with you for some of the planning because three quarters of my bridesmaids live here, and it's just easier that way. Plus, I never get to see you anymore, and that's so sad! You don't mind if I extend my stay a little, right?"

Jen wasn't actually asking permission. This was obviously already the plan. "Do I at least get to meet the guy first?"

Jen pushed a phone in his face. "Knew you would ask. Here he is. Benjamin Wu, attorney-at-law, sixth year at Calvin and Francis. Lives in Manhattan and that's fine, I'm willing to leave Brooklyn. But we're doing the wedding in Connecticut, so clear your schedule."

"Why Connecticut? How about Chicago for once?"

"His parents live there, plus we want that New England fall. Not to mention you travel all the time anyway, so I don't see why you care. And. And! His parents are super-duper duper rich." She put her hands out as if she were presenting a prize.

"Are you marrying him for his money?"

She snorted. "Relax. I promise with all my heart its true love. The money just means we're gonna have a full-on extravaganza. Can't wait. Bring a date for once, will you? Like a good one? I don't want Benny's family to know that we're weird orphans. There's nothing weirder than a man who's single at a wedding. Talk about my worst nightmare."

Parker's mind shouldn't have darted to Elliot, but it did. Who he should really call up was Tessa. Tessa would be a perfect wedding date. Well-mannered, dressed appropriately. Polite. *Happy to be there.* Wouldn't worry his sister or his friends. In fact, she was the kind of straight-forward, commitment-ready person Jen would approve of Parker dating.

But Elliot would probably blow him in the church annex.

Fuck, don't think about that now, fuck, Parker, you fucker.

And there was this other thing nagging at him. Parker had always taken care of Jen. He was the mature one. The one who had it together. But now roles were reversing, and dizziness resulted. What would Jen think of Parker chasing after a woman like Elliot? A woman who didn't even want him. Jen would think he was pathetic. That he needed to be taken care of like a child, looked after. And Parker didn't want Jen to take care of him, he couldn't stand the thought of it. That was his job and his job alone, always had been since the day his parents died in that car crash. And he wasn't going to relinquish the role now. Sometimes, you did things for family you wouldn't do otherwise.

Parker cleared his throat. "I'm seeing someone."

Pamela rolled her eyes but Jen hit him on the shoulder with her fist. "Get outta town, since when?"

"Since a few weeks now. She's a flight attendant."

Pamela straightened in her seat. "Oh really? I thought she was a photographer."

Parker cut her a look. "*No*, her name is Tessa and she's a flight attendant and she's very nice and successful and looking for a serious relationship, and Jen, I think you'll like her. Assuming she'll want to take the leap with me and go to Connecticut in six months."

Jen got up, setting down the scotch glass, and walked around the living room. "Parker, where the fuck is your couch?"

"Okay, so the plan is, you can come up some week and meet Benny and then I'll come back down again before the wedding so we can chill and hang out for a while. How does that sound?"

Jen hung on Parker's arm as they walked down the chilly street in Boystown heading to meet Rebecca and Pamela and a slew of Jen's old college friends who still lived in the city.

Parker was tired, and grumpy (as usual) and he kept checking his phone for a message from Elliot. Or a sign. Or something. But he only received radio silence. She wasn't even posting to her Instagram accounts. Something was up.

A pang of guilt hit him as he opened his phone one more time and saw a message from Tessa.

Sent you my schedule for next week, did you get it?

Shit. He hadn't asked Tessa about the wedding despite what he said to Jen. He'd only mentioned Tessa in a moment of self-preservation. And also, he didn't want Pamela spilling the beans to his sister about his little *thing* with a little certain curvy, beautiful photographer. Tessa was a safer bet.

"Park! Park. Jesus, are you even listening to me?" Jen opened the door to the fancy champagne bar.

Parker stepped in. "Yeah, yeah, something about ordering orchids for the table centerpieces..." His voice trailed off as they approached a table of women.

Rebecca and Pamela sat squished in the middle, Rebecca with a totally panicked look on her face. The rest of the women all stood and screamed, embracing Jen one by one.

"Oh my god, Jen, we never thought you'd do it! Lauren and I were just talking the other day and I was like you know what Lauren, I think of all of us girls, Jen is going to be the one to stay single forever. She just isn't the marrying kind. And wow, now look at you! Engaged! And to a fancy Manhattan lawyer, wow! I guess I was wrong. Margot's gonna be the sole single lady in the bunch, oh sorry, Margot sweetie, I don't mean it in a bad way. It's a compliment, like Beyoncé!"

A hand snaked up Parker's biceps, a voice close to his ear. "Wow, Parker, I haven't seen you in, what, five years?"

Parker's eyes closed at the overly familiar voice. "Kate."

"You haven't forgotten me then? Funny since I haven't gotten a phone call in a while."

"You're married."

"Divorced now, actually."

Kate grabbed Parker by the wrist. "Come. Let's get a drink at the bar."

***

Kate languished in front of the bar, her finger tracing the lines in the smooth, shiny wood, her feet turned towards Parker.

"What would you like?" Parker reached into his pocket to get his credit card. He already knew he'd be covering all the drinks for the night, so he might as well open the tab now.

"Prosecco. Or whatever you're having."

Parker ordered two Proseccos. "Well, when in Rome." He lifted the flute to clank glasses with her. The fizz sparked at his nose when he brought it to his lips.

But not half bad.

And Kate wasn't half bad either. Although she'd been one of Parker's whoops-a-daisies in his twenties. Like woops-a-daisy, how did you fall on my big hard cock in the backseat of your Volkswagen Jetta kind of woops-a-daisy. She was pretty, although much like Cameron, years of strict eating schedules, Pilates, and hot yoga twice a day had maybe sucked the softness out of her.

Parker was hard enough on his own. Not that he was picky about women's bodies, he liked them all, but he tended to prefer things a little...*softer*.

Soft like Elliot's thighs.

He breathed in fast and deep, clearing his throat. "What're you up to these days, Kate?"

She smiled at him, gesturing with her glass. "I'll tell you all about it if you take a seat with me over there."

Chapter 11

Parker was drunk as fuck. He didn't normally get wasted, but who knew Prosecco could be so good? He liked the bite of the bubbles, the small amount of pain with every crisp sip. He should've been drinking this all along.

And it was Jen's ad-hoc early engagement party, which was as good a time as any to cut loose.

And it was numbing his feelings about Elliot. Thinking about her made him ache with emptiness. He could lie and tell Jen that Tessa was his new girlfriend, that he had his emotional shit together, relationships in order, a shiny new date for her wedding. But of course it wasn't true.

Jen wouldn't approve of Parker dating Elliot. Uh-uh.

Kate sat on his lap in the corner booth, just the two of them. Her arm wrapped around his neck, heels dangling from his thighs, glass bouncing near his shoulder. Her tits were practically in his mouth so he had to angle his chin upwards to avoid their proximity. His arms were slack at his side so as not to touch her.

"I always thought we should've ended up together. After college," she said.

"I didn't go to college."

"I mean when Jen and I were in college, when you and I first met."

"I'm seeing someone, Kate." Although *who* the person Parker referred to was unclear even to him.

Kate bounced her leg on Parker's leg. "Yeah, I heard. A flight attendant. You could do better."

Kate had always been a snob. Coming from a rich family, driving around in her BMW three series at nineteen. She used to flirt with Parker. She'd stumble around his small apartment after frat parties, beer in her hand and tell him it'd be okay for them to mess around, even if her parents didn't approve of men without college degrees. At the time, it made Parker insecure. But also it reminded him that no matter how successful he ever got, he would never change. Would never become *one of those* kinds of people. People who thought they were better than others.

"I think you have that backwards."

"You're too square. It's why everyone wants to get in your pants. At least all of Jen's friends do. They all wanna see what kind of freak you are under the sheets."

"I don't know if I should be flattered."

"Maybe, maybe not. But I've always felt like you and I had a real connection, Parker. Wow, if I had known you were gonna be such a big shot, I wouldn't have dumped you for Carlos."

Ah yes, Carlos. The pre-med and eventual Mag-Mile plastic surgeon Kate would end up marrying and apparently divorcing. At the time he was dumped, Parker had felt bad, self-esteem at a low. He was taking scraps from Kate anyway. Her drunk after frat party tumbles. But after Carlos, Parker swore he would never again be used like that.

And he would *kind of* learn his lesson over the next fifteen odd years.

Parker patted Kate's shoulder. "I think it's time I return you to the table—"

But Kate squeezed his neck tighter, suddenly her voice reaching a desperate pitch. "Parker *nooooo*...take me back to your place. I don't have the kids tonight. I have so many regrets from when we were young. I masturbate to you sometimes. Remember all the things we used to do with my vibrator togeth—"

"Holy shit, it's the Parked Mechanic."

A flash from a phone camera exploded light over Parker and Kate in the dark corner of the bar. Parker shielded his face from the assault with his hand. At first, he was shocked, but then he realized *he was being recognized from his Instagram.*

"Bro! This is unbelievable." A tall, lanky man with curly hair and neon-yellow Vans approached him. He couldn't have been older than thirty. "I never see Instagram celebs in Chicago."

"What's he talking about?" Kate asked. "You're an Instagram celebrity?"

The guy in the Vans took out his phone and held it up to Kate so she could see Parker's account.

"Didn't think you were the type," she whispered into his ear.

"Listen, man, you gotta let me buy you a drink."

Parker waved the guy off. "Nah, no worries. The Instagram thing is a fluke."

"No, no, not just the Instagram thing. You know my friend. Elliot Sheer?"

Kate fell like a box of bricks from Parker's lap as he abruptly stood.

"Oh, shit, shit, shit. Kate, I'm so sorry."

"Parker, what the hell was that?"

Parker knelt down to help Kate up. She was discombobulated from the fall. He gently picked her up from her elbows, helping her get to her knees, brushing off her pants with her.

"Yeah, dude." The guy chuckled. "That is usually people's reactions when I bring up Elliot though."

Parker leaned over to Kate. "Hey, can you give me a moment? Thanks."

But Kate huffed, rightfully irritated with Parker. "Elliot, huh? Didn't know you were bi. I'm into it though. Hurry up and come back to me soon."

Parker rolled his eyes at the comment. Then he regarded the man in front of him, arms crossed. "So you know Elliot?"

"Yeah, been friends for years now."

"How about I buy you the drink?"

The guy shrugged. "Cool."

Parker sat with John in a quiet booth off the side of the hustle and bustle of the rest of the restaurant goers.

"Cheers." Parker held up his glass and John clinked. He looked a little confused as to why Parker was asking him for a drink.

"I'm not hitting on you. Sorry, you look a little confused."

The guy smiled affably. "Oh, yeah, I know that. You wanna talk about Elliot. It's obvious."

"Is it really so obvious?"

John shrugged. "She has that effect on people."

"Did she say anything else about me?"

John leaned forward, tapping the table a little bit. "Well, I probably shouldn't disclose too much, because you know how Elliot is, but look. I've been friends with her a long time, and we've all lived the party life together, you know what I mean?"

Parker hadn't ever really been a party-guy but he nodded regardless just to encourage John to keep talking.

"Anyway, it's not that we want her to settle down or something. It's just that…well, it's getting to be that time to grow up. To like, chill out a little bit. We worry."

"Tell me more. Be specific."

"Look, I know what you wanna know, so I'm gonna tell you. Elliot talks about you all the time. I told her to, like, grow up and try to have a relationship like the rest of us, but she won't listen. A real stubborn bitch."

Parker bristled at John calling Elliot a bitch but didn't want to scare the guy away with his temper.

But also: Elliot was talking about Parker. Talking about him with her friends.

And her friends were…*worried* about her? So it maybe seemed.

"What about Bruno?" It was petty of Parker to ask. Especially when he had quite literally texted Tessa right after seeing Elliot with Bruno.

"Bruno's not your competition, man. He's been friends with Elliot for years too. He's the bassist in that one bluegrass band, maybe you know them. He's way too hung up on someone else to go after Elliot. None of us would go after Elliot, actually, she's too fucking wild."

This time Parker did feel his temper rising. "That's not a very nice way to talk about your friend."

John nodded. "Love her, but we've been dealing with her antics for a long time now. She needs to chill the fuck out. I thought maybe a guy like you would be good for her. Then again, it looks like you're not so chilled out either."

He must've been referring to the fact that Kate had been drunkenly splayed on Parker's lap when John showed up. And that was warranted.

"I could be serious about Elliot. Real serious. If she'd let me."

"I get what you mean. She's been especially ragey since she had that fight about tearing that one dress. I'm sure she told you."

She had in fact told him. It was, like, the one thing she told him. "Yeah, she did."

"Anyway, she's getting sued now. Over the dress. Apparently, it was worth ten grand and made by a local Chicago designer. It's stressing her out. And she is not one to handle stress well."

Parker's interest perked. "Really? Who's the designer?"

"I dunno that kinda shit, dude. Here. I'll show you." John opened his phone and shoved a picture in Parker's face.

Parker raised his brows. "Oh, well then. I see."

⁝

"Yeah, I don't have another one of those dresses. It's what we call couture. It means one of a kind and it takes forever to make. *By hand.*" Rebecca handed the phone back to Parker.

She was sitting in her studio, measuring tapes around her neck, pin cushion stuck to her wrist, sketch pads spayed about.

"But hypothetically, you could make another one, couldn't you?"

Rebecca pushed her clear, oversized frames up over her short blue hair. "Why would you possibly want me to do this, Parker? What would be your *possible,* reasonable explanation?" Her voice was teasing, but also suspicious.

Parker ran his hand through his hair. "I'll pay you double whatever you charged originally."

Rebecca shook her head. Then closed her eyes with a sigh. As if she couldn't fucking believe what she was saying. "This is for that woman, isn't it?"

"What woman?"

"Don't play fucking coy. I know you're not into that flight attendant. You can lie to Jen but you can't lie to me. I knew this photographer was gonna burrow so deep into the crevices of your brain that you wouldn't be able to think straight. You wanna pay me twenty grand for some couture dress? For what? So you can take her to the ball and find her lost glass slipper and propose to her at midnight?"

"No, so I can stop her from getting sued."

"Oh Jesus Christ, sweet lord above." Rebecca stood up from her work bench, paced around. "You didn't even blink an eye at the words twenty grand. I didn't know it was gonna be this bad. This is bonkers. And what kind of person is she? Getting sued over one of my dresses? Wild."

Parker leaned against the wall, tracking Rebecca as she marched from one end of the workroom to another. "I …I want to take care of her a little bit. Do something nice. Then, maybe then she'll… You know…"

Rebecca stopped in her tracks. "No, Parker, I don't know. What will she do if you spend twenty thousand dollars on a couture dress for her so she doesn't get sued? *What will she do, Parker?*"

He shrugged. "Maybe then she'll settle down. Fuck, Rebecca, don't look at me like that. I can't help the way I feel."

Rebecca shook her head. "I know, babe. I know. God, I hate when you look sad. Reminds me of the face Avery gets before a big cry. Fine, sit down. Fine. I'll make the fucking dress."

Parker smiled at her.

She swung a measuring tape at him. "But no friends and family discount. Pay the going rate."

"There's   nothing   I'd   rather   do   more."

Chapter 12

It had been a long, long blackout period from Elliot. Parker hadn't heard from her in weeks. But, and he double checked his calendar for this, she'd be receiving the couture gown in the mail today.

He hadn't put a note with it, no indication that it would be from him. But he knew. He just knew. That she would know.

That he was watching her. And she was watching him.

Without seeing her for so long, his insides ached, empty and hollow with nothing but cold air blowing through. He and Tessa kept in touch. Or rather, Tessa kept the conversation going with Parker. And because he admired her tenacity (and because he was terrible at saying no), he tried to put his heart into it. But her messages were not the soothing balm they maybe should've been, all things considered. Still, he held a deeply ingrained belief: if he stuck with it, he could grow used to it. He'd grown to love other things, like scotch for instance. And being a mechanic. But his dad always used to say that life was about choices and not feelings. And that's what Parker did, he made *choices*.

Tessa was great, she was beautiful. She was forthright. She was communicative.

And she was available.

She even offered Parker a buddy pass so he could travel with her.

Which he politely declined.

Because today Elliot would get the couture gown replacement. And today he needed to be anywhere but where he was because he was way too antsy. Each little whistle of communication between them was another point on the score board. And he didn't know who would win the round.

So now he was at an airport bar. Not the business class lounge because the lounge by his terminal was claustrophobic, the drop ceiling a dingy yellow, the rooms eerily quiet.

Today he'd rather be out in the great wide open. The noises humming around him. The restaurant wasn't bad either. As far as airport restaurants were concerned.

He was seated at the bar by himself, nobody there yet, too early for the lunch time rush.

And Tessa was supposed to meet him in less than an hour. She wouldn't be around too long, so they'd agreed on a quick airport date. Parker was all for the idea as it meant there would be no pressure to fool around since there were hardly any private areas in airports. He glanced at his phone. Fifty five minutes to go. He sipped his tea.

He was going to ask Tessa to his sister's wedding today. It was the responsible thing to do.

Then why did you send that dress to Elliot?

He'd gotten Elliot's PO box from John. He'd had to promise him a tag on his Instagram. John was an aspiring SoundCloud rapper looking for his big social media break, and Parker was up to fifty thousand followers on Instagram by now.

Sometimes, he liked to lie to himself. He was merely being a good friend by sending the dress. But coupled with that fake-friendship, he wanted to give Elliot a reason to seek him out. He needed her to. He needed to give her a reason to find him. *Come find me.*

But all of that was very secret and something he wasn't even really admitting to himself, hiding his deep, dark Easter eggs far away in the back of his mind.

And there forever did he wish for them to remain.

Of course, he didn't want Elliot to find him now, *not today*. Today wasn't the right day because today was a day for Tessa.

Tessa, who deserved his undivided, undiluted attention. For once.

"Would you like anything else sir?" the woman behind the counter asked him. "Scone? Croissant?"

Parker surveyed the row of pastries under the glass next to the bar. He could surprise Tessa.

"Can I have one of everything?"

The woman's eyebrows went up. "Um, yeah sure."

"Can you stack it all up on a plate, like kind of artfully?"

"Uhhh, I sure can. This all for you?"

"I'm meeting someone."

The woman smiled. "Of course you are." Then she gave him the once-over.

Once the plate was in front of him, he realized he'd have to sit and stare at it for a while. He wasn't one for eating carbs, and actually he didn't even know what Tessa ate. He didn't know anything about her food preferences at all. He should've asked. When had he become impulsive?

Slowly, he reached out for a small chocolate croissant on the edge of the plate. Maybe just a bite then?

"How did you *know* I was starving?"

A large, expensive, *heavy* handbag plunked against the bar and a hand snatched the chocolate croissant from Parker.

He grimaced, his eyes closing briefly. Two conflicting feelings fluttered through his brain:

Oh shit and utter unadulterated joy.

How did she find him here? Could it really be a coincidence?

"I checked your schedule on your phone." Elliot spoke through a mouthful of croissant.

"My phone has a passcode."

"You unlocked it in front of me. Also, it's 1-2-3-4."

"Remember that conversation we had about boundaries."

Elliot tilted her head. "You're not happy to see me, Mr. Serious?"

Despite his better judgment he was happy. And he did see her. Oh, he saw all of her. She wore a white crew neck T-shirt, cropped to show some of her midriff and the bottom elastic of a grey sports bra. Her jeans were baggy again, ripped as well. And she had on black combat boots. Her hair was in two buns on either side of her head. No makeup, that he could tell anyway.

She offered him the rest of the croissant, but he held his hand up, declining the offer. "Suit yourself," she said, cramming the rest of it in her mouth.

She did *not* eat like a lady. Jen would laugh at her. Rebecca and Pamela would stare at her like she was some kind of science exhibit.

"So you hunted me down."

She smiled, swallowing. "That's right, but I have my reasons."

She got the dress. He knew it.

"You got a special package in the mail?"

She grabbed another pastry from his plate, raising a brow. "Huh? I haven't been home to check the mail in weeks. Why, did you send me something? Weed gummies?"

"Why would I send you weed gummies?"

"Iono. Have you ever fucked while high? It's so good."

He hadn't. He'd stopped ingesting marijuana years ago after a particularly bad experience with an edible. They made him irrevocably anxious. But the image of Elliot on his lap, lazily riding his dick in some kind of chair in some kind of hotel room nearby while they were both high out of their minds filled his brain. He'd take an edible if it meant he could do that. *Parker, no!*

"What is it you want?"

She reached up and ran her fingers through the front of his hair. "You had a weird…hair thing." He ran his hand through his hair after in an attempt to put it back as it was. He didn't want to admit that it felt good. "Anyway, I want to have a meal with you."

His eyes narrowed. This might have been a normal thing for a normal person to say but she was not one of those. "Like dinner?"

Elliot tossed her head back and forth. "Or, you know, like lunch? Irrelevant really. Time zone changes and all that."

He looked at his phone, nearly eleven a.m. "So…like now?" Fuck. This really wasn't good timing.

"No time like the present. But later is better actually. I don't like to rush. It's rude."

"I thought you didn't want to get to know me."

She nibbled on her lip. "I heard you ran into John."

He wasn't sure if he should be embarrassed or what. Had John spilled the beans about the dress?

"He showed me the picture."

"What picture?"

"Of you and another woman. Sitting in your lap. You really get around for such a prude. So many women go absolutely gaga for you, it's annoying, actually. Especially because you don't seem to realize it at all. But, I get it. Some people have a certain something. *Je ne sais quoi, et cetera.* You're one of those people. You know who else is one of those people?"

Parker thought for a beat. "Ina Garten?"

Elliot threw her head back. "Ha! I was going to say *me*. I have that certain something, too. Because it takes one to know one. Anyway, I guess that's why you always have some random blonde falling all over you."

Ahhh. Jealousy seemed to be a very real thing for Elliot. Sometimes, at least. It was the one thing that seemed to ground her. As far as everything else was concerned, she was as floaty as a helium balloon. A bright red heart balloon, drifting into the sun, pierced with an arrow.

Perhaps jealousy was the only thing that worked on her. Now there was an interesting, if not old-fashioned idea.

Parker wasn't one for jealousy. Not really. Sure he felt jealous when Elliot was holding that guy Bruno's hand, but compared to most people he was rather secure in his relationships.

Watching Elliot hang all over other people on Instagram. Well, of course that sparked some pretty intense jealousy.

He also jerked off to it. So, apparently that was a thing he was into.

"Kate." He cleared his throat. "That's Kate. An old friend." *Friend* was a generous description of Kate.

Elliot grabbed another pastry, this time one with powdered sugar sprinkled on the top. It puffed all over her mouth and cheeks, speckling her jeans with white powder as well.

Parker let out a gentle laugh, his thumb reaching for her face to wipe away the sugar from the corner of her mouth.

Suddenly, everything went slower as he realized what he was doing. Drawing his thumb away, he grabbed a napkin and wiped the dust from his hand. The touch grounded *him*. Reminding him that he wanted her. And that he'd been denying them both.

Elliot sighed. "So, do you agree?"

"Agree to what?"

"A lunch? A dinner? Etcetera, etcetera."

"You came all the way to this airport to schedule a meal with me?"

"Well…" Elliot looked sheepish. "I have a shoot in Tokyo, too. See it works out easy-peasy. And I've always wanted to go to Tokyo in the fall. So, why not?"

Parker rubbed his stubble thoughtfully. His gaze absently traveling to the hem of her cropped shirt. He'd never seen her tits. Except for the Instagram videos, which she hadn't been sending anymore.

Fuuuuuck.

"Fine, lunch. In Tokyo. Strike that. Make it dinner. I like ramen."

She smiled, but then her smile fell when out of nowhere two arms wrapped around Parker's chest.

"Oh my god, it's so good to see you!"

Reflexively, Parker's hand found Tessa's, now in the middle of his chest, her breath against his ear.

"You're early," he said.

She kissed him on the cheek. "It's great, right? Now we can get to the fun stuff ahead of schedule. Eeeehh! Did you get these for me? How did you know I love cheese Danish?"

Parker's gaze wandered over to Elliot. She had a curious expression on her face. Like she didn't quite understand the scene in front of her.

Tessa unwound her grip from Parker's shoulders but laced their arms together. "Oh, I'm sorry, did I interrupt something?" Her gaze darted from Elliot to Parker. Her smile didn't even flinch. But it might have hardened.

Elliot shook her head. "Nope. I was just leaving."

Tessa sat on the stool next to Parker. "Great, happy to hear that, *Elliot*."

Elliot's eyes narrowed but she didn't say another word, collected her bag, hoisting it to her shoulder. She grabbed a pastry and shuffled away.

"Did she take something from your plate?" Tessa asked, eyeing the ever dwindling stack of carbs.

Parker pushed the plate towards her. He spit out the truth before he could think to lie. "I have to be honest with you. I might meet her for a dinner."

Tessa looked at him hard but not surprised. "In what capacity?"

"I honestly don't know. I wouldn't call it a date."

Tessa shrugged. "Good, I like to know my competition. I'm going on dates, too, so keep that in your head when you're out and about. She doesn't scare me one bit." She smiled again and leaned up, kissing him on the cheek. "But I *love* these pastries."

Hmm. Something told Parker maybe she was a little concerned. But she was hiding it well. Very well.

Of course their relationship hadn't progressed at all in a physical sense. And they certainly hadn't had any talks on exclusivity, it was much too early in the game for that. And while, Parker knew that Tessa had needs too, he was less *compelled* to take care of them as he had with Elliot.

Maybe the dating process would offer him better clarity. The more he got to know Tessa in person, the more he'd like her...right? That's what he kept telling himself.

The more he'd want to strip down and slip under the blankets with her, her head beneath his nose, the scent of jasmine and lemongrass wafting in the air...

Tessa took a delicate bite from a cheese Danish, then wrinkled her nose. "Yummy."

And a blip of something strange roiled in Parker's belly.

Choices. Not feelings. Choices. Not feelings.

He admired how straight forward she was. How she was unabashedly willing to go after what she wanted. And furthermore, how what she wanted was the same as what he wanted.

As they were preparing to leave, he held out his hand to help her from the tall stool. Her fingernails were painted mauve.

Then, a familiar ring from his phone.

He didn't answer it, not yet. Because he knew who it was from. And he had other plans for Elliot now. Strategic ones.

But after Tessa and Parker parted ways. After they'd had an amiable lunch together. After he'd given Tessa a chaste kiss on the cheek and left for Tokyo. After all that, he picked up his phone and opened the appropriate app.

And there was, as he knew it would be, his message from Elliot.

"Make it dinner. Ichiran, Shibuya, six p.m. See you then, Mr.   Serious."

Chapter 13

"Spicy Tonkotsu Ramen is my absolute fave." Elliot slurped from her chirirenge, the creamy but spicy broth wafting from its shallow bowl. "Here, don't forget the egg."

Parker was crammed into the small wooden booth at the casual ramen spot. It would be the last place he'd visit before leaving Tokyo. A short trip, one that might guarantee jet lag, but then he had a whole two weeks off after that. He planned to take Avery to the art museum one of those days.

"Avery won't understand any of this stuff," Pamela had admonished.

"I disagree. I love the idea of our baby getting an art education early on." Rebecca had smiled at him.

But in the meantime, he had this time with Elliot.

He had stayed in a small apartment owned by his client in Shibuya so the ramen place was within walking distance. And while Parker, to the naked eye, was clearly an American fish out of water in Tokyo, in an emotional sense he enjoyed it. Even though the city was bustling like Chicago, it was organized and polite. Public transport running beautifully on time. People minding their own business.

"I like that we're on a date, too." Parker smiled at Elliot.

In response, she rolled her eyes. "So, tell me about Tessa." Elliot sneaked a peak up at him.

"You know everything there is to know."

"Do you like her more than me?"

Parker slurped up the spicy noodles. Was it the noodles, or was his whole body heating up. He set down his chopsticks. "No."

Elliot stuttered-slurped for only a second. "How is she in bed? Is she a real try hard? One of those women who wants you to pee on her, slap her around like a bag of old shoes?"

Parker chuckled despite himself. "What is *wrong* with you? You say the wildest shit."

Elliot sipped from her small glass of beer. "Yeah, well. When you're told your whole life to shut up, it feels good to talk out of turn."

Parker's brow furrowed at that. "Who's told you to shut up?"

"It doesn't matter. Tell me more. I want to know the gory details."

"You don't have to shut up around me."

"Ugh," she scoffed. "Shut up. Now, does she always match her bra and panties? She seems the kind, for sure. I'd bet money on it."

Parker picked up another clump of noodles with his chopsticks. "I wouldn't know."

"Oh, commando? Really? Hadn't pegged her for a commando girl. Too wholesome."

"No, I haven't seen her underwear." *Slurp.* He coughed at the spice. "Not yet."

Elliot's palms slapped the table. "*What?*" she hissed.

Parker glanced up at her. "Are you surprised? Have I given you any other kind of impression of myself?"

"So, it's not only me then who can't get the *D*. And here I thought I was special. Or not special."

"Elliot. What are you talking about? I went down on you in a hotel room just a few weeks ago."

"Does Tessa know about that?" A wild look flashed through her eyes.

"She's not intimidated by you, Elliot. And we're not exclusive." Then Parker paused. "Don't even think about telling her."

She blew out a puff of air. "Please, telling her. One: like I even could find her information—"

"I know you, and I know you could."

She shrugged. "Fine, you're right. I could easily find her. That's modern technology. Nothing difficult there. I'm just not *interested* in finding her, so sorry. If you thought I was jealous, you were actually wrong. I came here to give my blessing to you on your very holy and sanctioned union. Can't wait to see the babies."

Parker reached over, scooped up a clump of Elliot's noodles, brought them to his mouth. Even though Elliot wouldn't disclose anything about herself, not for the most part, he was beginning to understand her patterns. Beginning to understand when she meant what she said and when she didn't. This time, she definitely didn't. She was very much jealous of Parker's relationship with Tessa.

And that got Parker so *fucking* hot. And he had to get a handle on that, *today*. Now, he would enact his new plan.

"Don't eat my noodles. Get your own."

"I want you, Elliot."

Elliot looked up from her bowl, noodles hanging from her mouth midslurp. Then slowly, she sucked them in. "Huh?"

"I want you."

"You have a strange way of showing it."

"But the truth is I can't do this with you anymore."

Elliot's eyes looked mildly panicked, which Parker relished. "Can't do what?"

Parker indicated the space in between them. "We can't have this back and forth. Not with all this…" He considered his words carefully. "Tension."

"There's no tension, I'm as loose as a used condom."

He shook his head. "That's disgusting. Why did you want to have this dinner with me?"

Elliot set down her chopsticks and crossed her arms over her chest. She reminded him of a pouty child sometimes. "I was bored."

A lie. "What's the real reason?"

"Why did you *say yes* if you can't—" she held up her fingers in air quotes "—*do this with me anymore.*"

"Because I wanted to make you an offer."

Elliot raised a perfectly sculpted dark brow. "Oh?"

Parker rubbed the stubble on his chin. "After talking with your friend John, I realized something."

"What?"

"I realized that there are more options to this tension between us than the obvious."

She scrunched her face. "Which is?"

Parker sat back in his chair, also crossing his arms over his chest. "Let me lay it out for you. Tessa is the right choice for me. I might like you more, I might want you more, but you've made it clear that this isn't going to work out the way I want it to. And I'm not willing to throw good after bad forever. So, formally, I give up. I'm laying down my hand. But, still, because I'm a good person, I'm going to offer something valuable in return."

"Jesus, get to the point already. Since when do you come locked and loaded with a speech?"

"I'm going to offer you friendship."

Elliot's eyes briefly closed and the popped back open, that beautiful sea blue. "Ha! That's funny."

Parker picked up his chopsticks and resumed slurping up noodles. "Why's that funny?"

She leaned forward, her elbows on the table. "Because I was going to offer you the same thing."

He scrunched his brow. "Is that right?"

"Yeah. It is. I decided, you know what? Friendship is cheap. It's a lot cheaper than love. And I don't need you or any other guy making demands on my time and emotions. And if you aren't going to fuck me then, what the hell. Why not be friends? I have lots of friends."

"So we agree, then. Friendship. No more no less."

Elliot shrugged. "That's right, Mr. Serious. Friendship. More or less."

Elliot and Parker walked side by side on the quiet street. Parker strolled with his hands shoved in his pocket, a mild breeze blowing past them, a respectable space in between.

Parker pointed to the intersecting street. "I'm up this way."

"Really? Me too."

Parker raised his brows. "What're the odds?"

Elliot elbowed his side as they turned the corner together. "Yeah, what indeed. Hey, maybe since we're friends now you wanna come up and get that drink with me?"

"I already had a drink with you. On the plane." Parker cleared his throat at the memory of the exact details of that particular plane ride.

Elliot rolled her eyes. "So? It's an expression *having a drink.*"

"An expression for what?"

"For hanging out. Relax, Parker. I'm not going to put the moves on you. Friendly moves only."

Parker nodded thoughtfully. So far, his friendship plan was working. Elliot seemed much more amenable than previously. She actually seemed open to the idea of hanging out. He shouldn't let opportunities go to waste.

But opportunities for what? Could he really play these games? Try to win over Elliot.

Or was he simply acting normal by trying to get to know her and *she* was the weird one?

Next to him, Elliot twirled the ends of her hair, her eyes distant, like she was thinking about something too. She wouldn't tell him what, that was for sure. But the comment she made earlier, about speaking out of turn because she was always being told to shut up... There was something there. A nugget of understanding. He made up his mind. His mission was to find out more about her.

"Shochu?" he asked. "We can pick some up at the convenience store on the corner."

Elliot's eyes lit up. "Yes! Shochu. And we can also get some snacks."

"Didn't we just eat?"

Elliot pshed at him. "What's your point? Don't you ever eat for the pure joy of it?" Then she raised a brow. "Actually from the looks of you, I bet that's an entirely novel idea."

She was right. He didn't. But maybe...

He smiled. "For my friend, I can eat some snacks."

"Now, that's the kind of attitude I can appreciate in life, Mr. Serious."

Parker poured out another small shot glass of Shochu for Elliot at the small marble table on the balcony at Parker's rental. The apartment by American standards was luxurious but still relatively small and sparse, with modern and sleek stone floors and white and square walls and minimal decorations. The multitude of green plants in white pots gave the space a tranquil vibe though. Parker wondered who watered them since no one regularly lived there.

But it was prime real estate in Tokyo, and his client likely paid a pretty, pretty penny for it.

"You look too big to be a racecar driver. Aren't they all kind of like horse jockeys? Small guys." Elliot sipped at the shot. Her cheeks and neck were flushed a bright pink from the drinking, but her voice and words were sharp and lively. Her chambray button-up was one button away from being indecent.

Parker rested his ankle over his knee. "Well, I was smaller at eighteen. I grew four inches the year after I quit.

"That's why you quit? You got too tall?"

"I was already on the tall side for the job. But no. I quit because of the accident."

"Oh shit. You were injured? Like in those crashes you see on TV?"

This was where Parker always had a hard time explaining about his racecar driver past. He wasn't injured physically when he spun out on the track, his engine blowing up behind him in flames. He hadn't suffered anything more than whiplash. But mentally...something never quite healed.

He still didn't own a car to this day.

He shook his head. "My twin sister, her name is Jen."

"Twin? Okay, ya weirdo." Elliot snickered.

Parker smiled, then sipped from his drink. "She had just started college, and I was paying for it. She always had a better head for stuff like that than me. And since our parents died, it's only been the two of us. After the accident, I realized life was delicate. That nothing was guaranteed. And it didn't feel worth the risk to me anymore. So...I quit."

Elliot's gaze shifted back and forth, but then she snapped her fingers and pointed at him. "And that's how you became a mechanic. The racing world exposed you to the profession!"

Parker tipped his chin at her. "Great work, Encyclopedia Brown."

Elliot wiggled self-importantly on the small steel chair. "Okay, nerd. But, like, I'm kind of impressed that you're trying to roast me. My turn."

"Truth or dare."

"You know I'm gonna guess dare, Parker. You're all truths. I'm all dare. Très predictable."

"Then why don't you change it up?"

She straightened in her chair. "Why don't you?" But then she slumped down. "Because you're going to ask me something boring like *what kind of childhood did you have?* And it's going to ruin my whole night."

"Maybe I'll surprise you. Didn't you once tell me that I'm exactly what you expected and yet not at all?"

She smirked. "I was trying to be mysterious."

"Fine, and now you're being predictable."

"That's my prerogative. I choose dare."

"Now that we're friends, I dare you to give me your phone number."

She rolled her eyes. "Haven't we already played this game before? Why do you need my number when you can message me on social media? Hey, remember when you scammed me and gave me the Rentmires Carpet phone number instead of yours? Ha-ha. Good times. Honestly, props for that, it was a good joke. I like that about you."

151

"Are you shirking the dare?"

She sighed. "Fine. Give me your phone."

Parker dug his phone out of his pocket and handed it to Elliot.

"Tessa says she wants to see your big hard cock."

Parker tilted his head. "Funny."

But Elliot held the phone out to his face. "No, really. Hmm, she might be super drunk because there are some unfortunate typos. Like here she refers to you as exciting, but I think the word she was looking for was *uptight*."

Shit. Parker had been keeping things chaste with Tessa, but maybe Tessa was pushing the boundaries…

Elliot scrolled quickly. "Wow, I really wasn't the only one you denied. I don't even know how I feel about that. Guess I'm glad we decided to be friends."

Parker threw his hands in the air. "I went down on you in a hotel room! Does that mean nothing to you!"

Elliot tapped away, then handed the phone back to him. "Go on, give it a whirl. Try out my number."

"No need. I trust you."

"Really?"

He nodded.

"Risky move but well played, Mr. Serious. I didn't see that coming and now I'm going to give you points for a tactical surprise. But you can't get mad at me when you text this number and my weed dealer texts you back. She's hot, so you'll probably start dating her too actually. And not fucking her. Oh, it's my turn, isn't it? Truth or dare, my good friend."

Parker liked the way Elliot could talk herself into a circle and back. He liked how she was both saddled with wild trouble but also free from regret. He wished he could be the same. But Parker had always been more one to follow the straight line of the track.

Actually, a curved line was a more accurate description.

Elliot had curved lines too.

"Hello, Parker?" Elliot waved a hand over his eyes. "Truth or dare?"

Parker tapped his fingers onto the marble table. "Right. I dare you to…tell me about your childhood."

She chucked her shrimp rice cracker at him. "Boo!" she jeered. "Whatever, this game grows stale. You could've gotten me to do all kinds of lascivious things and you chose not to."

"I thought we were friends. Wholesome acts only."

"Even friends can flash their tits now and again. In fact, that was part of pledging in my sorority. I did it with my best friends from college, August and Olivia. You wouldn't think they'd be the sorority types but—" Elliot paused mid-chew when she said it. Parker did too. Then she swallowed, and spoke slowly. "Don't, Parker, don't you dare—"

But Parker wasn't going to let this one slide. "A sorority!" He laughed this time. Not a chuckle, but a real laugh. "*You,*

you Elliot Sheer, photographer to Instagram influencers and rich people, who doesn't live in an apartment, with the filthiest mouth of anyone I've ever met...*you*...were in a sorority?" He shook his head.

Elliot dramatically collapsed onto her chair, legs and arms spread, head fallen to the side, corpse-ish. "People change. A decade's a long time. C'mon! Stop laughing! It's not that funny. I only did it because my friends were doing it. I'm a dropout! I've got street cred."

Parker's shoulder shook. "Nah, you don't."

"Well—well, I bet Tessa was in a sorority, and you wouldn't make fun of her for that!" Elliot sputtered.

Parker shrugged. "Probably. And no, I wouldn't. Because she's her and you're you. You talk a big game but...Delta Delta Delta probably had you in matching sweatshirts, marching around campus."

"I only wear matching sweatshirts with Olivia and August on Christmas." She rolled her eyes. "What would you know about it anyway? Did you even go to college?"

"No, but I slept with my share of sorority girls back in the day."

Elliot leaned forward, putting her elbows on the table. "Ooooh, tell me more. Tell me about all the sorority girls you put your dick in. Wow, so cool, so exciting. You're so great."

"You wish, *friend*."

Her eyes glimmered. "Dare me to flash you. Do it, dare me to. I would've in my sorority days."

But Parker shook his head. She loved to bait him. "Nice try."

She fell back in her chair. "Ugh, fine. But it would only be fair since you flashed me on the airplane. And seems like in friendships, reciprocity is a pretty important factor."

Parker kind of admired her tenacity. Ridiculous tenacity but tenacity all the same. And plus, he was getting a little tipsy now. Not drunk, but he'd had enough to drink to lube up his rusty joints. Shake off the uptight grumps. And Elliot, as usual, was riling his dick up anyway.

And maybe she had a decent point. Friendship was about give and take after all.

Wait, he didn't actually want to be her friend. This was an elaborate ruse to get her to fall in love with him.

But he did want to see her boobs.

Suddenly he couldn't remember why he was so adamant about all his rules in the first place. He knocked back another small drink, the glass hitting with a hollow clank. "Fine. I dare you to flash me."

Elliot stopped mid-chew, her eyebrows up. "I truly can't figure you the fuck out."

He lifted a shoulder. "Besides, I don't think you'll do it anyway." This was an obvious lie.

But Elliot flipped her hair over her shoulder. "You're right. I changed my mind. I don't want to show you now. You don't even deserve to see."

Now she was really full of shit. But he'd play her game.

"Are you forfeiting truth or dare?"

Her gaze flickered. "I'm not forfeiting, I simply know some bullshit when I hear it. And you're full of it."

"Well, now I'm offended."

"You wanna know *why* you're full of bullshit?"

"Not really."

"It's because you think you have all the cards in the world to play. You think you can say and do whatever you want and I'll fall for it. Like goading me to take my shirt off."

"You want to take your shirt off."

"I know that! But I want you to want me to take my shirt off. For the right reasons."

Parker rubbed his brow. "I'm getting confused. Can we call a truce for now? You can keep your shirt on, and we can preserve our friendship."

Elliot pulled out her phone, lips pouting. "No, I'm leaving."

"Oh come on, Elliot. Don't go. I don't even know why you're angry!"

She stood collecting her handbag. "I just...I just don't like the vibes here, Mr. Serious. And I gotta jet. Besides, you should really answer your text messages. Tessa sent you like

156

fifty. Why she's waiting around for you is beyond me. Probably your annoying *je ne sais quoi.*"

"You don't know anything about the situation."

But Elliot was already turning away from him, walking briskly down the hallway, and he was following her. She swiveled, stopping at the doorway, Parker nearly bumping their noses together. "Oh yes. I do. You're basically using her. I know you're not as righteous as you pretend."

They were so close now. Like they were reliving the scene at his hotel room in that blizzard.

Slowly, he raised his arm to lean against the frame, tilting his chin so that he had her half caged in, his body towering over hers.

It wasn't meant to be intimidating. But he wanted to show her that he could match her in strength. That she couldn't drop bombs in his heart and walk out of his life as if nothing happened. That each action in life had an equal and opposite reaction.

When he spoke his voice was hoarse and warning. "Righteous? Righteous is the last thing I am, Elliot, if you had even any fucking modicum of an idea. And I'm going to say something to you as a friend, and I want you to listen very closely, do you understand?"

The smirk on her face told him she was a little intrigued. Instead of backing away from him, she let her fingertip trace the vein from his forearm to his biceps. Then she let it drop.

"What do you want to say to me, *friend?*" Her voice was a mere whisper.

"Don't ever get it twisted. I meant what I said at the restaurant. I want you. I want you very badly. I want you bent over the couch. I want you riding in my lap. I want you down on your knees. Like you deserve to be. Like you described to me in that filthy way of yours on the airplane." He paused, to take a breath, because he was getting heated. Worked up. "But I need more than that. So much more. And if you're not willing to give it, then you need to keep your tits covered in my presence. Keep your skirt from hiking past your thighs. Keep your mouth away from mine. You understand?"

She glanced up from beneath her jet-black fringe of lashes, and licked her lips. "That wasn't a very friendly speech, Mr. Serious."

He shook his head slowly. "No. It wasn't."

Her fingers trailed up from her waist to the top button of her shirt.

"After what I just said to you, you better not be unbuttoning your shirt."

She flicked one open. "You mean like this? How about like this?" Another one popped, and the beginning of her black bra peeked out.

His fingertips threatened to rip the crown molding off the door frame, his nostrils flared.

His gaze traveled to the swell and hollow of her tits, pushed up and out by the cups of her bra. He was always falling for temptation.

He squeezed his eyes closed and let his hand travel behind her lower back. Her breath hitched in his ear.

And then his fingertips caught the knob of the front door, twisting it open, the quiet snick wafting cool air in behind them. Grounding him back into reality. The door slowly winged out to the hallway.

"I'll get you back for this," she hissed.

"I don't doubt that you will."

Then, she whipped around and bounded out, leaving his cage empty. "Tell Tessa I say hi," she called into the air.

Chapter 14

"My phone's at one percent battery, but here's a clue. I'm in a city with baby palm trees and I'm staying in a weird raspberry. Come and find me, Mr. Serious. That's a friendly dare."

The line went dead before he could even respond, but it had been Elliot's voice on the other end of that line.

And although it was the first time she'd ever called him, he'd found out that the number she'd given him had indeed been the number to her drug dealer. But fate would have it that Elliot was getting drinks with her drug dealer at the very moment Parker called.

"This is Allie, not Elliot. But if you want Elliot, she's sitting right next to me. Hang on a second, what did you say your name was again? Adam Driver? Oh, Parker. Hang on, Parker. I'm gonna hand the phone over."

"I made this challenge too easy." Elliot's voice came through the phone.

"What do you mean easy?"

"I'm always with my drug dealer. She's one of my best friend. So, odds were good you'd get a hold of me anyway."

But ever since then, Parker had been receiving the occasional text from Elliot. Along with a barrage of texts from Tessa.

It wasn't that he didn't like an attentive woman, he definitely did. It's just that Elliot was so much funnier and, well, *meaner* than Tessa. And Parker kinda, maybe, sorta had a thing for that.

Although Jen was certainly unaware of Parker's feelings when she asked him when she'd get to meet Tessa, his date for her wedding. *Oops.*

So, moments like the moment he was in now, sitting at a barstool in his living room, looking at wedding invitations with Jen, secret moments like this with Elliot excited him. He never knew what kind of shit Elliot might throw at him.

It kept life interesting.

Also, she might've thought she was sharp, but Parker knew exactly where Elliot was.

"The serif font makes most sense for the kind of fancy wedding we're going to have. Don't you agree? That's what the wedding planner says." Jen looked up at him from the table of splayed out wedding propaganda.

Parker checked his phone one more time. "I gotta go."

Jen wrinkled her nose. "Uh, what?"

"Yep, sorry. Gotta leave."

"For where? The grocery store? You don't have anything in your fridge but a dying bag of baby carrots, six frozen lasagnas, and a case of Old Style."

"Heading out to Charleston. Order whatever you want on my card—"

"I don't need your money anymore, Parker. Stop trying to take care of me."

He nodded. "Right. Well, just in case." He snapped a card onto the table. "Anyway, I'll see you tomorrow. Or maybe tonight."

He headed towards the door when Jen called out, "Hey wait! You're not even going to pack a bag?"

"Nope!"

Parker sat in the lobby of the Blackberry, or as Elliot referred to it "the weird raspberry she was staying in" as he watched the wind rustle the stiff palms of the palmetto trees outside. The palmetto trees were the baby palm trees she was talking about.

If she wanted to stump him, she really should've tried harder.

He'd been able to catch a direct flight out from Midway. He wondered if Elliot had looked up the flight departures because one left exactly sixty minutes after she called. Parker had paid a fortune to get on it.

And he flew coach too, which was a thing he *never* did. His legs cramped, the man next to him tried desperately to start a conversation that Parker refused to engage in.

He was singularly focused on the fact that he was going to see Elliot and *soon*. And on turf he was very familiar with. It might not be hometown advantage but it was close enough. He'd been to Charleston enough times because of Cameron.

Parker stretched out his legs in the red leather couch nestled beneath an abstract map of Charleston. He had on his work boots and he hadn't even realized it. They made him look a little rougher than he actually was. A few people glanced at him with judgmental eyes as they strolled into the marble floored lobby.

None of his texts to Elliot were going through, and he imagined it was because her phone was off for either battery-related or purposeful reasons. But that was fine. Parker had time. He had all the time in the world. Sure, he had canceled his client for tomorrow to make sure he would actually see Elliot once he got to Charleston.

But clients let him do as he pleased.

Elliot, not so much. And he preferred it that way.

"Glad to see you made it safely."

Parker's gaze slid up the tanned and toned legs of Cameron Joy, who was standing in front of him, one hand cocked on a jutted hip. She was in all white, tight white denim, white tank, white long cardigan. Nude heels.

"What are you doing here?"

Cameron tilted her head. "I live here, silly. And I came to see you. You could've texted and told me you were coming."

"But how did you even know I was going to be here?"

Cameron sat down next to him on the red sofa. "Oh sweetie. On your Instagram story where you say, and I quote: *Here I am on the next flight to Charleston. I'll be staying at the Blackberry tonight. Bye!*" She waved her hand to illustrate the bye. "You shouldn't post your location like this, you're going to get stalkers."

"Nobody cares about where I am."

"Uh, seventy-three thousand Instagram followers would disagree with that statement. Anyway, now that you're here. Dinner? We could start up where we left off last time...I forgive you for that, by the way."

Parker shifted uncomfortably in his seat. Cameron absently fingered the sleeve of his T-shirt. "Why don't you dress nicer?"

"I live in Chicago. It's different from around here."

Cameron shrugged. "Well, I made us reservations at the usual place."

"Wait, what? No way, Cam. I'm not going with you."

Cameron's eyes went wide for a moment. "What? You can't be serious. And with what you did to me last time?"

Parker shook his head. "I'm sorry. I'm meeting someone."

Now her eyes narrowed, her voice escaping through gritted teeth. "Did you meet someone else?"

During their time together, Parker hadn't dated anyone besides Cameron. Even when he knew she was cheating on him. Even though he knew she was married. He couldn't bring himself to do it.

He was different now, anyway. And not exactly committed to any one person. Although he was trying to be.

"I don't want to get into a fight with you right now." He checked the time on his phone. Where the hell was Elliot?

"Parker, I don't like the way you're acting. You've changed."

"Change is good. Maybe you should consider it."

"For one thing, I don't remember you being such an asshole. In fact, you were the sweetest guy. What has happened to you?"

In mild frustration, Parker ran his hand through his hair. "I've changed my priorities, Cam. You used to be my first priority. I would've done anything for you. But I was never your first priority. Still wouldn't be now. So, I've fucking changed. You're not on my list of priorities anymore, and I shouldn't be on yours either."

"You're overreacting. Remember all the good times we had together? The good times we could still have? You used to fly to Charleston every weekend to see me. I could hardly believe it. I don't know any other man who could be so devoted, and now you'd have me believe you'd throw it all away."

"I'm not throwing anything away. You threw it—us— away. I'm moving on. Please let me."

Cameron crossed her arms over her chest, shaking her head. "Whoever she is, you've got it bad."

"This is none of your business."

"But you'll come back. You always do."

"Sorry, but not this time, Cam."

"I made our usual reservation. You love Stakes. It's your favorite."

"I don't even like that place. I went because you wanted me to."

"You were lying to me?"

"Hey! Catch!" With quick reflexes Parker caught a plastic bag filled with something unidentifiable. "Whoa!"

Without even a second glance at Cameron, Elliot sat down on the other side of Parker. She was wearing an oversized deep red V-neck sweater with bright red hearts printed all over it. The hearts were all impaled with steak knives.

"You figured out my riddle! I knew you would, you big old nerd. You're kinda smart like that."

Parker was so happy to see her, he smiled. "It wasn't a very hard puzzle."

"Um, excuse me." A voice snapped through his fog of happiness.

Oh, shit.

Parker inhaled, cleared his throat. "Cameron, this is *my friend* Elliot."

Elliot tossed her shining black hair over her shoulder. "Friend? You weren't calling me a friend when you had your tongue on my clit back in Pennsylvania."

Cameron gasped. "Parker, is she being serious? Is this …the woman? She's not even…" Cameron's voice trailed off and Parker wasn't sure exactly what Cameron meant to say, but he knew it wouldn't have been anything complimentary to Elliot.

"Well, I don't know if I'm *the* woman. But I'm certainly *a* woman. Who are you? An evil hag?"

Cameron gasped again. "I know the owner of his hotel. I can get you kicked out of here, if you can even afford to stay in a place like this."

Elliot crossed her legs. "Go ahead. Appeals to power in a corrupt society are for people without any inner power of their own. Besides being evil and a hag are actually two things I aspire to. We should all be so lucky."

Okay. That was a strangely fine-tuned philosophical thought from Elliot, but Parker had to agree.

"Aren't you going to do something about this?"

Parker had been staring at Elliot. His gaze shifted. "Oh, right. Cameron, you're still here."

Cameron adjusted the strap on her Louis Vuitton and straightened the hem of her bright white tank top. She shook her head. "You'll regret this. Big time."

"Leaving so soon?" Elliot said. "I thought you were going to hang out with us. Don't be shy, I'm pansexual." She turned to look at Parker. "See, there's something you can write down in your record books about me. Pansexual."

Parker nodded. "Got it."

Cameron pivoted on her heel. "This isn't over." And stomped away.

"Bye, my new best friend, evil hag!" Elliot called over her shoulder.

Parker exhaled. Jesus fucking Christ, that wasn't a good time. But also he kind of admired how Elliot wasn't put off at all by any of it. She so effortlessly dealt with all obstacles coming her way. Negative or positive things seemed to be exactly the same to her.

"Do you think she liked me?" Elliot asked.

"What's in this bag?" Parker examined the plastic bag filled with brightly colored gummies.

"Isn't it obvious? Drugs."

He threw the bag back at her and she caught it against her chest. "What?"

"You can't openly walk around with drugs."

"Relax." She opened the bag and took one gummy out, giving it a squish. "They don't even look like drugs. Besides, these gummies are derived from that new strain of cannabis that isn't illegal yet."

Parker's brows knitted together. "I don't believe you."

She patted him on the shoulder. "Believe it. I may not be the most academic human alive, but I know about weed." She opened the bag and plopped the gummy back inside. "Let's go to my room."

Parker and Elliot sat with legs crisscrossed on her bed, across from each other. He felt like they were two high schoolers at home without parents for the first time.

"To be honest, I'm a little nervous. I haven't smoked weed since I was a teenager." Parker was never one for doing drugs. He liked to drink socially on occasion but other than that, it just wasn't his jam. Particularly because Jen had been the more wild between the two of them. She'd done enough drugs to cover them both. Although she always seemed to have a good time at music festivals and raves and concerts. Parker didn't attend those events.

Elliot placed the gummy in the middle of his palm, then pressed her fingers around his so he made a first. "This is my thanks for fixing my camera. If you hadn't fixed the shutter then I would've lost that client. And she would've been *fucking pissed*. You saved me big time. The best way to show gratitude is with brain-altering substances, didn't you know that?"

Elliot's mention of her difficult clients made him wonder about the dress he sent to her. She should've received it by now, but according to John she also hadn't been in town very much. Maybe she hadn't checked her PO box. It was entirely possible. Or maybe she just didn't care. That was possible too, but seemed less likely.

Either way, he was with her now, and that's where he wanted to be.

"Fine. I'll take the edible."

Elliot clapped her hands together. "Hurray, we're going to have so much fun staring at the TV and eating junk food together. This is like my dream come true."

"We don't have any snacks."

"I'll send them delivery. Everything you want. Everything your high little brain can conceive of."

"I'll give you my credit card."

"Why? I can cover it. Did you not know I get paid super super good money for taking my silly little pictures on Instagram? I'm not against taking your money, but considering this is my way of saying thanks, you should let me pay."

Parker shrugged. "Fine, have it your way."

"Wait, are you trying to show off? Do you have a Black Amex or something?"

He did. "That's not it."

"You have a Black card?"

Suddenly, he was feeling shy. "I don't...*not* have one."

Elliot rubbed her chin, looking at Parker thoughtfully. "Huh. How about that? Anyway, you can buy me something later. This time it's on me."

Little did she apparently know, he'd already dropped twenty Gs on her.

Elliot removed another gummy from the bag. Hers was blue, his was yellow. "Cheers."

Chapter 15

The edible high hit Parker little by little and then all at once. It was much like the way he fell in love.

Also much like the way he fell in love, it was as though he'd dropped into a foggy, misty hell where his brain couldn't escape.

"It's only ten milligrams, you're gonna be fine." Elliot patted his hand on the bed, they were still sitting across from each other.

But Parker had a creepy-crawly feeling that everything would not be fine. For one, when Elliot would talk, he'd lose track of her sentence halfway through. But he didn't know how to tell her this was happening so he had to fake pretending to know what she had said. Which made him even more anxious, to the point where he felt like surely he must've looked grotesque and scared, eyes wide and flitting to and fro, wanting to shrivel up and disappear in the corner.

"I don't know about that."

"Here, have some chips." She shoved a bag in his face.

Weren't edibles supposed to make you hungry? The greasy smell wafting from the bag made him nauseous. Parker wasn't hungry, but he tried for Elliot's sake. Gingerly, he removed a potato chip and bit into it.

Then with alarm, he realized he couldn't taste it.

Then he thought maybe he couldn't swallow. He tried hard, nearly choking himself. Or what felt like choking.

"Oh my god, am I eating my own teeth?" he asked, horrified.

Elliot giggled. "Okay, well, I guess now I've accidentally gotten my revenge on you for Tokyo. That's too bad, I was planning a whole thing. But you really aren't having the best experience of all time."

"I think I'm dying, Elliot. I really do."

"Fair. Sorry for your bad karma. You deserve it though."

"Is it just me or does this hotel room feel haunted?"

"Oh boy."

"And are the knives on your sweater threatening to jump out and stab me?"

"Ooooh boy. I didn't give you a psychedelic, just a fucking edible, dude. You're gonna be okay, I promise." But Elliot picked up her phone and started tapping away, her brows drawn together, then she looked up at Parker. The whole thing might've taken approximately six thousand minutes— he wasn't sure as time was moving at in incalculable rate. "Hmm. So, I think I might know what happened."

Parker shook his head. "Tell me."

"Well, apparently, because this strain of marijuana isn't recognized yet by the law, these edibles might not have been...regulated in quite the right way. This article here says that from their independent testing of these drugs you could be getting as little as five milligrams of THC for an advertised strength of ten…or…" She bit her lip, making a concerned face. "As high as one hundred milligrams. Of THC."

Parker fell back on the bed. "Fuck. Fuck. Fuck. So, what you're saying is, is that I'm high as balls right now."

"Pretty much. Not only that but you're a newbie, so…I'm sorry. I didn't think this would happen. My friends and I take the regular kind all the time in Chicago since it's legal there. But we might be a little more experienced than you."

"Do the shadows on the wall look like monsters or am I hallucinating?"

Elliot removed the four bags of chips on her lap and stood from the bed. "Okay, Mr. Serious, I should call you Mr. Paranoid now, but anyway. We gotta get you out of here. What do you say we go for a walk?"

Quickly, Parker sat back up. "A walk? Like in a park?"

Elliot nodded. "Sure, like the one nearby. Hey, maybe we'll run into your lady friend. I think she liked me."

The sun was setting in downtown Charleston. He'd spent many nights there and he could attest that the sunrises were better than the sunsets. But right now, this sunset wasn't so bad.

Getting outside was actually something of a salve for Parker's hyper drug-induced paranoia. Suddenly the foggy feeling on his shoulders lifted.

"Outside is like magic," Parker muttered.

Elliot swung her arms back and forth as they strolled. "Nah, that's the weed chilling out. Pretty soon you're gonna feel right as rain. And you're going to be hungry as hell."

"The sky is like cotton candy. Like you could eat it." In front of them, the stripes slashed the horizon in pink and blue and orange. Behind them a dusky navy-grey. They were chasing the fading light of day.

She patted his back. "Now I know you're feeling better. Cotton candy, if only that was something I could acquire from the grocery store, then I could make all your immediate dreams come true."

As they strolled, a cool sensation began to swim down Parker's sternum and belly. And the haze lifted from his eyes. "You're right. I'm getting better."

"Good, the walk is helping metabolize the drugs. Now, you're getting to the good part." She gave him a mischievous smile.

They passed by the palms and gently swaying flowers in the manicured park. Only a few people were out at this time.

"Let's go sit on the bench for a moment. I have chips in my bag." Elliot gestured over to a bench.

They sat down, Elliot's knee bent towards the inside of the bench, her body turned towards Parker.

"So, you got about twenty-five percent more interesting today."

Parker scratched the back of his head; he was glad to hear this, but Elliot could be baiting him. His high was mellowing out to a pleasant glow now, but the hard edge hadn't fully been filed off. "Oh yeah?"

"Well, let me count the ways. One, you found me and waited for me all from a silly phone call because I forgot my phone charger."

"I have a portable charger in my pocket."

"Two, you were *once again* harangued by some random woman whom I can't for the life of me figure out how you'd possibly know. And of course there was the woman from the picture Jonathan took…"

"She's an old friend of my sister's."

"And so what about the random fierce hag at the hotel? She is quite the Real Housewife. That's not a knock. I happen to know that's not cheap to maintain and I'm jealous."

"Her husband is extremely wealthy."

Elliot leaned in. "She's *married?* Wow, who knew you had it in you? Lemme guess, you met her at a fancy bar and bought her a drink, and she took her wedding ring off."

Parker stretched his legs out in front of him, hitching one ankle over the other, crossing his arms over his chest. Now that his paranoia had faded, he was quite enjoying the attention from Elliot. Jealousy. A hell of a motivator. "Wrong and wrong. She's married to my client."

Elliot clutched at her chest in mock shock. "*And* a client. You're asking for trouble there."

"We're not together anymore."

"Not so sure she got the memo, Mr. Serious. And then, that brings us to the third and final installment of your love life."

You.

"Tessa." Elliot turned to mimic Parker's body language, stretching her legs out in front of her, ankle hitched over ankle and arms crossed.

"We don't have to talk about my love life right now."

"Don't have to, but will."

"I already paid the price with this terrible edible."

"But you feel pretty good now."

Parker checked in with his body: everything felt much less *wound up* than before, but also somehow happier too. A smile tugged at the corner of his lips that he didn't feel like he could suppress. Then that turned into full-blown giggles.

Elliot turned her head to stare at him as he bent over at the waist, giggling full heartedly with his belly.

"I see we've leveled up to the next portion of the high experience." She coughed out a few laughs as well, but smoothed her hand over her face. "Maybe we should head back then. I've been running around all day. I'm ready to lie down."

Elliot stood up, stretching her arms over her head and yawning. Parker followed her. But when she turned to go, he grabbed her hand.

"What?"

"I want to hold your hand while we walk."

Elliot scrunched her nose. "Ew, Parker."

He knew she wouldn't like the idea. But Parker wasn't going to get another chance like it.

To his surprise, she tilted her head at their shared clasp and then said, "Eh, fine. It's nice to have a little company tonight. If this is the price I have to pay, I'll take it."

He smirked at her. "Yes, what a heavy burden. Do we have any peanut butter and chocolate-covered banana chips in the hotel room?"

Elliot chuckled. "No, but we can get some. I'll go run into the grocery store right at the corner. You can wait out here if you don't want to be overwhelmed."

Parker thought that would be wise. He whistled to himself gently as he waited for Elliot on the mild night. And then a great sense of calm befell him.

Wow, where did that come from?

Elliot stepped out from the convenience store with a paper bag in her arms.

"I got some other stuff too because why the hell not?"

The outside overhead light from the store shone above her head like a halo. Like she was the goddamn Virgin Mary with an offering.

Not that he wanted her to be a virgin. Or a saint.

But it was more like she was mystical. Otherworldly.

He knew she wasn't. But the feelings swimming inside his chest were bubbling up throughout the rest of his body, rushing to his feet and fingertips.

He snatched the heavy paper bag out of her hands and placed it on the ground.

"Uh, what are you doing?" she asked skeptically.

But then he reached for the waistband of her jeans, drawing her towards him one step at a time. Her feet shuffled and then one stepped in front of the other.

When she was so close to him he could feel the heat radiating between their bodies, carefully he threaded his hands into her hair, his thumbs parallel to the line of her jaw, and he leaned in.

"How friendly is this? One out of ten." she asked, but her voice was weak.

At first he simply brushed his lips against hers. He could feel her sharp intake of breath. A sign that she felt something. This wasn't strictly sexual for her. Couldn't be.

And maybe it was only the drugs, but the light tickle on the sensitive skin of his lips against hers made his eyes roll back in his head. It was like finding the location of a phantom itch and scratching the hell out of it. He brushed his lower lip against her upper lip again, this time letting his tongue stroke lightly, licking at her. And she responded by catching his lips with her own, a proper kiss resulting.

It was slow and soft, until her tongue flicked out to meet his and then he slanted his lips over hers so that their tongues could meet, swirling and twining until he felt like he needed to catch his breath.

Her hands remained at her side, so he reached down, picking them up and placing them against his chest, hoping she'd let them roam around the hard expanse.

Meanwhile, his mouth sought hers, deeper in the kiss. It wasn't a sweet kiss, but it wasn't yet dirty. It held promise though, the way he was slipping into her mouth, the way a passerby could likely see their tongues through the corners of their open lips.

He wouldn't be doing this if he weren't so high. That's what he told himself at least. But the quiet moans humming from Elliot's throat egged him on. Also, who really gave a fuck about what anyone thought about him or her in this moment?

The only thing that mattered were the feelings that emanated from his chest. And that every single touch felt so good.

Her fingernails grazed up his chest, and she wrapped her hands around his neck, pulling him down so he had to lean even more to reach her.

Then abruptly she pushed him away. "We gotta get off this street corner."

He leaned in and licked the inside of her top lip again and stole another kiss from her mouth. For a moment, the kiss ignited again and he found his hands pulling around her waist so that his hard dick could press up against her belly.

She pushed away from him again. "I'm serious. Look at that, you got me all turned around."

"Since when do you care about PDA?" He looked in either direction at the barren streets and then grabbed her hand. "Come with me," he said, pulling her into the alley next to the store.

"What? Why? Wait, is what I think is gonna happen about to happen?" Elliot asked, but she eagerly followed him until they were shrouded in the darkness, nothing but a dim light streaming into the hidden alleyway.

Parker pushed her against the wall, his hands holding the tops of her arms. A smile curled on her lips, the thin light illuminating her white teeth. "Well, now that you have me, what will you do with me?"

He let his hand trail from her arm to her clavicle and then over the swell of her breast. Her breathe hitched, and Parker felt alive, more alive than he had in years. He also felt more in touch, more in tune with all his senses. And his senses were telling him that if he didn't feel the soft protrusion of Elliot's hard nipple brush against the sensitive middle of his palm, he would probably die.

She moaned when her nipple touched his palm, and he squeezed her breast lightly. "Oh God, Parker..." Her voice was so breathy.

He relished her swallowed moan when he took her mouth in his, in an indecent, mouth-fucking kiss, and he relished her small yelp even more when he shoved his hand into her panties.

He was the man with the magic hands after all. And it was about time she learned.

His fingers sought out her clit, grazing the hood of her lips and rubbing back and forth until she broke from the kiss, eyes rolling back in her head. "Mmm...yes, right there."

Good. Parker was a good listener, and most men really weren't. Women weren't that hard to figure out if you paid a little fucking attention.

"Right here?" he murmured. His voice was mocking although he wasn't trying to mock her. He ducked his head to her neck, his tongue flicking along the column of taut skin and she leaned her head away to expose herself more. All the while, he'd picked up pace with his fingertips, moving faster, pressing firmly in a circular motion around her clit.

"Oh fuck, yes, like that, don't stop, just like that..." Her words were coming out fast and choppy and her hips were rolling in tandem with his movements so Parker knew he was on the right path.

"Like this?" he applied more pressure, and then when she bit her lip, nodding, he flattened his palm and gave her a little slap, her delicate skin, hot and damp.

In response, she swallowed another moan. "Ohmyfuckingod."

A rustle beyond the alley distracted Parker, his eyes flitting left and right, reminding him and his elevated brain that he was straight up in public with his hands down Elliot's pants. Time to get this show on the road.

He roughly raked his free hand up over her belly and breast, squeezing hard but releasing quickly. Then he wrapped his fingers around the back of her neck before they traveled north too, grabbing a fistful of her hair right at the root. She gasped, chin jerking upwards, wetness rushing down her pussy all over his fingertips.

"Get there now, okay?" he murmured in her ear.

"What?" she practically whimpered, but she choked on her words when he redoubled his efforts with his fingers, wetness smearing across her clit. Rubbing furiously now against the roll of her hips.

"Get there *now,*" he growled, his hand down her pants moving franticly, his other hand grasping against her scalp for dear life. She whimpered again, and he leaned forward, letting his tongue slide over the folds of her ear. "Come for me while I rub your clit."

Her body tightened and froze, then choked sobs escaped her lips and she jerked as if being shocked with little electrical pulses against his hand. Until finally, her eyes went heavy, her body slack. He loosened his grip on her hair and her head fell back against the brick. He pulled his hand from her panties, scratching the flesh on her belly and hip as his hand traveled up her skin.

She looked at him with wide eyes, chest heaving. Her hands came to his jaw, pulling him forward, lips pressing against his. Then she released him. "Well. Okay then."

Her skin was flushed that bright pink again. The drugs had made her happier, friendlier than usual. Or maybe it was the orgasm. Maybe both. But she was softer. Didn't even protest when he clasped their hands together and pulled her out of the alleyway.

He was softer too, in the metaphorical sense. Wait, no. He was always this way, he just often faked it. He wondered if she faked it too.

He leaned down and picked up the abandoned paper bag of groceries, nestling it in between his arm and chest. Then he led her through the park. This time they walked into the dark night, the streets stretching out into blackness with happy, glowing lights lining the outer perimeter of the street. Their arms swinging gently between them. For the first time in a long time, Parker felt like he might feel...

Peace?

Wow, maybe he had really misinterpreted the effects of previous edibles. Maybe they simply took a little time to reach the right consistency. Maybe love was like that.

"What do you want to do when we get back to my room?" she asked. And he knew what she might be inferring.

"I don't know." He lifted her hand, kissing the back of it.

"What if we watch a movie?"

He smiled. This was the kind of time he wanted with her. Like partners. Like people who wanted to spend time together. "I could be amenable to that."

"What if we watch another movie afterwards?"

"I might fall asleep. I'm pretty relaxed."

"Me too. Are you spending the night?"

"Should I? Or should I sneak out at three a.m. like you do?"

She swung their connected hands back and forth. "I only do that because I have a relentless schedule. It costs a lot of money to stay this messed up so I gotta keep working. You can quote me on that."

"Your friend John says you won't settle down."

"Yeah, well, John should mind his own damn business."

"I think he cares about you."

They reached the entrance to the Blackberry and walked in. They waited at the elevator doors, which seemed to take over an eternity to arrive. From inside the elevator, Parker watched the numbers click down up at a time in orange highlight.

When the doors cheerily dinged open, they stepped outside. He realized they'd been holding hands the entire time.

Parker Donne had walked through a park with Elliot Sheer, while holding hands.

He looked up into the mirror in the ceiling, a thing he couldn't ever remember having done before, and there they stood like a bonded pair, connected at the hip. He reveled in it but only briefly, because the doors were already opening and she dropped his hand, the loss of her skin cooling his own as they made their way down a now liminal hallway.

"Do you remember my room number?" Elliot twirled around and then tossed a chip into the air, catching it into her mouth. Her hands went up like she just scored big.

"How would I know your room number?" It was 436, but for some reason he didn't want to sound like he cared too much. A lot had transpired between them, and it always seemed like Elliot was an inch away from being pushed too far. Maybe the weed paranoia hadn't all the way worn off yet.

Elliot strolled down the hallway. "Seems like something you might notice."

When they reached the room, he stopped without thinking about it. Elliot was ahead of him, but she slowed down, looked over her shoulder. Then a sly smile came on her face. She swiped her card out from her pocket and skipped over to him.

"I see how it is, Mr. Serious. You lied? To what end?"

Because he was all messed up in the head. Again the uncontrollable urge to smile swept upwards on the skin of his face. "I plead the fifth."

"It's okay. I like that you notice things."

The door whirred open and when they were inside, the shadows of before had faded. The room was cozy now with a beautiful white down comforter smoothed over the mattress, indented from their bodies where they had sat earlier.

The chips and bags of convenience store snacks were scattered on the floor and bed, but instead of grossing Parker out like it normally would, it made him feel like he was home.

Absently he dug into the paper bag in his arms and snagged open the bag of banana chips, grabbed a handful and shoved them into his mouth. Elliot giggled at the sight of him and she grabbed a handful as well, grotesquely chewing, making disgusting gnawing sounds with her mouthful. Parker copied her until they were both laughing.

Elliot swallowed, wiping her face and the tears from her eyes. "We're two monsters, aren't we?"

He glanced over at her, his stitches of laughter faded now. "If that's true, you're the most beautiful monster I've ever seen."

She stared at him for a moment, blue eyes wide, like she was seeing him for the first time in a long time. Then she laughed. "Oh, Jesus Christ. Let's order that movie, Mr. Serious. You like romance?"

What now, now that the high has worn off? What's it called the day after you're high? A low?

In the dark of Elliot's hotel room Parker consulted the red light of the clock on the nightstand. Six thirty in the morning. Hmm.

He hadn't checked his phone in hours. Elliot's phone lay on the nightstand next to his, plugged into his portable charger.

And Elliot lay on the bed, her soft snoring an uneven metronome in his ears. He wanted to go back to sleep, to pull her in close. But she was facing away, on her side, body spread like a fan, and besides.

They were just friends. Friends who kissed. And maybe did other things too…

They didn't kiss or do other things once they'd returned. They didn't talk about it either. Although Parker knew he'd been irrevocably changed. How much could one man take from one woman? She seemed to have a much higher tolerance for the unknown than he did.

Parker, naturally, feared death. The unknown was intolerable.

Slowly, he slid his legs off the comforter. He hadn't even gone underneath. He was in the same clothes as before. He felt grimy, but he also couldn't give any less of a fuck.

The only thing that mattered was the night. The night they'd had together.

They'd barely shared a word while watching the movie. It was an old movie, but one he'd seen as a kid. With Marisa Tomei and Robert Downey Jr. The actors looked so young, but when he'd first watched it they'd seemed so grown up.

He grabbed his phone from the stand. When was the last time he'd gone an entire night without checking his messages?

Of course there were messages from Cameron, angry emojis on fire and long written out blocks of text. It's funny how she'd never responded like that when they were together.

She used to make him wait, days, sometimes weeks, for a reply. And then he'd spin his wheels, desperate for her attention.

He didn't wait for Elliot in the same way. They weren't always in communication but he had this strange faith that they would see each other again and again and again. And as fate would have it, they always did.

Could it really keep going like this?

His phone lit up on the end table, buzzing with a phone call.

Tessa.

He hesitated for a moment and then grabbed the phone and stepped out onto the balcony to answer it.

"Soooo..." Tessa's voice had an excited ring to it. "Good morning, did I wake you?"

Parker grunted, but then cleared his throat. "No, I'm an early riser. Good morning."

"I have some news for you, Park."

"Oh?"

"Guess where I am..." Her voice was teasing a bit.

Parker shook his head, gazing out over the Charleston landscape, old but not ancient. "Ahh, the Arctic?"

Did it take him too long to respond? He might still be high. Or maybe it was the fact that he didn't really want to talk on the phone.

Inside, Elliot snoozed like a fallen angel who'd done enough work for Satan for the day. He chuckled at that. Yeah, maybe still a touch high? That edible had done a number on his good sense.

"Parker? Hello? Did you hear me?"

Parker snapped back to reality. "Sorry, you cut out for a second."

That wasn't entirely a lie. His brain had in fact cut out for a second.

"I'm in Charleston! Can you believe it?"

"Why! I mean..." He softened his voice. "I didn't know you'd be here."

Or that she knew he'd be there. But Cameron's voice rang in his head. Of course Tessa would also know where Parker was. She followed all his social media accounts, commenting under every post.

Hot as always.

Can't wait to see you.

Maybe you can give me a ride in one of those someday, wink wink.

Dammit. Cameron was right! He had really sold himself out, what was he thinking? He felt like a total fucking rube.

"What hotel are you staying at? From this picture it looks like the Blackberry. Fancy, I've never stayed there before. What's the room number, I can be there in twenty-five minutes."

Shit, shit, shit.

It wasn't that Parker was opposed to lying, but it did happen to be that he didn't actually do it all that often. And he was going to have to come up with a fast excuse now.

"I'm leaving. On my way out already."

Tessa's voice sounded pouty. "Oh no. But it's such a beautiful morning. I thought we could spend it getting breakfast then... I don't know, maybe spending a little time in the hotel room bed. Hint, hint. Just kidding, I know you like to take things slow."

Parker squeezed his eyes shut, hand to his brow. "I already checked out."

"At six a.m.?"

"I hate to be late for things." Despite himself, guilt settled in his chest. He also hated to disappoint. "But...yeah, breakfast. We should meet for breakfast. Before I have to go."

Tessa's voice lowered from its high register. "Great. Great. I'm at the airport now."

"I'll come get you." Fuck. The guilt was taking over.

He didn't want to go to the airport and he wasn't exactly in the mood for breakfast with Tessa.

But he couldn't ice her out completely. She'd get mad at him. And he didn't want to deal with that. He was starting to get the feeling that maybe he'd dug himself a little deep into this hole.

On the other hand...

He and Elliot had made some progress, but she was still wily like a fox. Skittish. One wrong move and she would flee from him. Block him from social media and all forms of communication. Or worse, wouldn't even bother blocking him, would just forget about his existence entirely.

And that thought hurt him deeply.

When he hung up with Tessa, he slipped back into Elliot's room.

She hadn't even moved. Her sweater was riding up her belly.

Every fiber in his being wanted to take off his day-old clothes, strip down naked, and get back into bed with her. He could strip her down too, pulling that sweater over her head, then pulling her pants off her shapely legs...yanking down the cups of her bra, assuming she wore one. Then he would tease her for hours and hours.

And she'd beg for it. Because she'd made it clear she wanted it. And because Parker knew what he was doing.

The thing was, she always left him wanting more. Although, if he were honest with himself, he was well aware that he could never get enough of her anyway. That was just the law of supply and demand. There was not enough supply of her in existence to meet his demand.

It was a shame she always disappeared when they were in some of their softest moments, like now.

His desire for her would grow, the flames stoked each time she ran away. Instead of the opposite happening, which would seem much more logical and reasonable. Which would be Parker's response to any other woman.

Elliot Sheer had him on a fucking hook.

And it was exactly where he wanted to be.

But an idea shimmered in the corner of Parker's mind. It felt a little disingenuous. Manipulative maybe. A little game-play-ey.

But, if he really wanted to have her wrapped around his finger, then he could sneak away. Slip off into the day like she did to him. Disappear like a curl of dust against the sunshine.

And, again, this was very wrong of him to think, but he could also, potentially, possibly *maybe* leverage his breakfast with Tessa.

He might not be head over heels for Tessa, but also, sometimes love grew slowly (or not at all) and he was still determined to give it a chance. Plus, there was Jen to think of. There was always Jen to think of and how she would freak out if she knew Parker was such a mess of a person. He couldn't—he *wouldn't* disappoint her further.

Because this thing with Elliot could blow up at any time. The whole situation felt like a ticking time bomb strapped to his heart. Part of him must love the thrill, or at least love *something*. Why else couldn't he stay the fuck away?

Before he could change his mind and let the memories of the night dilute his resolve, he collected his phone, washed his face in the bathroom, gargled some hotel-supplied mouthwash. And quietly, like a thief in the night, slipped out the door before the sun even rose.

Chapter 16

"**I** have a question to ask you."

Tessa was dressed in a bright blue sundress, thin straps with cleavage on display. She looked beautiful as always. She smiled coyly at Parker. "I have an answer."

Parker leaned forward, black coffee steaming in front of him along with an omelet and bacon and sausage. Tessa was eating a Belgium waffle with pecans and bananas. They were at a Waffle House. Maybe not the most romantic setting of all time, and maybe that's part of the reason why Parker still wasn't feeling the spark between them. More like a wet match.

Nevertheless, she would be a good wedding date. She wouldn't stand him up. She'd dress appropriately. Look beautiful. Soothe Jen's suspicion that Parker was lonely and made bad decisions with women who would never commit to him, easing her guilt about leaving him in Chicago. About their dead parents. About him paying for her way. And even more importantly, she'd get Kate off his back at the wedding.

Elliot would probably do the opposite of all of those things.

And Parker planned on being strategic. He sipped his coffee. "My sister is getting married in six months."

Tessa's lashes fluttered expectantly. "Yes…"

"And I was wondering if you'd go to the wedding with me."

She let out a big exhale in apparent relief. She reached out to grab his hand. "I knew it. I knew our time would come. Of course. Of course, I'd love to."

Parker smiled. Tessa was a nice person.

Then her face got serious. "But. Only on one condition."

Parker swallowed a bite of his Denver omelet. "I'm listening."

"We have to take a trip together before the wedding."

"A trip?"

She nodded. "A wedding date is serious. Meeting the family and whatnot. And so, we need to get to know each other in person better. And I know you have your whole thing about getting physical and *feelings* and all that. Fine. I respect it. But still, a trip. We live in different states. We don't have any other chance to interact effectively. I've been dealing with this for my whole career, and I'm sick of it. I want to be in once place together. That's what I want."

A trip. It seemed serious, but she was right. They both traveled all the time, and they lived across the country from each other. How else were two people such as they supposed to date? Parker set down his fork and knife and leaned back in his chair. "When's your availability?"

Maybe not the most romantic response on the planet, but Tessa pulled out her phone as if she were scheduling someone standby on a flight. "Well, I'll be in Ireland on Friday. Then Paris the following week. Hmm…also Amsterdam, that should be fun. But after that I'm off for a full two weeks. Don't worry about it, I can come pick you up first if you want. I love a layover in Chicago."

Parker felt a distinct rush of relief. A few weeks was a lifetime away. He wouldn't even have to worry about it. Big things could happen in a few weeks. Life-changing things. He'd learned that as a teenager. Plus, he was a busy guy, things popped up. Work things…personal things…

If he had to, he could even beg off for longer. Tessa would wait. Guilt bubbled in his consciousness.

The question was, why did he want her to?

Jen and Parker sat on the end of a hill overlooking a park across from them. Parker lived right next to it and they'd gone on a stroll.

"Why haven't you gone back to work yet?" Parker asked. Jen was staying with him for an inordinate amount of time.

"Why don't you have a fucking couch?" she snapped. Then she sighed. "My job went to work from home so I've been working from home. Maybe you would've noticed, but without a couch I spend most of my day in your guest room. And you've been quite busy lately, haven't you?"

There was a small desk overlooking a window in the guest room. He had noticed Jen had been spending a lot of time there, but as was his usual M.O. he didn't ask too many questions. Jen was going to do what she wanted anyway. He had vaguely wondered why she hadn't made her way back to New York, though, and he suspected that she wasn't lying when she'd said she wanted to keep an eye on him.

"Are you nervous about walking me down the aisle?"

Parker shook his head. "No."

"Do you think you'll ever get married? I don't want you to be alone."

"Will you stop worrying so much about me? I'm a guy. Nobody cares if I get married anyway."

Jen's gaze cut over to him. "You do."

He shrugged. "Maybe. Maybe not."

"Why don't you have this Tessa woman over for dinner? Or no, why don't we do a proper British tea?"

"British tea? We're not British."

"I know, but it sounds fun. I saw a recipe for English cream scones on the *Barefoot Contessa*. And besides, Tessa's well-traveled, right? She probably does all kinds of stuff like that."

Parker couldn't agree to this—obviously he didn't need to over complicate this thing with Tessa. He just wanted a decent wedding date. But now a trip...and Jen's wonky British tea idea... "She's busy, she can't stop by at the drop of a hat. Maybe someday I'll even have to move out to wherever she lives." He liked to speak in the future tense as if he'd be a completely different person once it arrived.

"You don't know where she lives?"

"Denver. Sorry. I forgot."

"You forgot where your girlfriend lives?"

"Slip of the tongue. She travels all the time. Easy to get confused."

Jen rolled her eyes. "Strange. Oh hey, can I borrow your phone? I need to check a work email and I left mine in your guest room."

Parker handed his phone over to her, and Jen furiously typed away. Then she handed it back to him. "Tessa's coming over on Friday. Done and done."

"What the hell, Jen?"

"What! I don't understand why you don't want me to meet her before the wedding. All your girlfriends have always loved me."

This was true, as Jen was happy-go-lucky, fun, outgoing…easy to love. Although, she could also, at times, be terrifying. Unlike Parker, who was always a little stiffer, a little harder to get to know. Love was more elusive for him than it had been for her.

"I'm going to cancel those plans with her."

Jen arched an eyebrow. "Why? What are you hiding, Parker? Are you up to something?"

The heat rose in his chest. "What are *you* hiding Jen? You were supposed to leave weeks ago. Isn't your fiancé looking for you?"

She straightened her spine. "Nice try on the conspiracy. He's been on a work trip. Mostly I'm sticking around to keep an eye on you."

Parker gave her a suspicious look, deflecting. He'd text Tessa when they returned, tell her there was a change of plans.

"Don't even think of texting her and changing plans when we get back," Jen barked at him.

"How did you—"

"Twin brain." Jen smiled. "Still got it. I can read your mind. Or at least part of it. Frequency is pretty hazy these days."

Parker pursed his lips. He could only hope so.

Chapter 17

Jen had set out a full English tea. Tiers of plates with cucumber finger sandwiches, petit fours, and tiny sandy biscuits filled Parker's dining room table.

"Why do you have this long dining room table but no couch? Tessa's gonna think you're a loser. I don't want her thinking you're a loser. She's gotta have a reason to stay with you. At least until the wedding." Jen filled a tiny little dish with sugar and another pitcher with milk.

"How much did you spend on all this stuff?" Parker asked. It certainly didn't fit his minimalist, modern décor. It was all stuffy and British.

And he'd been texting with Elliot. That was his secret.

Not normal texting. And not sexy texting either. But still, late night texting.

Elliot almost never texted him during the day, instead she would opt to send him messages right before she went to bed around two a.m. Of course she would wake Parker up, and he wanted to be annoyed. After all, he valued his sleep schedule and he'd always adhered to it as best he could, even with all the jet lag he'd typically have to endure (although lately he'd been taking fewer and fewer jobs.) He was already wealthy enough to retire four times over, he'd lived cheaply for most of his life and he'd begun investing early as well on account of his clients giving him investing tips. That had turned out well for him.

So, he had to ask himself what he was hustling around so much for?

Where would you go if you could go anywhere right at this moment? Elliot had texted him.

Nowhere, I'd stay where I am.

Which is?

Warm under this blanket in my bedroom.

What's your bedroom look like?

It was a weird inverted way to text a little dirty. But also there was something intimate about it. Emotional. It warmed him, spurred him on.

Part of the reason Parker kept up the travel was the thrill of potentially running into Elliot. Which seemed to happen so effortlessly. But she wasn't traveling as much lately as far as he could tell, which meant she was likely in Chicago. He didn't know where though. And he certainly couldn't ask.

"Um, hello. Park, where'd you go? You look like you fell into a trance."

"Huh? Oh, sorry." Parker blinked hard, his corneas burnt from the bright window he was staring out of without attention to anything. He shook his head. "What did you say?"

"I said I spent four hundred dollars on all this stuff. But don't worry, I used your card this time. Because Tessa's your girlfriend so you have to pay for this shit."

"She's actually not my girlfriend."

"What? But that's what you said."

"Technically speaking. Don't worry about it. We're taking a trip. A trip is serious!" Parker's nerves were jittering a bit but the conversation was interrupted by a knock on the door.

"I'll get it. I wouldn't want you to have to answer the door for *not your girlfriend.*" Jen wiped her hands on a towel and trotted over to the door.

"You must be Tessa. Wow, you're stunning." He heard Jen's voice from around the corner. He was in the kitchen fixing a scotch neat, when the voice that answered in return he realized *wasn't* Tessa's.

Oh fuck.

Parker stutter stepped in either direction until he realized he'd have to go out there. He booked it to his doorway entrance.

He was half elated, half completely fucking panicked. How was it Elliot could always make him feel two equal and opposite sensations simultaneously?

"You're expecting Tessa, well, this really was interesting timing." Elliot said.

"Ah, Jen, sorry, this is my friend—" But he was rendered frozen at the sight of Elliot.

She wasn't dressed as she usually was, in the jeans and oversized sweaters falling off her shoulders, casually revealing bra cups and bra straps. Or in all black with her hair tied up. Or in old ripped jeans with sneakers and stained sweatshirts. Or party dresses with a skirt that rode up the backs of her thighs. That he had pushed all the way up to her belly button.

Instead she was in a sparkling gown. White and gauzy with embellishments glittering at the hem.

Wow, she could've been a bride. She could've been fucking Cinderella. But no, wait, not any of those things. Parker realized those things didn't quite suit her.

She was like Jem from *Jem and the Holograms*. Jen used to make him watch that show every Saturday morning. He remembered it so clearly.

"What are you doing here?" His voice was soft when he spoke, his gaze tight.

Jen looked confused, but also seemed to sense that something strange was occurring right in front of her. "Hello, beautiful lady in a gown. Can I get you a scone, it's technically for the second course but I figure what the hell we're Americans and...uh, I didn't quite get your name. You're not ...Tessa, are you?"

"Her name's Elliot."

"Okay, pretty sure I can speak for myself." Elliot gave Parker a strange look but then smiled at Jen. "Sure, scones are my fave."

Jen moved from the doorway slowly. "Come on in, Elliot. Cute name."

Elliot followed Jen to the large table off to the left of Parker's kitchen.

It took a moment to snap Parker out of it, but he dropped his hands from over his chest and trotted after them. "Elliot can't stay," Parker hissed.

But Jen shot him a dirty look and handed Elliot a tiny plate. "Don't be rude to guests, Parker. You have so few, I'm just glad to see you have morefriends. Elliot, sit. We're actually waiting on someone else to join us."

Elliot raised an eyebrow. "Tessa?"

Jen looked surprised. "Oh, are you a friend of Tessa's? Is everyone friends? That's so great. Are we expecting anyone else? We have enough for quite a few people. I put it all on Parker's card."

"No, sadly, Tessa and I are not friends. But it's a nice thought."

Jen raised her eyebrows with a questioning look to Parker. But he shook his head. "Can you give us a moment, Jen? I really need to talk to Elliot about…"

"Work stuff?" Elliot supplied.

"Work stuff? You drive a Prius." He crinkled his brow.

"Not your work stuff silly, *my* work stuff. You told me on the phone the other night that your sister is getting married and she needs a photographer?"

It took a moment for the words to register with Parker. "Oh. Right."

"Elliot, you're a photographer?" Jen twisted around to look at Parker. "I didn't know you'd been paying attention to my wedding stuff! Tell me, Elliot, are you expensive because my fiancé is rich and kind of a snob and so is his family."

"Expensive as they come." She pulled out her phone and passed it across the table to Jen. "Here, you can grok my Insta and see for yourself."

Jen swiped the phone. "Holy shit, I follow this beauty influencer and you did her fifth wedding? Wild how many times she's been married."

"Uh, Jen. Again, I need to speak with Elliot al—"

"Hello, knock, knock!" A cheerful voice called from the front entryway. Parker's stomach sank.

Fuck. Fuck. Fuck. He had left the front door open in his Elliot-haze. Goddammit.

And Tessa had already trotted through the entry way and right into the dining room. "The door was open so I welcomed myself in."

Tessa froze at the scene already in progress in the dining room. "Oh." She covered her mouth. "Oh." Her eyes narrowed in on Elliot, then she pointed slowly with her index finger. "I see there are more than expected."

"This is Elliot," Jen provided. "She might do the photography at my wedding."

"That's right!" Parker jumped in. "Elliot's a photographer, and that's why she's here. She travels a lot, too. Remember?"

Tessa nodded tersely. "Yes, I know. How could I forget? You have an unforgettable face, Elliot."

Elliot preened at the words although Parker wasn't so sure they were meant as a compliment. "Thanks, my dad used to say that I have the kind of face that turns up in people's mirrors when the lights are off."

Jen snorted at that. Oh no. It was happening.

Jen liked Elliot.

And Jen would realize Parker liked her too.

And then Jen would know that Parker was a big old, everyday chump for Elliot. Like he'd been for so many wild women before her.

"Elliot's leaving actually," said Parker.

Elliot took a huge bite of the chocolate scone. "That's not true. I just got here."

"That's so rude, Parker." Jen placed another scone on Elliot's small plate. "If she's going to photograph the wedding, we have so much to discuss. Tessa, have a seat. I'm Jen, Parker's sister. I'm so glad you're here. I don't often get to meet Parker's...*friends*. And now look, full house. Please, sit. Sit. Have some food on this little teeny plate. Isn't it cute? It has little yellow daffodils around the center. I'm about to serve the tea."

"Thank you so much. I'm very happy to meet...*you.*" Tessa sat confidently on the wooden chair, crossing her legs and clasping her hands on top of the surface. Delicately she picked up a pair of tongs and placed two strawberries and a rectangle of dark chocolate onto her plate. Tessa bit into one of the strawberries. "Yummy."

Parker insides cringed.

Then Tessa glanced up at Parker. "Well, sit down. Since we're all *friends.*"

"Yeah, friend." Elliot smirked. Parker didn't acknowledge that but he did slowly walk over to the table with a grimace he was surely poorly hiding on his face.

"Don't mind him." Jen waved her hand as if she was waving Parker away. "He's overly serious."

"Oh my god, tell me about it." Elliot rolled her eyes, and she and Jen both laughed.

Jen's phone lit up on the table: *Benny Wu.* Jen's eyebrows furrowed together. "You know what? I have to take this, if you could excuse me for a moment." Jen shuffled out of the kitchen and into her room, closing the door.

A moment of silence passed and then Tessa flashed her bright white smile. "You must know Parker fairly well." The register of her voice hiked up.

"Nah, not so great. Well, except for that one time." Then Elliot leaned in across the table to Tessa and whispered. "That one time he went down on me in a hotel room."

Silence befell the room.

Parker's heart stuttered, his tongue tight in his mouth. "She's joking. She's…she's not serious."

Tessa raised her eyebrows and looking back and forth between the two. *Fuck.* Parker ran his hand through his hair.

But Tessa had already gingerly placed her strawberry back onto the plate. "Interesting." The words were tense, clipped through clenched teeth.

Elliot picked up the strawberry, popped it into her mouth. "Eh, don't even worry about it. It was a while ago. But Parker always accuses me of forgetting that it happened, but I didn't forget. See, Parker? I remember."

"How about that." Tessa sat back in her chair with surprising calmness.

"Elliot's *joking* like I said. She has a very odd sense of humor. So odd some might even say it's not humor at all." He shot her a murderous look, to which she smiled broadly back at him.

"That's right. I'm just joking. Sorry, gotta work on my tight five if I'm ever gonna get that stand-up career off the ground. You win some, you lose some."

Tessa's nostrils flared and she smoothed out the material of her skirt. "Well, what's past is past, isn't it? What matters is the future. Like the trip Parker and I are taking together."

Elliot looked at him. "What trip?"

Jen's door opened. She had a pasted on smile on her face, but Parker certainly wasn't going to be investigating that now. The air in the room was thick with tension but Jen flounced down in her chair on the table, unaware. "Ah, so Elliot. Can I ask you about this...uh beautiful gown you're wearing?"

Elliot smiled, lifting the hem of the flowing gown, examining the beaded crystals. "Well, funny story. Parker bought it for me. I looked up the cost and it was around ten grand, but I know for a fact that he had it made. So, I'm guessing he paid a pretty penny for it."

Jen reached out to touch a delicate crystal bead at the hem. "Wow, Parker, doesn't it remind you of Mom's wedding dress?"

Oh shit.

"I um...I don't remember."

Tessa set her fork down quietly on her plate. "You bought this woman a ...ten thousand dollar gown? Why?"

"I ...she was being sued." Parker stammered.

Jen tilted her head as if she just realized what he'd said. "Wait. You bought a wedding dress for a wedding photographer?"

211

Parker panicked. "There's—there's a lawsuit. It's complicated. I—I didn't though. I really didn't." He really had.

"Okay…" Jen said slowly, still trying to put the pieces together.

Elliot waved a hand. "Oh, no. That lawsuit was dropped. I talked her out of it. So now I own this dress out right. Question for the room, should I sell it and reap the profits or keep it and play dress-up at the airport?"

Jen's mouth was now open, and it seemed to be dawning on her that something very big was happening that she didn't previously know about. Knowing Jen, she wouldn't make this any better. "I don't think you should sell it," Jen advised. "I think you should take a picture in it, and tag the person trying to sue you. They call that synergy in my line of work."

Elliot nodded. "Right, right, right. Maybe I could tag Parker too since he's got so many followers. I've always wanted to get TheParkedMechanic involved in my photography. He looks like a model. Great for *my* line of work."

Tessa's teacup clattered to the saucer. "My apologies. I forgot that I have somewhere else I have to be. Urgently."

"Oh no, but you just got here," said Jen.

As Tessa stood, Parker stood too, chasing after her. "Wait, wait, wait." He gently caught her arm as she made it all the way out to his hallway.

He could still hear the muted chattering and giggles of Elliot and his sister behind the closed door, who appeared to be carrying on despite what was happening between Tessa and Parker.

Tessa's nostrils flared, her eyes glinting with irritation. Oh fuck. In this moment, every callous action of his was coming back to punish him. He deserved this.

Tessa wanted something so basic, so normal with him.

And he was acting exactly like...well, Elliot. Who tortured him.

She put her hands on her hips. "Stop. Don't say anything. I don't want to hear it."

Parker put his hands on her wrists, lowering them, holding them in between. "Listen. I didn't invite Elliot here. I know she keeps turning up everywhere, but I'm not orchestrating it. It's just kind of always happens." Kind of true, actually.

She shook him off. "Stop talking. I don't care."

"Oh—okay."

She glared at him for a moment. "Remember when we first met? When we had drinks at the hotel bar? Do you remember what I said to you then?"

"I do, I—"

"I said that I always go after what I want, and that I'm not interested in wasting time."

Parker rubbed his forehead and sighed. "Yeah, of course I remember."

"Well, right now this is feeling like a real big waste of time which supersedes me going after what I want. That little circus show in there isn't for me. And I don't believe it's for you either, but right now you're behaving like a fucking clown. Call me when you're ready for something serious. And when you have that Elliot women out of your system. Adults choose. They make hard choices. Maybe you should try it sometimes. Goodbye, Parker."

And with that, she turned on her high heel and swished down the hallway.

Parker stood in her wake, raking his hands through his hair. *Fuck.*

He returned to his apartment in a daze, but Jen and Elliot were laughing.

"Where's Tessa?" asked Jen.

"Didn't she want to stay for the cucumber sandwiches?" Elliot asked, picking one up.

Then he noticed his bottle of McCallan 12 in the middle of the table. They'd broken into his stash in a manner of minutes.

"Tessa had to leave, family emergency." He stared at Elliot, but she refused to meet his gaze.

Jen frowned. "Hmm. That's too bad, I had this whole thing planned." Then her phone lit up on the table again. "*Shit.* Shit. It's Kate. All this fucking wedding planning. My phone's been ringing nonstop." She picked up her phone.

"Kate, I'm kind of in the middle of some—wait what? What about the doves? Are you serious? Jesus, fine I'll be there in twenty minutes." She took the phone away from her ear, giving a rueful shrug. "Sorry, I gotta go. Wedding dove emergencies. Elliot, it was nice to meet you. You should stay! Enjoy the food, we have so much. Park, I'll see you later. We can talk then."

"Fine. Yeah. I'll see you later." He was too keyed up to care about Jen, his whole focus was on Elliot, who was still staring ahead at the tiered stacks of plates, fiddling with a crumpet on the center of her saucer. "

Once the door had shut, and it was just the two of them, Parker put his hands on his hips. "You wanna fucking explain yourself?" he asked.

She scoffed, her eyes narrowed. "Do *you?*" She had the nerve to get an attitude with him.

"Me? What have I done?"

She crossed her arms over her chest. "Oh, cut the shit, Parker. You think you're this perfect great guy, but you're clearly leading Tessa on. Poor woman. What's the point, you enjoy torturing innocent ladies?"

Parker put his fingers to his lips. "Shh. Lower your voice, my neighbors will think I'm a serial killer."

Elliot glowered but when she spoke again her voice was an angry hiss. "I'm doing you *and* her a favor, and you know it."

"Oh yes, doing me such a huge favor by showing up at my house unannounced in a *fucking gown.*"

"You sent me the gown!" Elliot paused as if she'd just remembered something. "Thanks, by the way. For sending it. It's the nicest thing anyone's ever done for me."

Parker stopped pacing abruptly, shoving his hands through his hair. He lifted a shoulder. "You're welcome."

"I was being honest though, I'm keeping it. That influencer dropped the charges against me, but I had to agree to shoot her house tour for free."

"Why would she even want to work with you again?"

Elliot shrugged. "People have short memories. They can only hold on to so much at a time."

He walked towards her, scraped the chair out and plopped down. His legs were splayed out next to hers, and while her legs were stretched out the gown ran well past them, almost as long as Parker's legs. And her eyes sockets appeared darkened, hollowed, as if she hadn't been sleeping. Her forehead etched with crinkles from the expression she was trying to mask.

"The whole thing really worried you. I can tell."

She shrugged again. "Nah, nothing worries me. Hey, dude. I fixed it. I ain't too proud to beg. And then I got a free gown out of it."

"And you wore it to my house."

"In that sense, it was a failure." She elbowed him against his ribs.

Parker shook his head. "I'm so pissed at you, but also…"

"You find it hard to stay mad at me."

"You're taking advantage of it."

"Look, I didn't know Tessa would be at your house today."

"You would've if you'd bothered to call or text or literally anything instead of just showing up. I didn't even give you my address."

Elliot fiddled with the ends of her hair. "But this has always kind of been our thing."

"What thing?"

"Just…showing up."

He scratched his head. "Hmm."

How did he forget everything when Elliot was around? He canceled clients. He forgot he was angry. He forgot he was fine.

"Your sister seems nice."

"No, she doesn't."

Elliot chuckled. "Well, she was cool as fuck about me showing up in a ball gown to your weird little lunch."

"She's always been that way." Parker scrubbed the scruff on his jaw, memories flowing into his consciousness. "We didn't have a lot of money growing up, but Jen is talented at creating a good time wherever she goes. We had some really top tier tea parties back in the day. She must've gotten it from our mother. And if you think I'm serious, you shoulda met my dad. Straighter faced than the King's Guard. But my mom…she was a blast. It's too bad she was a terrible fucking driver."

"You liked your parents, huh? It sounds like they were good to you."

"Of course. They were good. Really good. But now they're gone."

Elliot tilted her head. Her gaze a little blank. "Yeah, I feel that. I have the opposite problem. My parents stuck around, but they suck. Control freaks. And they definitely don't like me."

"You're not close?"

"Understatement."

"Do you still see them?"

Elliot paused. "I don't wanna talk about this right now."

Of course she didn't. But on this particular subject, he wouldn't push.

Then, Parker was startled by his phone vibrating in his pocket. He pulled it out.

Rebecca: You never told me how the dress worked out. I got a tag on Instagram, so I know it arrived.

That's right. Rebecca had been dying to know the outcome of her special delivery. Parker held up his phone. "Elliot, smile for the camera."

Elliot gave the middle finger. He snapped the pic and sent it to Rebecca. "Great, she'll like that."

"She who? Tessa? Wow, you're a bad person."

"Jesus Christ. No, not Tessa. Rebecca."

"Rebecca Martinez?" Her eyes went big. "Ex-fucking-scuse me? You know the designer of this dress?'

"How else do you think I got it for you?"

Elliot fell back against the chair dramatically, the back of her hand falling over her forehead. "Holy shit."

"She wants to know if she can post this picture to her Instagram."

"Rebecca Martinez wants to post a picture of *me* to her social media? Fuck yes."

Parker flashed her the picture. Elliot was slouched at the end of the chair, legs splayed wide, sneakers peeking out beneath the hem of the dress, middle finger flashing and a *don't give a fuck about you* sneer on her face that maybe some people would describe as sexy. Her makeup was simple, bright red lips, dark black eye liner and long lashes. Her lashes were long anyway, but now they were inky black and thick too.

Elliot nodded at the picture, unimpressed. "Ah yeah. That's me."

He locked his phone, setting it on the table.

"Should I go?" she asked.

He was taken aback by the question. And a little surprised at her timidness, which she'd never displayed before. He was surprised she thought he wouldn't want her here. Although she had royally fucked everything up for him so in that sense…he should be mad.

Of course, he wasn't.

He sighed, staring at her for a moment. He should kick her out. That was some shit that she would pull, and just like sneaking out in the small hours of the morning like he did last time it would give her a taste of her own medicine.

But that had hurt him to do.

And he wasn't like her at all. He was only like himself. And he wanted to be with her now, no matter how uncomfortable she'd made him. "Are you hungry? Maybe we can finish some of the food my sister prepared."

She shook her head. "I'm not hungry, but actually…I'm pretty tired. I came here from another shoot. Changed at Bruno's and everything. Now, I'm swamped."

"Why'd you come then? Why not stay home?"

She picked up the dress, swinging her feet back and forth. "I thought the least I could do is stop by and thank you in person."

"How'd you know it was me?"

She thought for a moment, then she threw her head back and forth. "Who else could it possibly be? I have a question for you."

"Go on."

"Do you have a bathtub?"

"Like in my condo?"

"No, like in your kidneys. Yes, obviously in your condo."

He did have one. It was installed custom because he didn't comfortably fit in a normal sized tub. But he had yet to use it. He wasn't one for relaxing. He was more for doing things. Running around. Working out. He nodded over to his bedroom door, which connected to the master bath. "Right through there."

She lowered her eyes and then raised them again. "Can I take   a   bath?"

Chapter 18

Parker paced around his dining table as the faint sound of running water emanated from his master bathroom. He nabbed a cucumber finger sandwich and downed the whole thing in one.

Elliot said her whole body was sore from too much photography. She lugged around equipment. She walked all over the place. The travel.

Parker could relate as a mechanic, often bent over and fiddling with items that required specific coordination. Although the soreness bothered him less because he took care to take care. He scheduled regular massages, he worked out and stretched, he watched his drinking (when he wasn't too stressed) and he slept regular hours. Plus, he actually *owned a place to live.*

He got a little sad when he thought about Elliot living like a vagabond, floating from one place to the next, her only central touchpoint a storage unit.

"Parker!" she called from the bathroom, panic in her voice.

Shit. He hoped she hadn't slipped and fallen or something of that nature.

He ran to the bedroom and opened the bathroom door, but she was just sitting there, bubbles covering the top layer of the water, covering all her naked bits except for her arms and calves and feet that were sticking out from the tub. Her feet were propped up on the side ledge as the tub was long enough that she could completely submerge if she wanted.

"What's wrong?" he asked, slightly out of breath. Maybe he'd been a little too eager to run in there.

"I need entertainment. Entertain me." She pouted.

He paused for a moment, then chuckled. He was in a good mood now. He'd deal with all the fallout from Elliot's arrival later.

For now, he was going to have a good time. "Well, I'm not doing any edibles, nor do I own any."

She shrugged, water sluicing and slushing around her. Those bubbles wouldn't maintain their form forever.

"Wait, hold on. I have an idea." Parker hustled out of the bathroom and back to the dining room where he collected the tiered plates and carefully brought them back, setting them on a small table next to the tub. "You need to take better care of yourself." He handed her a strawberry.

"Chill. I'm in a bubble bath. It doesn't get more self-care bullshit than that." She popped it into her mouth, chewing thoughtfully. "Hey, throw the next one, see if I can catch it!"

He smothered a grin, picked up another strawberry, then tossed it with an easy swing so it lobbed into the air.

Elliot's juked her shoulder left and right and then lifted halfway out of the bathtub, catching it in her mouth while simultaneously flashing her tits.

Goddamn. His jaw clenched, causing him to bite the side of his cheek. Her tits were large and somehow perky, light pink nipples that complemented the blue of her eyes and looked delicate and pale compared to her strikingly black hair.

She crashed back down into the water with a smug look on her face.

"You doing that on purpose?"

She looked down, the shadow of her inky black lashes fanning out over her cheekbones. "Yes and no. I dare you to take off your shirt." Her eyes twinkled at him.

Parker shook his head. "Tell me the truth about why you told Tessa about what happened between us in that hotel room."

She leaned back, crossing her arms over her chest, causing her boobs to hike up, and creating a deep valley of cleavage. "I dare you to take off your pants."

"Tell me the truth about why you wanted me to meet you in Charleston."

She let her head fall back of the back edge of the tub. "I dare you to get into the tub."

"You know what? Fine." In his socks and shoes and all his clothes, Parker stalked over to the tub and put his heavy foot in.

"Ahh! What are you doing!" she squealed.

Then another big heavy foot in, water splashing everywhere and soaking up his jean clad leg.

The he sat down, bending his parted knees so he could fit at the other end of the tub with her legs stretched out in between the wedge of space.

"Classic Parker behavior. We're in a bathtub and you're fully clothed. I've never even seen you naked before."

"Do you want to?" He lifted an eyebrow, smirking a bit. He was teasing her. He didn't mind making her beg a bit at the moment.

She sighed. "Your bathroom is so nice. Did you hire a designer or something?"

"Rebecca did it. She designed everything."

"Then why's there no couch in your living room? It's a big wide open space."

He splashed a little water at her. "Can't find the right couch to settle down into, that's all."

She splashed him back. "I'm being a good girl right now. I feel like I deserve a prize."

"Why do you say that?"

"Usually I'd be all over you, trying to get you naked. But look at me here, as pure as the driven snow. Like a little sweet birdie swimming around a puddle."

"What kind of prize should I give you?"

She smiled slyly then she floated at the surface and stretched over to him so that her chest was level was his. Naked and open in the steamy air.

"You really want to know?"

At this point, his dick was rock hard and aching. And Elliot's tits were in plain sight, wet and full and hot. He wanted to lick them. Put his hands on them. Slap them. Rub his dick on them.

Oh Jesus. He was really putting himself in exactly the position he both did and did not want to be in.

"Yes, I really want to know."

She circled a fingertip over the T-shirt covering his chest. It was dry on the top, soaked on the bottom where he was reclining in the tub.

"The truth is, I don't need to get you naked at all to do what I want to do with you."

His gaze darkened on her. "Is that right?"

Her finger dragged down to his sternum in a straight line down to his belly. All his muscles flexed at once. His heart rate jumping in response.

"Then what?" he asked. "Then what are you doing?"

She leaned in towards him, letting her mouth come so close to his they were almost touching. He lifted his chin to catch her in a kiss but she moved so that he couldn't.

"Tell me no, and I'll stop." Her finger traveled to the button of his jeans. "See, I don't even need to get you naked to get what I want."

He closed his eyes, his hands coming to her hips and tightening at the warm flesh.

"Okay then, Mr. Serious." Slowly, beneath the surface of the water, she undid the button at his fly. "Tell me no...go ahead." The whisper of her voice in his ear made him shiver.

She pinched the zipper between her fingers dragging it down. "Oops, look what I've done." Then her hand dove in, pulling down the waistband of soaked boxer briefs, finding him there. Hard and aching.

He gulped, his throat tight, his eyes closed. His hips were moving beneath her. His fingers flexing in her skin.

She grabbed his dick hard, stroking up and down, freed from the constraints of his pants and boxer briefs, but still fully clothed. "I'll take this as a yes."

Then she moved in the water from in between his legs to suddenly right above his hard, exposed dick.

His hands had moved with her, his elbows retracted to drag her closer. She pushed her hands against his chest. He might've been sweating but it was too hard to tell in the water. Her fingertips grazed upwards until they found the back of his neck, pulling hard on the hair there. He groaned.

"I'm gonna put your dick inside me now, Parker. And then I'm gonna fuck it. So you'd better speak up if you don't want it."

Instead, he jolted his hips so that the head of his cock hit her entrance. She nested down, and allowed it to breach the barrier.

They both groaned at the first slip of penetration.

"Push me down so it's all the way in." She moaned as she writhed on the, her hips rocking and her tits right in his face. He complied, and she sat on him, his dick buried inside her.

"Move, goddammit." He growled against her ear.

She licked the inside of his ear. "I knew you wanted to fuck me, Parker. Knew you couldn't resist. And my pussy is so fucking wet for you. Even in this bathtub I'm the wettest thing here."

She rocked forward, letting the shaft of his dick slip to the top of the head and then down again. Her pussy had fully lubricated every inch of him and he could feel her clenching around him.

Then she began bouncing in earnest, holding on tightly to his neck so that his head was against her sternum. She was grabbing on for dear life, up and down and up and down. Water spraying and splashing and threatening to fall over the sides of his deep tub.

"Ugh, fuck, god yes," she whispered.

He couldn't see anything and she was practically suffocating him with her tits but he didn't want it to stop. He groaned against her wet, hot skin. His clothes were sticky and heavy and suctioned to his body. He couldn't even move his hips. He had to submit to her as she fucked him. Used his dick for her own pleasure.

As she increased her rhythm, she swallowed hard, her eyes squinting. She released his neck, one of her hands slipping in between them. She was rubbing her clit now.

"Let me do that..." He panted against her, letting his tongue slide up and down her sternum. If only he could get to her nipples but he was too crushed against her.

"Nuh-uh." She shook her head. Her hand began moving so quickly the water was disturbed, splashing up around his shirt. Then suddenly, she gasped. "Oh god, I'm coming. I'm coming. Fuuuck."

She dug her nails into his shoulders which would've probably bled if he didn't still have his shirt on, and her whole body wrenched forward against him.

He couldn't fuck her like he wanted to. Couldn't move his hips up and down to come as well. Her whole body tightened, and little moans were coming out of her as if she were eating something amazing. And then she collapsed against him with one big exhale.

He was still rock hard inside of her but clarity was overcoming him. He rubbed up and down the slick skin of her back, gently. Soothing. She was breathing hard against him.

"You didn't come." Her words were muffled because her lips were against his skin.

"Shh. It's okay."

"Let's keep going," she said, and she straightened her back, putting her arms on his shoulders. "I'm ready let's go."

"Shh, shh." He soothed her more, fingertips grazing the sensitive skin of her lower back all the way up her spine. "Relax for a minute, Jesus Christ. You're so pushy all the time."

Finally, she let her weight rest against him, her spine curved, her head against his chest, her hair damp and wild. Makeup smeared all over her.

And when she was finally settled, his dick began to twitch deep inside of her.

"What was that?" she said, glancing up at him.

"Nothing…"

Then it jumped again, and her pussy responded with a little fluttering clench.

"What about that?" This time she pulled the collar of his shirt, stretching it to expose the skin of his collarbone and she kissed him there. The touch made his cock jump again.

She smiled against his skin. "Oh really?" And her kisses followed up his neck. Her hands made their way to the hem of his shirt and she yanked it upwards, forcing his arms over his head. His world muffled as she pulled it off him and then tossed it aside where it landed with a wet slap against the austere marble floor of his bathroom.

"Wow, your body is amazing." She leaned forward, grazing the edge of her teeth over one of his nipples, his hand clenched in the back of her hair, he fisted a handful and pulled her away.

"Don't even think about it."

She gave a little smile and then carefully, without removing his dick from inside of her she began to scoot his jeans from his waist, hooking her finger beneath the waistband and giving tiny little yanks.

"Kick your boot off. Lift your hips," she instructed. And then they both moaned when he did and jolted into her further. She began to ride him again, rocking back and forth, his jeans pulled off half way down his hips. His dick was out of his boxer briefs, only requiring another yank to get him fully naked.

Then she squeezed her eyes shut and slapped her hands down on his chest. "No, stop. We're getting you naked first. And we're getting of this tub."

She double down on the pulling until she was leaning all the way up on his shoulders and she managed to finally get all of Parker's clothing off. "Thanks for not even lifting a finger." She said, then her mouth took his in a kiss.

It started soft and luscious, her tongue flicking into his mouth, her lips catching his in an easy, soft pull. But then it quickly turned filthy, tongues flitting in and out, searching deep, lips barely touching.

Parker's heat was turned up to a thousand now. He would be sweating bullets if it weren't for the water. He groped Elliot's ass, squeezing tight, garnering a little yelp from her, then with a growl, he lifted her out of the bathtub, kicking off the pants and boxer briefs around his heel, leaving them to float in his enormous tub.

They were still connected, wet, and hot. And now Parker was overcome with the urge to fuck Elliot hard. And he would.

Instead of the bed, he walked out of the bathroom with her legs wrapped around his waist and he reached behind them closing the door. Then he slammed her back against the closed door.

"Shit," she yelled in surprise, but he didn't give her a moment to catch up, because he was fucking her ruthlessly now.

"Fuck, fuck, fuck..." she half moaned half panted. Her head rolled back, bouncing against the door. "Fuck, yes, yes."

His dick surged in and out of her. He grunted with each thrust and her whole body jolted upwards. Her hands were limp around his neck. He wanted her to come again but couldn't get to her clit.

"Touch yourself." His voice came out hoarse but he didn't slow down, continued to fuck her hard against the door, the only sounds in the house her quiet rhythmic moans and the pounding of her back against the wood.

"I..." She licked her lips. "I can't...I can't move."

"Do it now." He growled. "I need you to come now."

She nodded, strained. Then her hand traveled between them and it almost seemed as if she was struggling to stay conscious. Until she began moaning his name. "Oh, Parker...Parker...it's so good, don't stop..."

Her hand was working steadily, he could feel it scrape against the crisp shorn hair above his dick. She was getting wetter too, gushing now around him.

One hard thrust in. "You better come soon."

"Ah..." she cried out, swallowing. Her hand slapping at her own clit now. His mouth went to the side of her neck, and he began licking up and down her neck and ear in a crazed panic.

"It's happening." She bit her lip. "I'm...I'm..."

Parker's thrusts grew erratic. Pressure building within him. He was about to come too.

"Take it..." He sounded aggressive, almost mean and it surprised even him. "Take it now." And with that, he surged against the wall, pinning her there, her hips rocking against him as he came inside her, hot and fast.

Her whole face scrunched up and then she let out a loud gasp. "I'm done, I'm done, I'm done." The words fell from her mouth in rapid fire.

With a few more brutal thrusts, he was finished. Emptied out, slowing to a halt until he collapsed against her.

Realization melted over him like an ice cube under a hairdryer. They both were frozen in their position. Panting. Coming down from however high they'd flown together.

Maybe he'd made a huge mistake? She was going to leave him after this, he was sure of it.

He rested his forehead against hers. They were slick and hot from the bathtub, but now the cool air was wrapping around them. He didn't want her to catch a cold.

Slowly, he pulled out of her, wincing a bit, his come dribbling down the inside of her thigh. Then he lowered her gently to the ground. He'd gripped her so tightly his hands were a little stiff. That worried him too. She'd have bruises.

"Sorry..." he murmured.

"For what?" she asked.

"I was holding onto you pretty tight. Your thighs and ass are all red. And you hit the wall pretty hard while we were...uh..." He scratched the side of his head.

To his surprise, she placed a light kiss on his cheek. "I liked it. I wanted it. Don't forget that. I'm gonna grab a towel."

She wielded around him and headed to the bathroom. After a moment she returned into the bedroom, still naked, wiping off her hair. She tossed a towel to him too. He wrapped it around his hips and then sat on the edge of the bed running he hands back and forth over his hair. She wrapped the towel around her chest as well and then sat next to him.

"Can I borrow some clothes? Wearing a gown on a train loses its novelty fast."

Parker stirred at the end of the bed. "You could stay for a few. I don't have anywhere to be today, and Jen's out with her friend." He cringed at the sound of his own desperation. Under what circumstances did Parker really believe Elliot might stay with him after *that*.

Her lashes fluttered as she looked to each corner of the room, fiddling with the corner of her towel. "I'm on birth control."

Shit. Why hadn't he considered asking her that before? The height of irresponsibility. "I'm sorry, I should have used a condom."

She shrugged. "I could have mentioned it. I have one in my bag."

"This is unlike me."

"STI tests?" she asked.

His heart rate went up. "Haven't had one in over a year but…uh, haven't needed to."

She nodded. "Okay. Well, I'm negative. No STIs…I had chlamydia a few years ago. But everyone gets that. And I wouldn't lie to you about that kind of thing."

"Sure."

There was an awkward silence. "Clothes?" she asked.

"Oh." He stood from the bed, walking over to the closet. He thumbed through his racks. He usually only wore T-shirts and jeans but Rebecca had supplied him with cashmere sweaters and tailored button ups. He removed a navy cashmere sweater from a dresser, giving it a good shake. He'd only worn it once before. Then he located a pair of extra-soft grey sweatpants. She'd have to roll them or they'd be way too long. And maybe she'd have to tie the drawstring super tight, but they'd do.

He pulled on a pair of sweatpants too.

"I recognize those Pumas."

He turned his gaze. Elliot's face peeked around the frame of the closet door. She was referring to the shoes resting on the top of the dresser, away from his other shoes which were organized in a wall cubby. "Got them with a racecar sponsorship almost twenty years ago. Lucky shoes. I survived a car crash in them."

"Interesting definition of luck."

He emerged from the closet and handed the clothes to Elliot.

"Thanks." She let the towel drop and Parker turned around, his back facing to her. Suddenly, it felt...wrong to watch her change. She wouldn't have minded if he watched, clearly, but to him, changing represented an intimacy that he knew she wasn't willing to share.

"All done, stranger."

He spun around. She had rolled his sweatpants all the way up at the waist so the ankles came halfway up her calves. The sweater could've been a dress but she'd tucked the front into the sweatpants. She'd tied her hair up in a knot on the top of her head too, the likeness of a child who'd been given oversized clothes to wear while playing in the dirt.

Unbearably cute. That's what she was. Weird but playful. A small pang cut into his stomach. He really didn't want her to go, but he definitely couldn't ask her to stay again.

She stepped over to him, her hand going to his waist and drawing him near. "Thanks for the good time." She pushed up on her tippy toes, kissing him on the cheek.

Behind them, his bed was precisely made, with folded, tucked corners and fresh sheets. His housekeeper had been in that morning, but he made the bed every morning too. If only he could snatch Elliot up by the waist, and hide her beneath those covers, their legs tangled like webs. He'd turn the heat off so the air was cold but their bodies were hot, smashed together.

Then they'd doze off, and wake up lazily in the morning. Eat cornflakes in bed together that he'd ordered delivery. Laugh about nothing in particular. Parker would do the dishes. Make them both coffee. He didn't know how she liked her coffee.

And he'd fuck her again. But gently this time. Long and lingering. Until they were tired again. Rinse and repeat.

But instead she was leaving. Like he knew she'd do.

"Okay then…" She lingered by the entrance of his bedroom doorway. "I'm out."

He cleared his throat. "I have a question for you."

She raised an eyebrow. "Yeah?"

"Truth or dare."

She chuckled a little. "Maybe another time. I'm late for something." She turned on her heel and walked to the entrance, he close behind her. "Thanks again."

He stared at the door even after it closed shut, as if he could will her to come back. Will her to return. But after a minute, he scrubbed his hand down his face, padding over to his kitchen.

He pulled out a glass and poured a big serving of scotch. Bigger than it needed to be. In two gulps he'd almost taken down half.

He stalked back into his bedroom, drink in hand and looked out the wall-length glass that overlooked the Chicago skyline. The lights of the city twinkled in the night sky, and sometimes he was overwhelmed with how high up he really was. He didn't have the penthouse, but maybe one day, when the owners moved out. He'd already tried petitioning for dibs. He thought the larger apartment would be a better home to raise a family.

He sighed, downing the rest of his drink. There was an emptiness after what had happened with Elliot. An emptiness he couldn't fill up with drinks or work or friends. It couldn't be done. And he couldn't be settled. He wanted to keep her in one place, but she slipped away over and over.

When she was with him, time became a different element entirely. Nights went by in a matter of seconds, and when she was gone time dragged slower than a tortoise, days relentlessly long.

He walked into the closet to gather the wet towel he had dropped there and then back to the bathroom. Where they had...

There were puddles on the floor still. Fading wet foot prints of what had occurred. The only thing left of Elliot.

Until, in the corner of his eye he saw something.

There, on the bench Rebecca insisted he have for "utilitarian and decorative purposes" was Elliot's dress, strewn about like a woman in repose who had been gobbled up by the rapture.

He went over to it and picked up the delicate white fabric. Something dropped to the floor. He leaned over to pick it up what appeared to be a small scrap of light pink lace. But then he realized what it was. His hands bunched over the material. Elliot's underwear.

He took the items and brought them to his own closet, and with care he folded them both into the top drawer with his cashmere sweaters.

Then he took out his phone with a new feeling of determination.

I choose you he typed.

But   then   he   deleted   it.

Chapter 19

P arker was casually walking down the elevated strip of space in the KLM business class lounge at O'Hare airport, typing a message to Tessa, *hey can we talk*, when suddenly he tripped over something, practically face-planting onto the hard floor.

He turned around, irrationally angry and looking for whatever had tripped him only to see a familiar pair of sea-blue eyes looking back at him beneath a black baseball cap.

"What'd you do that for?" Parker asked, dusting off his shirt as if that somehow would help him recover from embarrassment.

Elliot lifted a shoulder. "I dunno. Just something I do."

"Well, it's a fucking hazard."

"You wanna take me to court?"

The words sounded suggestive somehow. Parker pursed his lips. No. Absolutely the fuck not. "It was nice seeing you, Elliot."

"Hey! Wait, wait, wait! Where you going?"

Parker stopped in his tracks and then slowly turned around. "It's an airport. I'm going to a terminal."

"Ha-ha. Wow, when did you become so rude? Sit down. C'mon. I haven't seen you in forever."

That's right. She hadn't. And that was no mistake on Parker's part.

After she'd left his apartment, left him there spent and alone, he'd set out on a mission to forget Elliot Sheer. A one-man pilgrimage to stop going after women who didn't want him. Not in the right way.

He'd blocked her on all social media. Rebecca had been sitting on the couch next to him as he did, her hand patting his shoulder. "You're doing the right thing," she'd reassured him. "You're never going to get to the place you want in life if you keep going after the wrong women."

Pamela had passed by with Avery on her hip. "Believe me, this is what I've been telling him!"

And in his head, he was coming around on Tessa too. *Choices. Not feelings.* Now that he'd eliminated Elliot as an option, all of a sudden everything felt a little easier.

"Oh my god, I didn't ask for your banking password, I asked you to sit down. Stop being so dramatic. I thought we were old friends."

He sighed and made his way over to her table, pushing her feet off the other end of the booth chair, then scooting in. If she was going to make him end this *thing* they had together in person, then fine, he would do that. He didn't want to hurt her, but he had to do what was right for him. What was right for his future.

"We need to have a talk, Elliot."

Elliot leaned forward. There was a cappuccino steaming in front of her. She was wearing a black T-shirt with some band name on it that he only vaguely recognized. She seemed so much less mature than him in every way. Why was he wasting so much time with her? "We always need to talk. It's like your whole thing."

He shook his head. "Can you ever take anything seriously?"

"Can you ever not?"

He was about to say something cutting back to her but then he remembered that without even thinking he was getting sucked into her little games. And he wouldn't get sucked back in this time.

"Where you headed?" she asked him before he could even recover.

"London."

"Get out of town."

Parker looked left and right. "I am out of town."

"Nah, that's where I'm heading too. You're flying into Heathrow then. Gimme your ticket."

"What? No."

"C'mon." She held out her hand with a come hither motion. "Lemme see if we're sitting next to each other."

"We're not. This airplane has pods anyway, so it doesn't matter, we wouldn't even see each other. Total privacy."

Elliot pulled out her phone. "I'm in 3D."

He gave an exasperated look then he dug his phone out of his pocket. "Fine. Three C."

She clapped her hands together. "Ah-ha! You're next to me but you have the window. Don't try to fight it, Mr. Serious, we are destined to run into each other. It's cosmic serendipity and there ain't nothing you can do about it."

Parker needed a drink. A stiff one, but because there wasn't anything directly in front of him he reached out and took her cappuccino. He took a big slug. It was the perfect temperature.

"Well, help yourself."

Parker set the mug back down, scratching at his brow. He'd lost track of the thread of the conversation in an instance of time. Time to take control. "Okay, you know what? Elliot, listen closely. We're over. Whatever was or wasn't between us is done. I can't do this with you. I don't want this with you. Do you understand what I'm saying?"

Elliot tilted her head to the side. "No need to be so grim about it."

His head fell back. She wasn't going to acknowledge what he needed her to acknowledge. She was going to keep running in circles with him until the end of time if he let her. "We can't talk anymore. We're not friends. Got it?"

She leaned back in the chair, crossing her arms. "What's gotten into you? I thought we had a great time the last time we saw each other, and you ghost on me out of nowhere?

And now I'm supposed to disappear like some kind of bacteria that you took some penicillin for? What the fuck, Parker? What the fuck does that mean?" Her voice was getting louder, eyes wider.

But Parker was going to stand his ground no matter what it took. He leaned forward, lowering his voice so that she had to pay attention. "We're not going to do what you want to do, Elliot. I'm not going to sleep with you and sleep with other people. I'm not going to pretend to be your friend and be fucking in love with you at the same time. I'm not going down this road with you, not now, not ever. This isn't a fucking game to me. This is real. This is my life. And you don't take it seriously enough. So you can't be here with me anymore. I need to hear that you understand. I need you to say you're going to stay away."

Elliot's eyes had widened. "You're not in love with me. I know you think that, but it's not true."

Parker sat back in his seat. Silence permeated between them for a solid minute of time. Somehow, the longest and fastest minute of his life.

"You don't get to tell me what I do or do not feel. Not now. Not ever. I've had enough of your shit."

With that, he shot back the rest of her cappuccino, the taste bitter in his mouth, and slid out of the booth. He had to get the fuck out of there and stat.

When Parker boarded the plane, he knew his luck had turned sour. He'd specifically looked up the airline to ensure that he would be taking the red-eye with the pod seating so that he could get some good rest before his long day of work with his client's collection of BMW M8s. Also, he had a whole week off soon. He wanted to ask Tessa to spend it with him in Denver. He would tell her that she was right, and that they wanted the same things. They would go on that trip before Jen's wedding.

Denver was where she lived. He knew where she lived even if maybe he'd forgotten at one point. He'd only forgotten because of all the *distractions* he'd been allowing into his life, which he wasn't allowing anymore.

But now he might be in trouble, because these seats weren't pods. These seats were regular old seats. No dividers at all. Only large tables in between. And Elliot was already seated. Her baseball cap pushed down, her legs splayed, her arms crossed.

"You're in my seat." Parker grunted at her.

She glanced up from under the rim of her cap. "Get fucked."

He rolled his eyes but he wasn't going to fight her for the seat. Not this time. They were already in a bad enough position as it was.

"Fine, be that way." He settled into the seat next to her.

"Fine, you fucking asshole, I will."

Don't take the bait. Don't take the bait.

But inwardly he was fuming. She was the most irritating woman in the universe. After all the shit she'd put him through, she didn't have the right to be mad at him. She didn't care about him or his well-being or about anything he wanted.

And now he was putting up some boundaries, and fine, she could be salty about it. Her anger was fine with him. Fine. Fine. *Fine.*

"Sir, madam, would you care for some champagne?" The flight attendant leaned over them with a tray of sparkling wine in flutes.

"No," Parker said the same time Elliot spoke. "Yep."

The flight attendant's eyebrows went up. Apparently they both were coming across a tad bit harsh. "Please enjoy, madam." They delivered the flute to Elliot.

"I've changed my mind, I would like some champagne, please."

"Very well. Please enjoy, sir." The flight attendant handed Parker the glass.

Fuck it. Fuck everything. Fuck being well rested for his client. Fuck keeping his shit together. Fuck being tightly wound Parker Donne.

Fuck it, he was getting wasted on this plane.

"Cheers, dickhead." Elliot put her glass out to him.

He barely acknowledged her, his eyes cutting to the side. Instead, he threw back the glass in one go. "Excuse me, can I have another? Actually, make it two."

Perhaps for normal passengers, the staff wouldn't allow this kind of behavior. But Parker had the highest miles status anyone could acquire, so they often allowed whatever he wanted. "Right away, sir."

The flight attendant delivered two more glasses to Parker. "Scotch too, thanks."

The flight attendant nodded; if he was suspicious of Parker's behavior he didn't indicate it.

"Are you out of your mind? This won't end well for you." Elliot murmured to him.

He knocked back one glass of champagne and then the next. "You don't know shit about me, Elliot."

Which was true. Or maybe it wasn't. They had spent a lot of time together. But fuck it.

Elliot sipped at her glass. "I know some bullshit when I see it. You're full of it right now. But okay, good luck."

The flight attendant appeared with the glass of scotch.

"Next one, make a double. Thanks."

Elliot set her glass down on the divide between them. "Well, this should be a lovely fucking flight."

Thirty minutes later and Parker was wasted. As a big guy, it took quite a bit of liquor to do the trick, and well, by god, he had managed to put back *quite a bit of liquor.*

But it didn't make him feel better like he thought it might. Or had he actually thought that it would make him feel better? Maybe he was actually trying to feel worse. Maybe he was punishing himself. Yes, that was more in line with the Parker he knew himself to be.

Punishment.

Which was what he deserved for getting mixed up with the likes of someone like Elliot Sheer. Who wanted nothing but to toy with him.

It was Kate all over again.

It was Cameron all over again. But worse somehow. Because he loved Elliot, madly and deeply, and in a way he'd never really felt or known before, and she still didn't want him. Elliot didn't even have a husband as an excuse. She simply didn't want to be with Parker. And somehow that felt like a much bigger insult than all the rest.

"What's wrong with me?" The words came out of his mouth before he could stop them. They weren't slurring so much as they were thick, and pathetic sounding.

Jesus fuck, Parker get it together.

"I think you downed six drinks in thirty minutes on a red-eye. That's the best diagnosis I've got."

He considered her words, through his haze of drunken anger. "Yeah, you're not wrong."

Elliot's eyes went skywards. The lights were low on the plane, and the only sound was the white noise of the circulating air in the jet. "I can't believe I'm going to say this. But." She slumped forward in her chair. "I think we need to have a real conversation."

Parker looked over at her for the first time, his eyes adjusting in the darkness to her face. She'd taken the hat off and her hair was a mess. There were dark circles under her eyes. There always seemed to be dark circles under her eyes.

"You always look tired," is what came out of him.

She sighed, exasperated. "Why must you always bring that up? Lots of people are tired."

He pointed towards her. "It's in your eyes. Dark circles. You don't sleep enough. You'd sleep better if you had your own apartment."

"How the fuck would you know?"

"Because home is where you rest your head."

"Wow, you're drunk."

"Yeah, but being drunk doesn't preclude being correct."

"No, being drunk means you're honest. But I never asked for the truth."

He narrowed his eyes at her, sipped the watered-down end of a glass of scotch. "Should I be a liar? Like you?"

"Fuck you. If anything I'm painfully real."

"Maybe you think so."

"What's that supposed to mean?"

"You lie to everyone, but most of all, you lie to yourself."

Her head fell back,. "Oh yeah, and what am I lying to myself about? That I'm in love with you, Parker? Is that why you gave me that confession at the lounge? You want me to admit to you that I'm in love with you? That every night when I lie my head down on my pillow, I think of you? Psh. Please."

He nodded. "That's right. I do think you're in love with me. And I think you're a huge fucking coward." He opened a bag of potato chips and took one from the bag. Then he remembered that first time on the plane together. When she told him she hadn't eaten all day. Her eyes had been tired then too. They were always tired. He pointed the opening of the bag towards her. "You want?"

She glared for a moment and then took the bag from him, shoving her hand in it and pushing some chips into her face. Talking with her mouth full. "Well, you're wrong about all that. Some people can't handle reality."

"Fine, if that's how you want to play it." He turned his gaze to the front of his seat, watching the simulation of the plane crossing over the water. "Like I said. We're over. Starting now."

"You can't be serious," she scoffed.

But he crossed his arms and closed his eyes. He vowed to not so much as turn his head in her direction for the rest of the flight. It wasn't worth the pain.

Not until she could be honest.

And if he wanted to reconnect with Tessa soon, he needed to completely shift his focus.

Luckily, the drinks were catching up with him and slowly he could feel his conscious brain receding into the ether, drifting into darkness, enveloped by foggy, useless thoughts.

And when he awoke, hours had passed. A flight attendant was checking the rows. Elliot was sleeping now, and it would be time to exit the plane soon. They were landing in a few minutes.

As the plane got louder, Elliot came to as well. He could only tell from the stirring of motion to the side of him, but he kept his eyes transfixed on the skyline on the screen in front of him.

And when the plane landed, they left as if they were two strangers, walking down the corridor in a straight line, him behind her. And when the baggage claim turned on he stood at the other side of the carousel so he couldn't so much as see her.

Even though when her bag passed him with its ET emblem, he had the urge to grab it and bring it to her. To grab her hand and hail a taxi and go to her to whatever hotel she was staying at. Diving beneath the covers and holding on tightly.

But instead, he white-knuckled his own suitcase and turned on his heel and got the hell out.

He was serious this time. He didn't need Elliot Sheer for fuck all.

That is until he realized something once he got in the cab and went to pay the cab driver. "Um, actually I don't have any money on me. Shit."

The taxi driver, unimpressed, didn't appear to like that answer.

"I can send you payment through my phone?"

The taxi driver accepted and luckily Parker made it to his hotel.

But of course he was missing one important thing.

His fucking wallet.

Fuck. She'd stolen his fucking wallet.

Again.

Chapter 20

Parker collapsed onto his bed in the fancy hotel in London.

He was only able to check in due to the various copies of his personal records he had on his phone and thank god for that. But still it made shit a hell of a lot harder.

Elliot had basically committed a federal offense.

Worse yet, all the commitment he'd had before to stopping things with her was withering as fast as a lily in the hot sun of the summer because the game was back on. He was never in control of the game. This wasn't his game Elliot was playing. This was Elliot's game he was playing.

And she made the rules. The house always won. Which meant, he was a loser.

AKA hungover as fuck, and it occurred to him that he had a very, very legitimate reason to contact Elliot.

And just like that, he was itching to do so. Just like that everything changed.

He wondered where she was staying. He wondered where she was working. He wondered what she was wearing.

He'd make her come to him. He would take control. She wasn't going to play him. Not this time.

Okay, fine. Let's be real, he'd go to her too.

He tugged on his collar. His T-shirt was a soft and worn black material. Why was this making him so hot? He was so determined to be rid of her for good and then one simple criminal act on her part made him absolutely maddened with desire.

He picked up his phone again.

I'm staying at the East Lipton Hotel. Be at the downstairs bar in twenty or I'm calling the cops on you regarding a stolen wallet.

For stretches of long minutes there was no response but he watched his screen the entire time, knuckles white and tightened around the frame. And then typing bubbles appeared.

Say please, Mr. Serious. Or I set all your shit on fire. You should be nicer to me next time. I'm not very reasonable when I'm angry.

He smiled a little. He wanted a response from her. The last thing he could stand was her apathy. And now he knew she felt the same about him. He typed back at her without rush.

See you soon, sweetheart.

***"Did you walk here in those shoes?" Parker asked Elliot as she sidled up to him at the downstairs bar of the hotel. It was lightly crowded, low lighting with easy jazz music floating around them.

"Don't be silly." Elliot propped her hip up onto the stool next to Parker's and then slid onto the seat, the tops of her thighs peeping out of the black trench coat she wore tied tightly at her waist. On her feet were sky-high black stilettos. He feared for her life in shoes that high. "I ran."

Parker was hungover from the flight, a dull ache in the back of his head, but nothing seemed to matter now that Elliot arrived. He really was a glutton for pain and punishment.

"I'd say we should have a drink but I think you've done enough drinking for a while." She bounced her heel so it rubbed up against the bottom of his pant leg.

His dick began to harden. Goddammit. She could do this to him and only her. Lately he'd noticed that other women had no effect on his libido. He could only get it up when he felt invested emotionally, and for whatever reason, he held stock in Elliot's emotions.

"I'm here for my wallet, and then you can go."

Her eyes glittered. "Did you think I'd let it go so easily? You must think I was born yesterday. I'm not giving this to you until you give *me* something."

He crossed his arms over his chest. He shouldn't play her games. He didn't even have to play them. He could be intimidating if he wanted. She stole his wallet, she was in the wrong, not him.

But he liked the mirage of power she was casting. He wanted to play. Why did he always want to play? Why did he forget Tessa in a moment's notice? Why did he forget quite literally everything else existed in the presence of Elliot?

What was fucking wrong with him?

The eternal question.

He was about to decline, to stand up and talk to her reasonably, march back to his hotel room alone, but she re-crossed her legs in front of him, flashing bare skin all the way up to her...

He squeezed his eyes shut so hard they stung. She was naked under the trench coat.

Of course she was. Why would he expect anything less? Or more, as was the case.

"I hope you didn't show up here...wearing something inappropriate." His words were stern.

She licked her lips. "Oh, I'm not wearing anything at all."

Yep. He nodded. "What do you want from me?"

"I just want your friendship again, Parker. That's all."

"You want my friendship but came here in nothing but heels and a trench coat?"

She picked up a menu. "Hmm, I could go for some fries, how about you? They call them chips here."

Inwardly, he sighed. "Order whatever you want."

Elliot waved and the bartender took her order. Then she flipped her hair over her shoulder. "You think I wore this for you? Maybe I've got a meeting with someone else after this."

Shit. Of course she was playing with him. Right? But then again…one could never really know with a woman like Elliot. Regardless, bile rose up in Parker's throat. Jealousy was so potent. He wasn't engaging in her social media anymore so he'd inoculated himself from her dirty private videos.

He wasn't going to watch those anymore. These were sexy, but they caused him pain too. And since they'd grown closer and closer, he was less inclined to share her.

Not that she was his to share.

But if she were, he *wouldn't.*

"Do you have a meeting with someone else?"

She smiled. "Of course. I'm on all the dating apps. You wouldn't understand because you're much too serious for something as frivolous as a hookup app."

That made him a little hot under the collar. She really was going to meet someone else.

No, Parker. Don't take the bait.

"If you care so much about our friendship, why'd you come to my house and try to ruin my date with Tessa?"

"Did I ruin it?" A large plate of fries appeared before them. Elliot grabbed a bottle of malt vinegar and splashed it on top. She took one hot fry and bit in. "Or is Tessa so fucking desperate and you so deep in denial that I'd bet money you could pick right back up where you left off. All aboard the oblivion train."

Parker took a French fry too and ate the whole thing. It was searingly hot and salty. Carbs and grease. Fuck, when was the last time he'd had French fries? Years at least. Like committing a crime.

"Don't play with me. You know what you were doing. Plus...later that night...we..."

She leaned forward. "We what? Fucked in your tub? Fucked against your wall? Yes. I remember. Like how I remember when you licked my clit. Like how I remember when you kissed me at night by a park. Like I remember how you pulled your dick out for me on an airplane. See? All friendly things."

"Fuck. I can't figure you out. Do you or do you not want to be with me, Elliot? Enough with the games. You say you want to be friends but then you purposely cause drama, and all we do together is mess around. And sometimes, *sometimes* it feels like you feel what I feel too. Like I'm not the only one in this. So, take me off the hook already. Yes or no."

Elliot flicked one of her fries back on the plate, crossing her arm over her chest. He didn't want to notice that the motion spread her coat open a little more, revealing more of the swell of her breast to him. She definitely wasn't wearing a bra either.

"I don't fucking know."

The answer surprised him.

"What don't you know?"

She shook her head. An actual sincere look on her face. "I don't know what I want with you, Parker. You're right. It's not just friendship. But I don't…I don't know what else."

He held his hand out. "Hand over the wallet."

She squeezed her coat again. "No."

"Why not?"

She released her hold, slumping in her chair. "Because you'll make me leave once I do."

He didn't say anything at all for a full minute. He didn't know what to say. Elliot wanted to stick around him, but she wouldn't give him anything else. But something was changing with her. He just didn't know what yet.

But also, she still looked tired. She'd come all the way here in nothing but a coat and heels, the heels quite unsafe to walk in in Parker's assessment. And she looked so tired.

He hated that she always looked so tired but it was also none of his business. She was a grown woman. She could figure out her own sleep schedule.

But he wanted to take care of her. Pull her under blankets and sleep with her tucked beneath him. Why couldn't he have the things he wanted when he wanted them?

He grabbed some fries and shoved them in his mouth.

Elliot giggled.

"Wha?" he asked, mouth full.

"You're eating like a barbarian." She grabbed some fries too, shoving them in her mouth.

He chuckled, then he grabbed most of the plateful, shoving them in his face so they were sticking out like little potato knives. "Lieghkdis?" His words were muffled.

She chewed her fries, laughing, covering her mouth while he struggled to eat everything.

Finally, they were both quiet again, the plate of fries decimated.

Give up the fight, Parker. You're never going to win.

"I want to give Tessa a chance," he said to no one in particular, his gaze downward.

Elliot put a hand on his arm. "Then go ahead. Do that."

"You know it's not that easy. I want to be transparent."

Her hand ran up the length of his biceps to his shoulder, her fingertips playing at the end of his hair near the base of his neck. "I guess things were different when I was married."

His eyebrows went up. "The fuck. You were married?"

"Yeah, but it was forever ago. I was only twenty one…"

"You were young. That's basically a kid."

Her fingertip traveled to the sensitive shell of his ear. His jaw tightened involuntarily at the touch. "He was forty-two. Rich. Hot. Or at least I thought so. My parents were properly upset, but for all the wrong reasons. They'd controlled me my whole life, and they saw the writing on the wall. Never let me do a damn thing. Expected me to follow the path everyone else was following, even though I had this idea that I wasn't like everyone else. And not in a fun talented way, but in like a fucked-up, I-don't-belong-in-this-world kind of way. So, when I met Barry—that was his name, Barry, can you believe it?—he was...like an escape. I dropped out of college and moved in with him in his fancy apartment in the city. He bought me my first camera. A nice one too. He thought it'd be a fun *hobby*. He became exactly like my parents, nothing more than a transfer of control. He didn't want me to work, so I didn't, as far as he knew. But secretly, I started futzing around with photography. He got so mad when I said I wanted to start my own business. So, I stopped telling him...and he was completely fine up until the second I gathered all my things and disappeared one night. Stashed away as much money as I could in a secret account. Spent nights in a storage unit. Ignorance really is bliss. Maybe you aren't the man anyone thinks you really are, Parker. Maybe you're an unknowable entity for everyone. Except me. I know who you really are. As for the rest, what they don't know what won't hurt them."

Parker needed time to process what she'd said, but he didn't have time. Life was too short. "I'm in love with you."

Elliot's hand dropped away from him, cool air replacing touch. "And maybe you should wonder if you're ignorant too."

He turned his head. "Then tell me what I don't know about you. The good, the bad. I'll love you anyway."

For a second, the way the light reflected against Elliot's blue eyes, Parker could see a sheen of tears. But then she smiled. "I'll tell you everything you want if we can go back to your room."

Not for the first time, Elliot and Parker made their way on an elevator to a hotel room. The truth was, he was addicted to the excitement of it. He was addicted to the adrenaline rush in his belly each time they fought and then made up.

He was addicted to the feeling he got when he broke the rules with her just a little bit.

He was addicted to her smell. He couldn't smell it yet, but he would, the scent of jasmine and lemongrass wafting from her jet-black hair.

They walked down the hallway in silence, numbers flashing like street stripes one after another until they made it to his room.

Even before the lock had whirred and the door barely opened, they were locked together in a kiss, Elliot's fingers struggling with the belt at his pants, his hands ripping open her jacket, letting it fall heavily around her shoulders, the belt still knotted but loose across her belly. His own belt hung open, pants undone.

Parker broke away from the kiss, dropping to his knees, parting the coat further with his hands, lifting up to run a tongue along one of her nipples. She moaned, her head falling back, fingers coming to thread into the hair at the back of his neck. He gave her nipple one loud suck and then traveled to the other.

When he kissed down her belly, she grabbed him by the collar. "Nuh-uh, my friend. You have to show patience to get your mouth on this pussy. You have to earn it."

He would've done anything for it at that point, his mouth was practically watering.

"How?"

She pointed. "Stand up, against the wall."

He did as he was told, standing against the wall across from her, her body a naked vision in front of him. Her nipples were hard points on the large swell of her breast and her pussy was shaved bare. He wanted to bury his face in her, making her come until she squirmed. But for now, he would follow directions.

She strutted over to him, still in her heels and jacket, but barely. Then she pushed down his pants and boxer briefs so they fell at his knees, his erection springing to life in front of her. "I've been dying to suck your cock ever since I laid eyes on you."

Parker bit back a moan, trying to stay conscious.

She dropped to her knees, and wrapped his cock with both her fists watching as she pumped him up and down, slow and steady. He had to swallow hard to hold himself still.

"Your dick is huge. I've never seen anything like it. Good thing I already know it fits. The question is, can I get it as wet as my pussy? Dripping and hot."

"Jesus, fuck…"

With that, her mouth enveloped his aching, leaking head, lips suctioning over and tongue flicking along the sensitive slit.

The light flickered in his brain, he really might die from this alone.

Then she reached further down his dick, her mouth sucking in big long strokes. All he could see was the top of her head, the tops of her breasts, and her feet behind her at the back of her bent knees.

"Look at me when you do that," he panted.

And instantly, her eyes popped open and he could see the pale blue of her eyes fringed with dark, sooty black. "Like this?" she asked, popping off his dick and licking up and down, until the whole shaft was glistening, ruddy.

"Don't play with me," he growled. His voice came off like a warning.

She gave a pouty look. "I don't know what you mean…" And she let her tongue barely flick out to the head of his cock.

"Don't make me discipline you."

At that her eyes glittered, and she gave him an innocent look, tilting her head to the side, her hand stroking up and down his shaft. "I don't know what you mean. Is this not enough." She kept eye contact with him as she ducked down and sucked in one of his balls, her tongue swirling around. "Isn't this what you want from my mouth?"

"You know what I want." He bit out.

She rose up on her knees again. "Show me."

"Open up wide." He said, grabbing onto the base of his dick and leveling it with her mouth. "And finger yourself. And don't stop until I tell you to."

"Or what?" she asked, flicking out her tongue for a small lick on the head.

"Or I'm going to spank the hell out of your ass."

"What if I want both?" she said, eyes glimmering. "What if I want—"

But before she finished talking, he shoved his dick back into her mouth, hand at the back of her head. He held her there lightly, seeing how she would take it, but on her own, she took him all the way down to the root, choking a little, but the delicate muscles of her throat working even harder to swallow him up.

"Good…that's it…" he murmured. He pushed a little on the back of her head. "Is that okay?" he asked. He wanted to keep playing the game, but also, he wanted her consent.

She nodded around his cock, humming. "Morhg." She moaned.

"More?"

She nodded again and he began to move with his hips, holding onto either side of her jaw with his hands, fucking her face gently.

"Fuck, yes. Fuck yes. Look at me when I fuck your mouth. Look at me."

She was suddenly the most compliant woman alive.

"And rub your clit. I want you to be moaning my name when I blow my load all over your face."

Her eyes went wide, watering a little bit now as he rocked in and out of her. "You thought I'd be nice and come down your throat, didn't you?" She hummed around his dick. He pulled out slightly, easing the rocking of his hips but she dove in for more, bobbing her head up and down in a flurry.

He had to put both his hands behind his head so as not to pass out this time. His dick was sensitive, jolting at the wet rush of her tongue. Pressure building in his abdomen. "You can suck that dick as good as you want but I'm still gonna shoot all over you. Maybe your tits too if you're lucky. Faster. Suck faster and rub your clit faster."

Her eyes fluttered shut, and her bobbing became distracted. She was about to come.

Abruptly, he pulled out.

"No…" she panted, leaning for it. But he held her back, his hand on her shoulder. "Come for me, Elliot."

His hand frantically stroked his cock, as she leaned against the support of his hand. It was hard to concentrate when he was so close to popping off but he had to hold steady so they could come together. They had to come together.

Little mewls sputtered from her mouth until suddenly a loud moan broke free her eyes shuttering closed.

"That's it, that's a good girl." He tried to sound soothing but his voice was broken when he began coming too, pleasure shooting through his body, muscles tensing and hardening, hand working. He let out a grunt and then thick ropes of come slashed across her face and tits. Dripping off her nipples as he'd promised.

She was still coming her body hunching over, her chest heaving, until finally her eyes opened and she practically fell onto him.

He pulled his shirt over his head and gently wiped at her cheek and the bridge of her nose and then folded the shirt over to wipe the come off her nipples and sternum.

With the post-orgasm clarity, suddenly, guilt rippled through him. *Shit.*

He tossed the shirt over to the floor, picked up his boxer briefs and yanked them back on. Running his hand through his hair, he looked at her. She was looking at him too...her eyes still wide, her mascara smeared all over her eyes and cheeks. Oh shit. He had gone too far.

But she asked for it? But he'd never shot a load on a woman's face before. He'd only fantasized about it.

"That—" she stood "—was fucking amazing." Then she pressed her body to his and kissed him hard on the mouth. She still had the fucking coat and heels on.

He broke away from the kiss. "Let me get you some clothes. You can hang your coat up at the entryway. And take those heels off, Jesus fucking Christ."

He rummaged in his suitcase to find her something suitable. At this rate, she'd have his whole closet. She let the coat drop in a pile on the ground and then she toed off her heels, picking them up and setting them on the small table in the corner of the room. She sat at the end of the bed, her ankles crossed and swinging a bit. Waiting for him.

He found a soft T-shirt and a brand new pair of boxer briefs. He kneeled in front of her, slipping her feet into the leg holes of the boxer briefs.

"Lift up ..." he murmured softly, and she did as she was told until he pulled the waistband all the way up to her belly button. She looked kind of cute in the navy shorts.

"Hands up…" He continued in a similar fashion with the T-shirt, pulling it down over her bare tits, covering her soft belly. She shook out her hair once he had it on her, her hand going to the hem of the shirt and knotting it at her waist so she wasn't drowning in it.

"Don't move." He went to the corner of the room, removing the fancy bottled water. "Here, drink this." He handed the glass bottle to her. She gave him a confused look.

"Why?"

"Because you worked hard, and it's important to rehydrate."

He'd meant it in earnest but she started to giggle again, shaking her head slightly, fingering the neck of the bottle. "I didn't expect this from you."

He sat down next to her, took the bottle, cracked the seal and twisted off the top and handed it back to her. "I love you."

He'd already said it, so what the hell. He meant it, after all, even if he said it without hope and without measure. Knowing she'd never say it back no matter how she felt in return.

She hesitated before taking the bottle back from him. But then she did, taking a huge gulp, and letting out a big exhale. The weight of her head settled on his shoulder.

"What do we do now?" he asked.

"We could fuck again?"

"I'm gonna need at least twenty minutes before we do that."

Her cheek scraped against his as she lifted her chin. "Really? That's not much time at all."

He wrapped an arm around her and drew her near. "Maybe we can sleep."

"Yeah. Maybe that's not a bad idea. You have an extra toothbrush?"

Parker stared at the dark ceiling, Elliot tucked into the crook of his arm. She was snoring gently. He knew this about her. She snored. She also set a timer while she brushed her teeth so she didn't short herself. She also flossed.

They flossed together, leaning over the bathroom sink. A supremely unsexy thing to do. Elliot pulled either side of the string of floss down to form a gruesome frowning face, causing Parker to laugh.

They laughed together.

He also ignored Tessa's phone call. And her text in response to his *hey can we talk* message. He ignored the call from Rebecca and the one from Jen. He also didn't post to his Instagram. TheParkedMechanic wasn't posting to his usual travel stories. His DMs were constantly loaded but would remain unchecked.

He'd woken up in the middle of the night, warm and sated, no sign of a hangover, no sign of jet lag. He'd reached over and pulled Elliot to him. She rustled quietly and then her eyes fluttered open a small smile playing on her lips.

"You weren't who I was expecting to see…" Her voice was heavy with sleep.

"Dreaming about some other man?"

"No. I was all alone."

He pulled her towards him and kissed her softly, a kiss that evolved into more kisses, which evolved into her running her hands through his hair, his mouth slanting over hers, and her leg hitching up over his hip.

When her pelvis ground against his enough times, he lowered the waist band of his boxer briefs and pulled down hers, and entered her slowly, one inch at a time. She writhed at the end of his cock, hips rocking as he so achingly slowly entered her.

Her voice reverberated in his ear. "Mmmm…mmmmm…yesss…" she breathed in a gentle hiss like a kettle warming up on the stove.

Until finally he was fucking her in earnest, slowly, gently, but earnestly. Arms wrapped around her rib cage, skin rubbing up and down, mouths clasped together. His hands traveled to her front, to squeeze the swell of her breasts, pinching her nipples lightly, then running down her belly and brushing against her clit.

"Mmmggmmm…" Her hips surged when he did that, and so he continued, the callused skin of his index and middle fingers petting the hot, silky skin.

Until finally, she came, slow and long and painstakingly delicate.

He came too right after. His hips snapping, his arms folded tightly around her rib cage, cleaving her hard against him.

And then it was over. And he was awake again. This time she was out cold.

He glanced over at the hotel clock. Six thirty in the morning. He would have to leave in an hour. He should get up now to make it to his client's garage.

But something…stopped him.

He grabbed his phone, scrolling past the missed calls and messages. Noting one from Cameron: *You can't avoid me forever, Parker.*

He texted his client's car manager.

Sorry, last minute emergency. Have to reschedule for later. Will refund you price of travel.

His phone lit up, the garage manager. When he answered, the man on the other end of the line was already talking a mile a minute about a vehicle that needed fixing. Parker switched his phone from one ear to the other.

"Calm down. Put the phone up to the car and let me hear for myself. Do you have the stethoscope in the tool kit I requested? Yep, put the phone close so I can hear the chattering noise."

The other mechanic did as Parker asked and Parker listened intently, but he already knew the diagnosis. He'd heard that exact pitch of rattling before. "With this model of Ferrari, the timing belt fence on the main pulley is spot welded in place. The spot welds have a tendency to break which is why the fence is making that weird sound. Re-spot weld the pulley fence, and you'll be good to go."

He clicked off his phone after that, not interested in the response. He grew less and less invested by the day in the business of cars.

Which was funny given how hard he'd worked to grow it. How much he'd sacrificed for it. How big of a part of his identity it had been for almost his entire adult life.

And now he couldn't even bother to make an appointment he'd already traveled across the world for.

Elliot was still with him, sleeping soundly, her steady heartbeat fluttering at the pulse point on her neck.

She was still with him for now. And that might've been some kind of record.

He drifted away until his eyes opened again, the clock read 9:30 and Elliot was still asleep. The latest Parker had slept in in over fifteen years. Like a rebirth.

But it was time to get up. Slowly, he removed his arm out from beneath Elliot's ribcage so as not to disturb her. He picked up the hotel phone and quietly ordered room service so that Elliot could be slowly awaken by the aroma of coffee, tea, fruit, oatmeal, omelets, sausage and bacon, croissants and an extra order of beignets. He'd never had them, but he knew she'd like them.

He would try them today.

Before the silver trays of food arrived, he dropped to the floor to do his usual routine of pushups and sit-ups. Then he jumped in the shower, cleaning off the sweat of sex and liquor from the night before. Cleanse. Renew.

When he stepped out, towel slung around his hip, he half expected Elliot to have vanished, leaving nothing but rumpled down comforter in her wake.

But she was still there. Sitting up now in the bed, phone out in front of her, eyes squinting, hair messy. She glanced up at him and smiled and he was half tempted to jump her fucking bones again.

But the knock on the door indicated the room service had arrived.

The room service attendant rolled in the cart. Parker tipped them accordingly and then he opened all the various silver dishes.

"What's all this?" mused Elliot. She sneaked out of the bed. And to Parker's surprise, she sauntered behind him, wrapping her arms around his belly, squishing her face against his back.

A surprisingly intimate gesture. Although her physical touch was always painfully intimate when he thought about it.

"Just a little breakfast."

"Little? You've got enough here for seven people. Don't you have to be at your job bright and early?"

He smiled at that. The only way she would know anything about his job is if she'd been secretly following his Instagram still, which he knew now that she was.

"The guy canceled on me. So, I've got the day all freed up."

She twirled around him, sitting in a chair next to the table of food, snatching up a piece of bacon and chewing thoughtfully. "What a dick. It's so rude to cancel last minute like that. I hope you charged him an arm and a leg."

He shrugged. "All in the name of business."

Elliot poured cream into a saucer of steaming coffee. She took her coffee with cream, no sugar. He took a mental note. "Well, I don't have to be anywhere today. I'm a free agent."

"Don't you have a wedding to shoot?"

"Not until tomorrow. I came early so I could see a guy."

He sat down across from her, tossing two bags of black tea into a mug, pouring hot water over it. "Which guy?"

She sipped her coffee. "I'll never divulge that information."

Parker was going to believe it was him, even though he had no way of proving it. No way of knowing how she would know where he was. Those were questions best left unanswered.

"We could walk around the city." Parker cut open a flaky croissant and buttered it thickly. He hadn't had a pastry in so long. He took a big bite, reveling for a moment in how good it actually tasted. The flakes fluttered to his tiny saucer plate. Decadent.

"Do we have to *do* stuff?" Elliot rolled her eyes. Her hand traveled over the many plates of food, settling on an omelet. She speared a big hunk of egg, shoving it in her mouth. "How about this? We hang out here, do nothing. Go downstairs to the restaurant, eat lunch. Come back here, do nothing. Then go downstairs and eat dinner."

"So, do nothing all day? We're in London, There are a million sites to visit."

She blew air from her mouth. "Psh. Fuck that."

"Won't you get bored with me in this tiny room all day?"

She glanced up under her thick, sooty lashes. "I could think of a million ways to keep busy, Mr. Serious."

He felt the upward tug at the corner of his mouth. "I'm not opposed. I have diversified interests, that's all."

"What's Jen do for work?" Elliot hiked her feet up on his knee, crossing one over the other.

He was a little surprised by her interest. "She works for a financial consulting company."

Elliot nodded. "That sucks. Too bad, she seems really cool."

Parker shrugged. "I don't think it's her dream job exactly, but we grew up poor, and it was the two of us against the world. She wanted financial security. But she's good at a lot of things."

"I really like her."

Parker smiled again. "Do you?" He tapped the top of her toes with each finger. Elliot wiggled them in response.

"Yeah, she's kinda weird. I totally crashed your get-together and she didn't even bat an eyelash. In fact, we've been texting."

Parker almost choked on his sip of tea. "You've been texting Jen?"

"Yeah, of course. She hired me for her wedding."

Oh shit. How could he have forgotten something like that?

"Is that a problem?"

Parker shook his head slowly doing the math. "You know I invited Tessa to the wedding, right?" And this was technically true. He *had* done that.

But he wanted Elliot to object to it. To give him a real, damn good reason not to be with any other woman. She would *have* to object to it after all that had passed between them.

Elliot dropped her feet to the ground. "Of course. Who else would you bring?"

He leaned back in his chair. What had he expected from her anyway? And what did he expect of himself?

He'd left Tessa on the hook. Again. Hadn't even texted her back after *he*'d initiated contact. All Elliot had to do was turn up anywhere and at any time and suddenly he'd be incapable of saying no. Even when he thought he could do it, like when he'd walked out on her at the airport, she'd turned around and played him again.

Wait, had she played him? Or had he willingly agreed to every single action he'd committed in this big wide universe? The latter was the truth. The former just a farce to avoid accountability.

But Parker had never been in this position before. He wasn't exactly a serial monogamist but he always stuck with one person. Until recently. Recently, it felt like his past was exploding in his face, and all he could do was chase one ungettable woman anyway.

"You could be my date." He sipped his tea, gazing at Elliot over the brim.

She laughed. "Don't be silly. I have to work the event. I can't be your date. I'm not a good multitasker." Then she quieted down. "You go with Tessa. Forget about me, Parker. You take this thing between us too seriously, and you're not the only one who'll get hurt in the end. I will too."

"I'm not going to hurt you, Elliot. Fuck, I'd do anything for you. Can't you see? I'd fucking ruin my whole life for you if you asked. Just ask."

"I don't have to ask. That might be the problem."

Chills ran up the length of his arms. "Something is drawing us together. Something cosmic. Magnetic. Why are you fighting it?"

Elliot tapped her nails against her mug. "I go to weddings all the time. And the one thing I notice the most about them isn't the flowers or the cake or the dress. It's the lie. The lie that everyone so sincerely commits to when they're standing in front of half a million people proclaiming their love. Half of marriages end in divorce, so this isn't mere opinion, it's cold hard fact. My own did, and I lost almost everything. Why even bother with the façade? I'd rather be free. Free and out of denial."

"You act as if being with someone means you can't be free."

She glanced up at him, head tilted. "Doesn't it? The illusion of me is better than the real thing. I know how to market myself well. The truth is, I'm sad, all the time. I'm not this carefree good-times person. You only see one side of me, and, yeah, that's certainly part of me, but it's not all of me. The rest is only for me. I'm doing you a favor."

He dropped from his chair to his knees in front of her.

She looked alarmed. "What are you doing?"

Then he gently grasped her by the elbow at either side, exerting pressure until she scooted off the chair as well. He leaned back so he was resting against her thighs and pulled her legs around his waist, holding as tightly as he could.

"These are the real airplane games, aren't they?" he said into her hair.

Her voice sounded distant and breathy. "What?"

"It's not that we've been chasing each other through the sky for months and months. It's that in the end, we were always designed to lose. Like a pyramid scheme. Destined to fail. I'll give you everything, I'll give you anything…"

"I don't know what you're talking about." But her words were strained. Throat tight.

"And, when it's all over, you'll walk away with all of me."

Her fingertips ran through his hair, scratching at his scalp. But still he ducked his head and pressed his cheek against her chest. Breathing in heavily: lemongrass, jasmine, salt, skin. The scents he would remember. "And I'll have nothing."

Because Elliot didn't just not want to be with him. She felt that being with anyone was the equivalent of a prison.

And Parker felt that being with someone was the only thing keeping him to the ground. He wanted her to ground him.

She wanted to fly in the sky.

And they weren't going to find common footing together.

Chapter 21

The ski lodge wasn't so bad. It really wasn't. And Parker wasn't sure what he'd been so afraid of in the first place. After all, his first night with Tessa on this trip had been...well, fine actually. They'd stayed at her place. She hadn't made a move on him, instead scootching against his hip and grabbing his arm to wrap around her waist as they slept. One again, he appreciated that she was going slow, although he knew physical intimacy neared. And he'd agreed to it, giving her the sense that he was ready.

But who wouldn't want to spend the night with a beautiful woman in her pristinely organized home? Parker's home was organized as well, if not mostly empty. Still, he appreciated cleanliness.

Tessa even cooked him dinner the first night of his visit in Denver. She'd worn an apron with her name embroidered and the phrase "Don't forget to kiss the cook." Fitting for the purposes of Parker's visit.

But they were going to do more than kiss, and as such, Parker had to prepare himself both physically and mentally. They were in an adult relationship now and not some drug- and sex-fueled cat-and-mouse airplane game that he'd been playing with a certain someone else.

A certain someone else who didn't even have her own apartment, let alone a clean one. Wow, what had Parker been thinking? He asked himself that almost every day and especially on this day as he and Tessa were to have their first night at the lodge.

He wasn't the biggest fan of skiing— and Tessa was a pro—but he'd always been naturally athletic enough to get by. His muscles and his general aptitude and strength were things people revered about him. But little did they know he valued them insofar as he had to use them to get by. Those aptitudes had nothing to do with what he held on the inside.

If given the option, Parker preferred acts of the mind over body. Even as a mechanic he was using fine-tuned skills both physically and intellectually. And it's certainly how he also viewed his relationships.

Tessa knelt down over his shoulder, passing him a peppermint tea where they sat in the lobby of the ski lodge. She rested beside him and sipped her hot chocolate with tiny marshmallows. "I can't believe you're finally here. I knew you'd make the right choice. I was a little worried there for a minute. But deep down inside, I'm an optimist."

Parker had gotten his shit together since his last unfortunate interaction with Elliot, and this time, no really, *this time* he wasn't going back to her no matter what kooky fun games she cooked up. He had already blocked her once and then unblocked her. This time he didn't block her.

283

Instead, he acted as though she didn't exist. He didn't check his messages. Didn't check his social media feeds. He put her text messages on invisible. That way, she wouldn't know she was blocked. Apathy was a much better approach than action. That way, she wouldn't be triggered to fuck with him as she often did the minute he was getting his shit together. Which again, he had done since he'd last seen her.

He *had* made a few regrettable tactical errors however. Like when he maybe accidentally checked a few of his messaging platforms to see if maybe she had *tried* to reach out. Surely, she'd be freaking out because he wasn't around. Or she'd want to send him things that reminded her of him. Or she'd want to chat, like she had so many times before late at night.

So Parker ignored the heaviness in his heart when he'd found that no, she hadn't messaged him at all. Not on social media...not on his phone...

Not even a message scrawled by an airplane in the sky...

He wouldn't be checking again.

"We should get dinner at the lodge and turn in early tonight." Tessa's happy voice broke his incidental brooding.

He cleared his throat. "I absolutely agree."

She leaned in, letting her forehead press against his before pressing her lips to his. No tongue, a peck. He mentally sighed in relief. *Why couldn't he be normal?*

Tessa was someone who put in the work, and for Parker that meant a lot. Elliot only cared about the good time. Didn't think anything else mattered. Tessa knew this wasn't true. And she wouldn't flake on him. And in return, he wouldn't flake on her. Not anymore.

"Actually, let's head up now." Tessa leaned forward, resting her mug against the end table. The tea hadn't even cooled, steam wafting from the dark brim.

"Before dinner? Aren't you hungry?"

Tessa lifted an eyebrow. "Yes, but not for food."

Parker's stomach flipped. "*Oh.* Right, of course. We should go upstairs then."

She grabbed Parker's hand and led them to the elevator, waiting at the helm for the doors to open. Parker tugged at his collar. He didn't fucking need Elliot Sheer. He had everything he could ever want in the palm of his hand.

Their room was cozy and warm, the walls actual logs. There was a fireplace in the room too, which Parker appreciated because he wasn't much a fan of the cold after having lived through so many brutal Chicago winters.

As soon as they entered the room, Tessa turned Parker around, pushing him against the door, her breath hot against his cheek. "Parker, I really don't want to rush you, but I'm going to get right to it, if that's okay with you?"

Parker scratched the top of his head. "Okay."

She broke away from him with a mischievous smile and began unbuttoning her plaid shirt until she was in nothing but a pink bra. She stripped off the shirt and then held it out to her side letting it drop to the ground. Then she undid the button of her jeans, shimmying them off and kicking them away. Her underwear was a matching pink, just like Elliot knew it would be.

No, fuck. Don't think about Elliot.

"What do you say we get this show on the road? I'm not really one for foreplay." She tossed her curly brown hair, exposing a smooth shoulder.

He pasted a smile on his face and nodded. "Yep."

She scurried to the bed, slipping beneath the heavy navy comforter. "Baby, I am so ready for you."

"Gonna...gonna grab a condom."

"There's no need. I'm on birth control."

Parker stood, looming over his suitcase, guilt flickering in his chest. There was no way he could sleep with Tessa without a condom after he'd slept with Elliot without a condom. He'd gotten tested right away too. He'd learned his lesson. He wouldn't fuck anyone without protection again. Or wouldn't intend to. Like how he hadn't intended on fucking Elliot, bare skin to bare skin... He shook his head as he removed the small square package from his suitcase. What the hell was wrong with him?

"I like to be extra safe." Parker smiled at Tessa, ripping off the package and concentrating as he removed the rubber circle. He held it up against the light because he realized in that moment that he was going to have to figure out a way to get hard. And fast. "I got chlamydia once a few years ago…"

"I assume you've had that treated," Tessa gave an awkward laugh.

He hadn't even taken his clothes off. Quickly, he stuffed the condom back in its opened package and pushed it into his pocket.

"Is everything all right?" Tessa's voice was high and tight, and her anxiety was warranted.

He glanced up at her. "I'm very…sweaty."

"That's okay."

He shoved his hands in his pocket. "It's just that I want our first time to be…nice for you. And I think maybe…maybe I have to take a shower first?"

"Parker, I swear I don't mind."

"I know you don't. I do. It's important to me. I'll only be a minute." Time to himself. A few moments to collect his thoughts.

Tessa swallowed hard, but then smiled. "Of course, do what you're comfortable with."

Parker stepped into the small lodge bathroom and shut the door behind him. Before he could talk himself out of it, his hand went to the front pocket of his jeans. He wouldn't message Elliot. He wouldn't text her or anything. He would just check his old messages. For a little dopamine hit, that's all. Hadn't he read an article about dopamine once? It caused happiness, didn't it? It was a thing certain kinds of brains chased. He had one of those brains, he was positive.

He scrolled through them until he found what he was looking for. Naked pictures of Elliot, sprawled out, close-ups of her tits, dirty things she'd sent him. Instant erection. Yes! That's what he needed. *Good work, Parker. That was smart thinking.*

But then, before he could stop himself, his hand went to his cock, first tugging lightly, sensation shooting through him and then pumping in earnest as he stared at her pictures, rereading her messages.

His hand paused as he scrolled past one message from her in particular.

Is it weird I kinda miss you?

"Rrhhmm." He had to squeeze his lips shut to stop the groan from escaping, hand furiously stroking now. Then the only thoughts on his mind were of Elliot on her knees in front of him, her eyes wide and intense, blue like the sea. His hand was wet before he knew it, the last of his come dribbling over his hand. He slowed to a stop and his body went slack against the countertop.

Oh shit. Why'd he do that?

He gave himself only a moment to recover before jumping into the shower under a jet of cold water. He didn't deserve to wait for it to heat up. He was an asshole. A grade A asshole. He deserved whatever pain was coming his way. And he'd ruined the only erection he was going to get that night. *Why the fuck did I do that?*

To Parker's disappointment, the cold shower warmed up nice and toasty, and his skin buzzed in a zappingly refreshing way when he stepped out of the stall. The outer feelings didn't line up with the inner feelings though. And for some reason, he wanted to be miserable inside and out. As if that alignment would somehow neutralize his unruly brain. Would justify his existence in a way that nothing else did.

He grabbed a towel, rubbed it up and down his legs, cock limp again. He picked up his phone one more time. He could try it again, and this time not blow his load.

But instead of pictures, he opened his new messages, the ones he'd been avoiding, along with Elliot, for the past weeks. Pamela had admonished him the other day for "turning into one of those Instagram influencers." And he'd brushed her off at the time, but she was right. Here he was, unable to ignore his messages.

He scrolled past small-potato brand deal offers and random messages until a message from John got his attention. He hadn't spoken to John in quite a while.

It was dated yesterday. He opened it.

Have you seen Elliot lately?

That was all the message said, but Parker's hands went cold. He shouldn't answer this message. He should delete it. Ignore John too and anyone else who had anything to do with Elliot's circle. Hell, he'd skipped watching a Steven Spielberg movie the other day so he wouldn't have to think about E.T.

But his fingers itched to answer. Why would John ask him this?

"Parker?" Tessa knocked on the door. "Are you okay in there? I'm not trying to rush you, but it's been a while."

Shit.

Quickly, he tapped a reply.

No, I haven't. What's going on?

Another knock on the door. "Did you hear me?"

"Coming out right now!"

Then another message from John appeared. *Dude, she's been missing for like nine days.*

It took exactly ten seconds for the message to sink in.

Parker burst out of the bathroom, his heart pounding, vision blurred, chest heaving. Was there a brick on his chest? He balanced himself against the wall, one hand out and one hand on his knee, bent over as he tried without success to catch his breath. Maybe his heart had exploded. The doctor had said they would keep an eye on his heart. Maybe this was how he died, here on the floor, with a woman he didn't love.

"Oh my god, Parker!" Tessa's voice was a distant sound, but then he felt the warmth of her hand on his back. Everything else was all black.

"I think..." He could barely get the words out between breaths. "...having...heart attack..." And with that, he collapsed to the ground.

Chapter 22

The hospital discharged Parker an hour later with a diagnosis: *panic disorder.*

The doctor had patted his back as Parker sat like a child at the end of an examination table. *Have you considered an anti-anxiety medication?* Tessa waited in the waiting room, but when he was all cleared to leave, he meandered over to her sheepishly.

"You're okay." She looked genuinely relieved as she set down the magazine and uncrossed her legs.

He settled into the small chair next to her, legs spread, his hands clasped together in between. "I feel a little silly. I guess panic attacks can feel a lot like heart attacks."

"No, don't feel silly. People have panic attacks on the plane all the time. I should've known better! I even have protocols to talk people down while we're flying. But you looked so…"

He nodded his head with a grimace. "Yeah, I know."

With a gentle but prodding tone, Tessa asked, "Why do you think it happened?"

Elliot. The fact that she was missing. The fact that he would die if he never saw her again. The fact that he didn't want Tessa no matter how much she wanted him. No matter how much he tried to force it. But mostly Elliot. Where was Elliot? He had to find Elliot.

Instead, he shrugged. "According to the doctor it's called a disorder because it doesn't make sense. But he also recommended that I take it easy." He scratched his head. "I'm sorry, I have to cut our trip short." Much was implied with that last sentence. He didn't want to cut their trip short, he wanted to cut their relationship short. Would Tessa get the hint? Would she let him off the hook?

She rubbed his shoulder soothingly. Guilt swirled in him mixed with sharp bursts of fear whenever Elliot crossed his mind. "Of course. I totally understand. We'll do whatever you need to do."

He looked at her and gave a weak smile. "Thanks. Just need to rest for a while, I think."

Then her hand paused. "But this is about that Elliot woman, isn't it?"

He arrived back to Chicago on a mission to find Elliot. He hit up all the spots from her Instagram, every bar, every best friend: Allie, Bruno, John. But of course none of them had seen her, and they were as worried as he was.

"I mean, she's gone missing before but usually no more than a week or something. Maybe when she's hooking up with someone," Allie said to him at the bar where she bartended (a day job from the drug dealing), making Parker bristle. She passed a small bag over to him filled with white powder. "Bump?"

He even talked to Bruno. Although Bruno seemed unsurprised to see him. They had never met before but apparently Elliot had told Bruno about Parker, a fact that made something swell in his chest. His chest was mostly filled with panicked dread but now with a tiny sliver of bittersweet happiness.

"Elliot always has a room here. She knows that. You can look in it if you want but she doesn't leave much behind. I don't ask her where she goes and I don't ask her when she's coming back. It's like a respect thing, you know?"

Parker didn't know. He was always asking Rebecca and Pamela where they were going. They all shared calendars. Same with Jen. How else did you know that everyone was safe and alive and where they might be at all times and not dead on the side of the road from a car crash? How else!

Still he searched the room. The walls were blank, the closet almost completely bare except for a few dresses hanging on hangers and several pairs of sky-high heels neatly lined up on the floor. All he found was a piece of paper with a few numbers scratched on it. Hmm. Had she left it for him to find? No, but she wouldn't do something like that, would she?

I mean, she would...

He thanked Bruno afterwards and Bruno did that guy thing that guys do where they pulled him in for a hug after they shook hands. Parker was taken aback, and awkwardly he patted Bruno on the back. He didn't have many male friends, despite working with mostly men. He'd never much enjoyed their company, but suddenly, he wanted nothing more than to be Bruno's friend.

"I worry about her, man." Bruno pulled away, rubbing his eyes. Was he crying?

"Elliot says you two are good friends."

Bruno nodded. "Known each other since preschool. She proposed to me when we were three, but I turned her down." He shrugged, laughing a bit. "She was a nightmare even then."

Parker begrudgingly smiled at that but worry outweighed anything else. "Allie says she's disappeared like this before?"

"Yeah, but not for this long. I don't know. She'll turn up. She always does. But still...still...wish she wouldn't pull this shit...wish she'd chill out. We're getting too old to play these games."

Parker knew exactly what Bruno meant. And, if Elliot was still gone by the end of the week he would call the police, despite her friends' wishes for him not to. Apparently, they all believed she'd show sooner rather than later.

"Besides," Bruno had said. "Elliot hates cops. Even if they found her, she'd probably get herself arrested for assaulting an officer."

That much Parker could believe.

After his visit with Bruno, Parker went home. Even though he really didn't want to, it was time for him to tell Jen what was going on. And more importantly, Elliot said she and Jen had texted. Maybe Jen had heard from her. Parker could only hope.

"Can you stop pacing? You're gonna bother the baby." Jen looked up from the kitchen table as Parker paced back and forth in front of his wall-to-ceiling living room window.

"Avery likes it."

"Well, I don't. Can you fucking relax?"

Parker made his way to the kitchen and gently covered Avery's ears with his palms. Avery was resting in the travel basinet Parker kept available at his place. "Language," he hissed.

Jen pshawed at him. "What is going on with you?"

Parker cracked his neck and then his knuckles. He was lucky to have Jen. To have family who cared about him. "I had a panic attack at the ski lodge."

Jen's eyes went wide. "Well, are you okay? I don't think I've ever seen you panic about anything."

Parker thought about his answer for a second before answering. "Elliot Sheer."

"Excuse me?"

"I had a panic attack about Elliot Sheer."

"I thought you were there with Tessa. Isn't she your girlfriend slash not girlfriend?"

Silence fell between them which Jen broke. "I fucking knew *something* was up! Why didn't you tell me?"

Parker shifted uncomfortably. "I'm telling you now."

Jen wiggled her finger at Parker. "I knew there was some sketchy shit going on with you and Elliot. Anyone with a pulse could tell. But I thought you wanted someone to settle down with. Like Tessa. No offense to Elliot but like…that chick…doesn't quite seem all put together if you know what I mean. Don't get me wrong, I like the woman but—"

"Elliot's missing."

"*What?*"

Parker scratched his head. "And see, the thing is…" He took a big breath. "I think I'm in love with her."

Jen's jaw dropped. "What?"

"Well, maybe I don't think it. Maybe I know it."

"You're in love with a missing woman? Parker, she could be dead. She could be locked away in some serial killer's basement somewhere. This is serious. This is dark. This is serious, dark, and twisted. We can't live our lives like true crime podcasts, we're too boring for that."

Parker winced at the thought. "Her friends say she does this a lot, that she ghosts on everybody from time to time and they don't hear from her or anything. Although, never for this long. They're all certain she'll turn up sooner or later. Have you heard from her?"

Jen shook her head. "No, but I've been busy with other wedding details. Rallying the bridesmaids. Trying to organize an out of state wedding And I'm gonna be real with you. She does seem the type to do some spontaneous shit like that. Remember when she randomly showed up here that one time? And hey, if this is something she does every now and then, then maybe you shouldn't worry too hard. I bet you she's on a getaway trip in Cabo sipping margaritas and sleeping with strangers. Sorry, but it's true. I don't know her that well, but what I do know of her…let's just say she doesn't seem much like the settling-down type."

Parker raked his hand through his hair. "You could be right." As much as he hated to think about it, to think about any of it. "I will find her though."

Gently, Jen asked him the next question. "If you're in love with Elliot, what *the hell* are you doing with Tessa? It's not like you to play women this way. And I won't stand to have some kind of fuck boy for a brother. I'll have to have you murdered. Oh shit, maybe we are living a true crime podcast."

"I might be in love with Elliot, but she's not in love with me. Or if she is, she won't admit it. You know how dad always used to say, 'You're only as good as your choices, not your feelings.' I thought I was making a good choice with Tessa, instead of following my feelings for Elliot."

Jen's brows went up. "You know, for a dead guy, Dad gives some pretty bad advice."

"What's that supposed to mean?"

"Dad was wrong. Plus, are you kidding me? Choices? He gave you the middle name *Lance-Loves-Laurie* and my middle name is *Laurie-Loves-Lance*. Talk about a man who followed his feelings, especially when it came to love. He was so goddamn in love with mom. *Your* feelings matter. They always have. Even if things can't ever work out with Elliot, it doesn't mean you should be with a person you don't love because they sound like the right practical move on paper. I joke about Benny's family having a lot of money, but if I'm honest with you, I hate it. His family is so fancy and they scare me. There's no special finance job or graduate degree in the world that can compete with old fashioned snobbery. But it doesn't matter. Because what matters is how I feel. And how Benny feels. Same goes for you."

Parker nodded. "You may have a point." Avery fussed from the bassinet, reminding Parker to resume the gentle rocking which was working to soothe him too.

"Fine. Good." Jen crossed her arms. "So, what are you gonna do? Build a search and rescue squad? I assume you're going to dump Tessa."

"Oh, I think it's safe to assume we're over." The words came out like a reflex.

"You sure about that? You'd be wise to make it all very, very clear."

Parker scrubbed his scruff. "You're probably right."

"And what about Elliot? Aren't you scared?"

He nodded. "I'm going to find her."

"Is there anywhere she mentioned in particular? Anywhere she could be hiding out?"

Parker fell back against his seat, rocking Avery's bassinet with an outstretched arm. "I don't know. I've already gone everywhere I can think of. Maybe I'll run into her at the airport again."

Jen's phone illuminated on the table. She was constantly getting calls and texts and emails either from work or from Benny or from her many wedding organizers and participants. Her gaze fluttered downwards towards the phone.

"Take it." Parker inclined his head.

"Oh my god, no. I'm not leaving you in your time of need."

But the gears in Parker's brain were churning now, his thoughts folding inwards on themselves. "It's okay. You have a lot going on. I'm just glad to have had you around for this long."

Jen rose from the table. "I've been glad to be here, too. Okay, I'm gonna take this call, then. Benny is moving all our shit into a storage unit for our honeymoon and then we're moving to Midtown, which is maybe the most out of pocket decision I've ever made. It's about to get messy. Listen, I know this isn't resolved, but I want you to be happy. Especially before my wedding. I don't want any sad, weepy faces staring at me as I walk down the aisle." Then she squeezed his shoulder and turned to head into the guest room.

Parker sat with himself and his own feelings for a few minutes until suddenly he knew where Elliot was. Shit. He should've thought of this right away. He googled the set of numbers she'd left in her room.

A place she only went when things got really dire. Which they   almost   never   did.

Chapter 23

Had Elliot left the number for him to find in her otherwise empty room or was it mere coincidence?

One could never really tell with her.

At any rate, he googled it and it turned out to be a phone number plus a few other digits. It wasn't too hard to figure out from there. And voilà, he'd found her secret spot which happened to be fifteen minutes from his apartment. He just wasn't sure in what kind of state he'd find her.

He ordered a car, and the short drive stretched for an eternity before he arrived at the storage facility. After paying, he walked up to the large interior door of Unit 136 and knocked loudly.

"I know you're in here." *Knock knock knock.* "You might as well open up. I'm a mechanic but I also have some lock-picking skills."

He kind of did. And he had his Swiss army knife and he'd watched enough YouTube tutorials to pick a lock or two. And barring all that, he'd break the door off its fucking hinges.

He pounded a few more times when suddenly the door swung open.

And there she was, right in front of him. He was so happy to see her he could almost cry. He wanted to swoop her up against his chest and press her tightly against him. He wanted to put her over his knee and spank her.

But mostly he wanted to know what the actual hell was going on with her. For once, he wanted to know her. The whole her. And not just the bits and pieces she indecently flashed.

Her eyes had darker circles than he'd ever seen, probably from sleeping in her storage unit. And she wore a long red sweatshirt with a decorative Christmas tree that read *The Holiest Christmas Cunt* with no pants, socks pulled up to her knees, hair in a messy topknot. Behind her a space heater noisily blew hot air. He wondered how she managed to run electricity into the unit, but knowing Elliot...she was crafty.

She rubbed her face with her sleeve. "What the fuck do you want?" But before she could turn away, he grabbed the middle of her sweatshirt and yanked her against his chest, his arms crushing her body in a desperate, aching embrace.

"I thought you could've been fucking dead," his voice reverberated hoarsely against her hair. Acute pain deep inside his sternum poked mercilessly at his heart.

Her chest pushed against his in a deep inhale and exhale. But then her arms crept around his sides in a reciprocal squeeze. And they stood in silence while an invisible second hand ticked on and on into the ether.

"I am dead," Elliot's voice broke the moment. "Just not in the ways you might think."

Finally, he let go, pulling back, examining her tired eyes. "Then let me in. I've been known to revive an engine or two."

He was a little afraid she'd shove him back out the door and slam the door in his face. But she didn't, she waved her hand like a maître d', inviting him in instead.

Parker stepped awkwardly into the storage unit. Amazingly, it was cozy and like an apartment. She had draped lights along the ceiling, candles burning in tall glass candleholders, a few tables and a rack of clothing all filled with sweatpants and sweatshirts.

"How do you have electricity in here?"

"I watched a YouTube tutorial on how to live in a storage unit and ran an extension cord along the power cable in the hallway."

Yep. Definitely crafty. "Everyone's looking for you."

She gestured at the couch in the center of the room. He sat.

Hmm. Comfortable. But *still*, he was pissed at her.

She collapsed next to him, burrowing beneath a fur blanket that'd been slung over the top cushions. Next to her a small end table contained a book folded open on its face and a mug with steaming water. On the floor was a hot plate with a kettle.

Despite the fact that it was a storage unit, and despite all the fire hazards that made Parker extremely nervous, it was surprisingly nice what Elliot had done with it. But why would she live here?

"Why's everyone looking for me? They know I come and go as I please. Maybe *you're* looking for me."

"So I guess you're never accountable to anyone? You've never disappeared for this long before. What's going on?"

Elliot shrugged, picked up her mug. "You want some tea?"

"Where are you showering?" Parker asked.

"I joined a gym, and I go every morning. Isn't that so healthy of me?"

Parker grimaced. "Is this a money thing? I have money, Elliot, I can help you. I can get you an apartment. Hell, you could... you could..." He was about to say *stay with me* but then wisely stopped himself. Even if he could treat her in some kind of roommate capacity, he knew things with Elliot never went as he wanted them to. He had no power here, as per usual. And more than that, he didn't want power. He wanted trust.

Elliot sipped her tea quietly before speaking again. "I don't want an apartment. I have enough space as it is."

"You still look tired."

"Thanks, I love when people point that out." She rolled her eyes, setting her mug down. "Fine. I'm depressed, you happy now? I've admitted it. Would you like for me to cut a whole emotional vein and bleed all over you so you believe me enough to fuck off? Can't I say *leave me alone?* Isn't disappearing enough of a message? Maybe you could actually respect my wishes."

"You're right. You should be able to be alone. But if you're depressed, have you considered that maybe you *shouldn't* be alone?"

She used her hand like a mouth to mock him, repeating his words in a high-pitched whiny voice. "*If you're depressed, have you considered that maybe you shouldn't be alone?* Freedom. I have total freedom. I don't owe anyone shit."

"You're confusing freedom with isolation."

She shrugged. "Freedom means independence."

"Independence isn't all it's cracked up to be. There's no such thing as making it on your own. Everyone gets help. We all need other people."

She glared at him, but he wouldn't be deterred.

"Okay." He stretched his arm out along the back of the couch, settling in. "I have an offer for you."

She tilted her head. "I don't need anything."

"You don't know if you need something until I offer it."

"Ugh, what, then?"

"I'll sit here with you. I won't say a word. And you can rest your head against my chest."

Elliot scoffed. "Why would I want that?"

"Because every time you fall asleep with me, that's what you do. You curl up right here." He patted his chest. And also, he was tired too. He could use a nap. Or the longest sleep of his life.

She let out a big sigh. "I'm not leaving."

"You don't have to leave."

"And I'm not talking to my friends."

"Nobody says you have to. But I'm telling them where you are and that you're okay."

She thought about it. "Fine."

He lifted a shoulder. "Well, come on then. Make yourself at home."

At first she gave him another disgusted look, but then she fell towards him, burying her head into his chest, inhaling deeply into his shirt. In return, he wrapped his arms around her. He could still make out the faint smell of lemongrass and jasmine. She apparently hadn't changed her shampoo. The familiarity warmed him from the inside out.

Within minutes she was snoring. Parker carefully stretched his hand over to the end table where he'd placed his phone to message all her friends, including August and Olivia whom he'd never met but knew were important to her.

She's here.

And he sent out her location, letting them know that all was well. At least for now.

Parker awoke from the sound of a quiet knock. He breathed in deep, squeezing his eyes, and then slowly his mind returned to him. The hot weight on his chest smelled of jasmine and lemongrass. He adjusted slightly and she moved on top of him, with a little grumble.

Knock knock knock

This time Parker opened his eyes. Remembered where he was. With Elliot. In her storage unit. Space heater. Hot plate. *A fire hazard.*

When the knock came again, he finally sneaked his way out from Elliot's body and traveled to the door. Unsure who could be outside, he opened it slowly and saw the tall form of Bruno.

"Hey…" Parker said in a quiet voice. "She's sleeping."

Bruno responded in a similarly quiet tone. "Ah, gotcha. Can I come in? I brought food." He held up a plastic bag filled with Chinese takeout boxes.

Parker's stomach rumbled in response. He hadn't eaten in hours, he realized. He moved so Bruno could step inside when another person stopped in front of the door. A woman with a nose piercing and platinum blond hair cut short and shaved on the sides stopped dead in her tracks.

"Elliot?" she said. "Shit, thought I was gonna have to look all night for the right unit—this place is huge."

Bruno shushed her from the table as he set out the boxes of food. "Shhhhh."

Parker recognized the voice as Allie's. He nodded. "Elliot's asleep inside. C'mon in."

Elliot's head rested against the back end of her couch, snoring quietly as Bruno, Allie, and Parker settled around the table.

"We should wake her up. Elliot loves this restaurant," Allie said, snapping apart her chopsticks.

"I think we should give her a few more minutes," said Parker. "She always looks so tired."

"That's because she's an insomniac." Bruno shoveled some Szechuan chicken into his mouth. "Drives me bananas when she's constantly roaming around the apartment at night."

Parker picked up a spring roll. A little greasy for his usual fare, but he bit in and found it to be delicious. "What keeps her up?"

Bruno shrugged. "Drugs?"

Allie laughed, her mouth full. "Nah. She doesn't do any stimulants. Not that I *sell* coke or anything. I just do it on occasion." She elbowed Parker as if the distinction were important for him to know. "I think she's traumatized. She got married too young and she totally cut off her horrible conservative family. That kind of shit can do a number on someone."

Parker nodded. Trauma was one thing he could understand.

"I tried to get her into therapy," said Bruno. "My mom's a therapist. Would've given her a great referral. But no dice. She resists all our best efforts."

"I can fucking hear you," a voice thick with sleep came from behind them. Parker looked over his shoulder to see Elliot splayed out on the back of the couch. She dragged herself from the cushions and raised her arms over her head in a big long stretch, her mouth opening almost comically wide in a yawn.

"You're the best of times and the worst of times, Elliot. And that means it's time to seek treatment," Bruno said, pulling out a small stool for her.

She plopped down and opened a box of fried rice, pulled out a spoon and took a big bite. "Ohmygodsogood," she mumbled, mouth full. "Food tastes so good right now."

"That's because you haven't been eating right. I see those Little Debbie cake wrappers all over that table. Classic Elliot." Allie pointed a chopstick in Elliot's direction.

Elliot rolled her eyes. "Back off. Is this a fucking intervention?"

"Dammit, I knew we forgot to organize something," Bruno murmured through a mouthful of food.

Parker huffed a little bit of a laugh. It was fascinating watching Elliot interact with her friends. They all seemed to view her as some kind of errant teenager. Someone they worried about but were never able to hold accountable and kept around anyway. Or maybe they viewed her like family. Probably closer to that.

But why Elliot was so hell-bent on pushing everyone away all the time. In a world where life could be lost in a flash, it seemed almost tragic. Not almost. Completely. Parker scratched his head.

"For real, Elliot," Allie said, breaking into Parker's thoughts. "You need to see a therapist. This is the worst bout of depression you've had so far."

"Do you guys mind not talking about this shit in front of…" Elliot whispered conspiratorially, "…*him*."

Bruno pointed his thumb. "Who? In front of Parker? Why shouldn't Parker know? You talk about him all the time. She does by the way. Get over yourself."

Elliot shoved her face full of food. "Okay, rude."

"No, he's right, Elliot," Allie said. "I'm not saying you need to settle down and get married at this exact second or something but your commitment issues are getting out of hand. You're not the only person in the world to ever get divorced. It'd be one thing if you didn't have an obsession with this guy, but you do. So, either get with him or don't but stop playing this game. It's exhausting even as a viewer."

Elliot squeezed her eyes shut, but Parker was sure his eyes on her were burning a hole right through her. He crossed his arms over his chest in what was likely in a smug way. "Tell me more, Elliot. Please."

Her eyes cut to him with a glare. "Ha-ha. I didn't invite you here, remember?"

"You didn't invite anyone. But here we are."

Suddenly, Elliot threw her chopsticks down into her carton of food. "I've lost my appetite." Then she shoved her feet into a pair of slippers behind her, grabbing a large coat off the couch and pulling it over her sweatshirt. Of course, her legs were completely bare.

"Are you seriously leaving right now?" Bruno's face was incredulous. "And dressed like that?"

"I do what I want." Elliot huffed.

Bruno turned to Parker. "Do something," he mouthed.

Parker shook his head but got to his feet. "Elliot, you're not walking out like that."

"Excuse me. You don't get to control me."

He gained distance to her in just a stride or two. "Nobody's trying to control you, but you'll get hypothermia if you walk outside barely dressed. It's not cute." And with that he knelt down and threw Elliot over his shoulder so she was hanging from his back.

"Motherfucker, let me down!" she yelled, hitting her fists against his back.

"Ah ha ha ha that's what you get for being an asshole and scaring all your friends." Allie pointed her finger in mockery.

"Shut the fuck up, Allie."

Parker placed Elliot gently on the couch, where she hugged her knees tightly to her body. "I hate you guys."

"Good," said Bruno. "You're lucky Parker is big enough to pick up your delinquent ass. I sure as hell am not gonna risk my back for it. I'd've let you freeze. You should send him a thank-you letter."

Elliot glowered at him. "Ugh, I really hate you guys."

"I don't give a shit." Allie smiled at Elliot. "So, where are we all gonna sleep in here?"

"Excuse me, you guys aren't sleeping here."

"Yeah, I think we all are. You can't be alone. This has gone on long enough. And if you won't leave, then neither will we. You owe your friends at least this much. We worry about you," Bruno said as he passed a folded blanket over to Parker. Parker glanced at the side of the room and got an idea. He walked over to the far wall of the room.

"How about all these fold up tables? Why do you have so many?"

"Wedding expo stuff," Elliot said, but continued to pout.

Parker unfolded four tables. "We can sleep on these. It's not ideal but she's got an entire bed set wrapped in plastic right here. Elliot, you can sleep on the couch. Bruno, Allie...we can make these tables less stiff by piling them with pillows and blankets. I'll have to use two or I'll hang off the end."

"See what we'll do for this friendship." Allie put her hands on her hips. "I'm going to sleep on a fucking foldup table in a goddamn storage unit on the South Side of Chicago. I went to Brown for god's sake."

Bruno gave her a look. "You sell weed for most of your income."

"Yeah, and I own my condo. What about you, music man?"

Another knock echoed at the door. "Oh shit," Elliot sat straight up. "We've been caught by management."

But Parker strode to the door and opened it. In front of him stood two women, about the same age as Elliot, one with neat brown hair tied back into a ponytail and one with hot pink bangs. They both wore Christmas sweatshirts like Elliot's except one read *The Brightest Christmas Cunt* and the other *The Prettiest Christmas Cunt.*

Elliot arose from her seat, her jaw slack. "August? Olivia?" Then she quickly ran to the women, all three embracing at once in an aggressive hug. Parker stumbled out of the way.

"I can't believe you're here," Elliot's voice muffled inside the envelope of the hug. They'd each flown in from the east coast.

Finally, the one with the brown ponytail pulled back. "I had to leave my cat to fly out here. Jack is watching him, but you know how much I despise leaving Holiday."

The other one with the pink bangs, put her hands on Elliot's shoulders, then stroked the hair at Elliot's temple. "Let me look at you, god, your hair is so pretty for such a horrible bitch. Henry is right, you are the *most* unhinged, Elliot!" Then she rubbed tears from her eyes. "You had us really fucking worried! Are you kidding me? If you ever do this again, I swear to everything that's good in this world...Thank god for plane guy or we wouldn't have any clue where you even were."

Elliot nodded, this time sniffling and wiping away tears too, but also chuckling. "I'm sorry. I'm sorry." Then she turned outwards gesturing towards the woman with the brown hair. "Everyone, this is August." Then she gestured towards the woman with the pink bangs. "And this is Olivia."

"Nice to meet you both in person," Allie said, closing up the Chinese food boxes.

Bruno smiled. "All right, we'll get some more tables, then. We can pretend like we're having a grade school lock-in."

Elliot grabbed a blanket, pulling it around her shoulders. "But Parker has to sleep on the couch with me."

Bruno looked skeptical. "I don't know if he'll fit."

A glimmer of a smile passed over Elliot's face. "Oh, he fits all right."

"Ugh, you disgust me." Bruno scrunched his face.

Allie snickered. "Don't know what you were expecting."

"She'll never change," August added.

"Who would even want her to?" That was Olivia.

Heat crept up Parker's face, but inwardly he smiled. And then he grabbed Elliot's blanket, ready to spend the night in solidarity.

Chapter 24

Parker's face must have been bright red, huffing and puffing, sweat streaming. He was in good shape, but running with Pamela was always a risk. After she had Avery, she'd given up long-distance running for a while. But now she was back and training for the Chicago Marathon and Parker made the mistake of going on a run with her.

Avery was crawling like a pro now. Parker had made cranberry scones for the occasion, which he realized was an error because babies don't really prefer scones. Then he realized he was mimicking Jen's off-the-wall high-tea party when Elliot had shown up. He was forever wanting her to show up.

"Handwritten letter," Pamela huffed as they headed down the Lakefront Trail. "That's how you make sure things are really over with Tessa."

"But we weren't even officially together. That seems so…"

"Impersonal?"

"I was gonna say old-fashioned."

"Yeah, but that's what makes it more final than a normal breakup. Especially if you're gonna be a coward and ignore Tessa's calls."

Parker jumped out of the way of a woman with a doublewide stroller. "I'm not ignoring her calls. I already told her I needed some space for...well, forever. It's over. Honestly, it never really got off the ground in the first place. But she just wouldn't leave me alone. So, *then* I ignored her calls. *Boundaries.* Setting boundaries is different than ghosting. Now that I've had some time away from it, I'm wondering what the hell she was ever doing with me in the first place."

"Make a right at the stairs. There's no explaining attraction. And people's trauma makes them act in weird ways, and we *all* have our own personal trauma. You included. I hope you apologized."

"I did, but an apology packaged with a forever goodbye isn't the easiest pill to swallow, I guess."

Pamela elbowed Parker so he'd move to the left as they huffed down the stairs. "Send the letter. Letters are final, there's no possibility for a rapid reply."

Of course, sending a letter wasn't conventional, but perhaps it was necessary. A marking of a new passage.

On the other hand, Elliot hadn't asked anything of him, naturally. She hadn't asked him to be with her or to be exclusive or to stop seeing Tessa. But after all they'd been through, he *had* to assume that finally, yes finally, now was the time that they were going to get serious.

"Let's take Columbus and head to Grant Park," Pamela panted.

Parker grunted in agreement, his mind elsewhere.

Elliot couldn't really in good conscience want Parker to be with another woman, could she? He wasn't into polyamory and as far as he knew neither was Elliot. Or maybe she was, but his impression of her was more that she didn't want to commit. She was terrified of the idea.

When he'd woken up in her storage unit, he was a lot less cramped and stiff than he expected after having slept on his side all night scrunched up with Elliot tucked inside the curve of his body. It was a nice couch.

They'd all gone out to breakfast after that, piles of scrambled eggs and pancakes and steaming hot coffee refills, conversations about August's cat Holiday and her boyfriend Jack and Olivia's engagement to a man named Henry who was apparently August's brother (the gossip was flowing!) until suddenly, the sun was setting again and Parker's fingertips slipped away from Elliot's, and everyone returned to their usual spaces. At the very least, it got Elliot out of the storage unit.

He had to end all this drama with other women. The cat was out of the bag with Jen, she knew about Tessa and Elliot. He could not go on this way any longer. Just because someone seemed like the practical and right choice for his life, didn't mean he had to choose them or that life. Sometimes, one had to chase after all their sky-high feels.

Pamela and Parker rounded a corner of green, square hedges at the park. Parker slowed down, hands on his knees. "You go ahead," he called to Pamela. "I'll catch up."

Maybe Elliot wouldn't commit. Maybe she would never give him what he really wanted and needed.

But maybe she would.

Ultimately, Parker wrote Tessa a letter.

Dear Tessa,

I'm sorry that it's come to this, but in the end, we simply aren't meant to be. You deserve someone who wants to chase you through the sky. Someone willing to follow you on any journey. And I'm not that man. I hope one day we can be friends.

Wait, no. He backed up deleting the part about being friends. He wasn't going to lie to appease others or his own false sense of self. Honesty.

For the sake of both our well-being, I think it's best we don't maintain a friendship. But please know I wish you only good things, as you deserve.

Best,

Parker

With an unexpected rush of relief, he folded the paper into an envelope and scrawled out Tessa's home address in Denver. Certainly more permanent than a text or email.

Then he called Jen.

"Is someone dead?" That's how Jen often answered phone calls. The flames of trauma might fade but they never extinguished.

"Not someone, something."

"Is this a riddle? Hurry, I'm driving."

"I won't be bringing a date to your wedding anymore. I'll be alone. As usual."

Jen sighed. "It's for the best. But hey, at least I didn't lose my photographer."

"Elliot. Yeah."

"I won't pry right now, okay? But Parker, don't worry about me so much. Worry about yourself and what you want for once."

Parker raked his hand through his hair. "Right."

Parker blocked Tessa on all social media and on his phone. If she reached out to him, he knew eventually he'd break. His nice-guy persona would compel him to do "nice" things that weren't actually nice at all. He'd give in to the temptation of trying to make her feel better or pretend to be friends just so he wouldn't hurt her feelings *or* his self-esteem, and that was supremely fucked up.

Instead, it was time to make things work with someone who was, in fact, terrible for his self-esteem.

He'd made his intentions clear to her, and in an act of complete surprise, Elliot had turned up at his apartment the day after Jen left to go back to New York before the wedding.

Parker was watching baby Avery, a large baby mat unrolled in the middle of his empty living room. Babies were nice in the sense that they didn't really require couches. They were totally fine to roll around on the furniture-less floor all day long.

Still, he practically jumped to his feet when he saw the text from Elliot.

"Let me into your building."

She was here? Where he lived? Again? This was the second time she'd shown up, only now he wasn't harboring any delusions about a relationship with Tessa. Now he was harboring delusions about a relationship with Elliot.

No, Parker, not delusions. You fell in love.

Plus, who could resist him in combination with a baby? Certainly not one hundred and ten thousand followers on Instagram. Elliot would give in too. She would.

When she buzzed to get in, he opened the door and his brain took a minute to register what he was seeing.

Elliot had cut her hair. And Parker knew what that meant, having grown up with Jen for all those years of his life.

Change.

Elliot's hair was short right at the chin. And she had bangs now too, blunt and straight across. Two parallel black lines framing her beautiful face. Sea-blue eyes even brighter juxtaposed against midnight black.

And he was nothing but a drunk sailor lost in Lake Michigan.

"You gonna let me in?"

Parker jerked. "Ah, yeah. Wow, come in."

Elliot sauntered past him, lemongrass and jasmine wafting behind her. Wait, no, she smelled different now. A new scent. He'd have to get closer to find out.

"Oh, whoa, there's a baby here!" Elliot exclaimed. Then she dropped her boho bag on Parker's table and flopped down next to Avery.

Parker warmed at the sight and followed to sit beside her. "This is Avery. You like babies?"

Elliot stacked some blocks with Avery and glanced over to Parker. "Do I like babies? Baby, I am a baby."

Whatever that meant.

But when Parker handed Avery a piece of cut-up banana, which Avery smashed in fist, then let drop all over the baby mat, the glee in Elliot's eyes wasn't lost on him. And it was nice because it didn't matter if Avery made a mess because Parker had fully baby-proofed his place.

"So. To what do I owe the pleasure?"

Elliot fiddled with a block with the letter P on it, flipping it to and fro then finally rolling it over to Parker. "I...uh...I was in town."

"Right, you do *live* in town. I know that you do. Remember?"

Had Elliot actually blush at that? Bright pink flared across the bridge of her nose.

Parker picked up the block, squeezing it in his hand. He wanted to push Elliot. He always wanted to push her. But pushing was delicate business. "Something's changed with you."

She lifted a brow. "How do you know?"

He tilted his head. "You cut your hair. That's what Jen used to do after a big life change."

Elliot chuckled to herself, fiddling with whatever she could grab then passing it over to Avery, who chewed on the block and then passed it back. Elliot smiled.

"Are you nervous about something?" Parker asked. She was behaving so out of character. Coquettish and coy. And not at all like the Elliot he knew. He needed answers.

"Fine. If you must know, I came over because I missed you."

Parker raised his brow. "Is that right?"

"Yes. I missed you. But don't go getting all...I don't know...*effing weird* about it."

"Effing?"

"*Not gonna swear in front of a baby*," Elliot whispered in response to the questioning look on his face.

He smiled, shaking his head. She was something. "I missed you too. I always miss you when you leave. I wish you'd never leave. I wish you'd stay. Stay here with me."

Elliot chewed on her lip. It was a huge thing for him to say, to tell a woman to move in with him. But he and Elliot were past niceties.

"I ended things with Tessa. Obviously."

"Of course you did," she whispered. "Because you're in love with me."

Avery giggled in the corner, absently grabbing onto Elliot's hand and examining her red-lacquered fingertips as if they were foreign objects. Again, Elliot smiled.

Parker stood up and ventured over to the kitchen counter where he'd set a bottle out to warm. He tested it on wrist before returning, cross legged on the rug, Avery leaning against him, grabby hands clutching the bottle. "I think you're in love with me too," he said. "I think that scares you."

"Lots of things scare me. Plenty of things don't."

"What do I have to do to make this work with you? Cards on the table. I'll do anything. But you know that."

Elliot shifted on the floor, tucking her hair behind her ear. Nibbling her lower lip.

"Your hair looks beautiful. It suits you," he said softly.

She glanced up at him. "I cut it myself in Bruno's bathroom."

"You're talented with hair then."

She shook her head. "Not really. I kinda lost my shit and hacked it off with some dull scissors and then Allie told me I looked like an art school dropout and forced me to go to this fancy hair stylist in Lakeview who fixed it for me."

Parker reached out, fingering a lock of hair. "Guess it worked out in the end."

She held his gaze. "With the help of others. Things usually do."

Avery's gurgles distracted Parker from the moment. He dropped his hand. "You okay, little one?" But Avery had begun fussing, tiny hands swiping the bottle, sending it to its side. Spilt milk. Then the crying began.

Parker got to his feet, knelt to collect Avery in his arms, lifting the crying baby, and rocking back and forth. "Hang on, okay?" He nodded at Elliot.

But Elliot stood, brushing off her pants, and for a moment, Parker was sure she was going to saunter away. She reached out her arms. "Give Avery to me. Go on. Hand 'em over. I've got the magic touch."

Parker raised his brows but shifted Avery to his hip and transferred the baby to Elliot's outstretched arms. Elliot cradled the baby close to her, rocking back and forth, humming gently.

Within a few minutes, Avery de-escalated from a code red scream to quiet cooing, now sucking on a thumb and staring wonder-eyed at Elliot's face.

Elliot bounced, humming a soft but tuneless song. Avery's chubby little hand reached out and grabbed her hair. Elliot chuckled in response. The inside of Parker's chest clenched tightly, heat blooming from his sternum up to his neck and jaw then creeping to his cheeks and eyes.

His eyes. A bright sting. Oh god, they were burning now. But why?

Oh my fucking god.

Colors blurred. Tears overwhelmed and threatened to spill from the ledges of his lids. Parker couldn't remember the last time he cried. Had it been at Jen's grad school graduation? No... he'd been fighting off Kate's advances the whole time...

It'd been before that. Had it been at his parents' funeral?

Not there either. He hadn't cried at the actual funeral. There had been too much distraction, too many tasks to check off the list. Too many hands to shake. And Parker had to show Jen that it was going to be okay. That she could still have the life she wanted. Even if maybe he couldn't.

And then the memory came crashing down on him like a piano falling from a seven-story walk-up. Four weeks later. After his parents' funeral. When the chips had fallen. When the dust had settled. When the cremains had been safely sealed away. That was the last time he'd cried.

Jen had already packed up for her first day at university and Parker was left alone in the empty house their parents had owned.

He had to leave before the realtor arrived. The mortgage wasn't paid off, and they were moving out. The insurance money wouldn't cover the remainder. Parker had waited though, he'd waited until the very last possible moment to go.

His eighteen-year-old orphaned self had splayed out on the floor like a fallen angel in the middle of his family's empty living room. The radio played loud pop tunes. Without the available absorption of furniture or rugs, music echoed hollowly all throughout the room.

He'd stared at the blank popcorn ceiling above him until the limitless canvas of off-white morphed into so much artwork of a family he'd never again have. His life would be divided into two parts. The before and the after his parents died. The person he was supposed to be and this other person he was going to be instead. Loneliness. Isolation in a world stuffed to the brim but almost nobody left who was part of him. The desolation that burned his insides would be nothing but a faint echo compared to the pain he'd feel for the rest of his life, having nearly lost it all. Having lost almost every last damned thing. And the knowing anticipation of that pain burned even brighter.

Hot tears had rolled down the corner of his eyes, wetting his temples, ears and sideburns. He'd snarfed and hiccupped, blinking hard as more and more tears welled up and overwhelmed him until his chest was heaving and the delicate skin of his eyelids were red and raw.

Fuck life, he'd thought. *And fuck this.*

And while he was lying there, he fantasized of another life. Maybe somewhere else, in some other space and time and dimension where people were dancing, together, happily to that reverberating music. But in that moment, he was left to lie there alone, still and empty. And he'd cried like he'd never cried before.

Until this very moment where he stood, a full grown man in another empty living room. His own. Parker shuttered his eyes, but the tears rolled hot and smooth down his cheek in present day. And it was as if he existed in two spaces at once, a split screen of time. One where he was eighteen, and one where he was thirty-eight.

The last time he'd cried, his parents had died. Now, where he stood, with Avery a new life, and with Elliot, a new love, the tears had found him again.

"Parker?" Elliot's voice broke through the wisps of clouds that were forming around his brain, memories floating across the equator of time.

He glanced up; her head was tilted as she swayed back and forth with Avery. Her face a questioning but gentle smile.

"C'mere," he rasped, wiping at his eyes with the bottoms of his palms.

Elliot swayed over, closing the gap between them, her unfocused humming growing louder as she drew near. She shifted Avery to one hip, the baby laughing gleefully when she leaned in and blew a raspberry on Avery's shoulder. Then she wrapped her other arm around Parker's waist, pulling him close against her hip. Encouraging him to bounce and sway side to side too. His hand enclosed around her waist and soon enough, all three were swaying and bouncing together in the middle of the room.

Dancing.

"See, it's not even hard…" Elliot whispered.

"What are we even dancing to? There's no music," he said.

Elliot's fingertips soothed the skin at Parker's back. "Oh, there's always music playing somewhere."

And there was. In that empty room where he'd been all by himself twenty years ago. He was dancing to that music now. *They* were dancing to it now. And for the first time in two full decades, Parker felt a little less alone.

That night, Elliot stayed over.

When Pamela arrived, there were Elliot and Avery, leaning against the wall, Parker's iPad splayed out in front of spread legs, Avery tapping at the bright colors that splashed by, with Elliot's assistance.

"Who do we have here?" Pamela mused as she swished passed. "I'll be asking you about this *later*. Ahem."

After Avery and Pamela left, a curl of anxiety twisted up his abdomen. Usually, this was Elliot's cue to disappear. To poof into the air like so much dust.

But instead she picked the dirty dishes off the floor, where they had eaten instant oatmeal, and rinsed them out in the sink. Then she spun around, arms braced against the counter. "Got any pajamas? Or I could sleep naked."

He rubbed the stubble on his chin, a small smile lifting his cheeks. "Dealer's choice."

When she lifted her shirt over her head and let it flop to the ground as she walked, he followed like an obedient puppy, pulling off his own T-shirt and unbuttoning his pants until they both made their way to his bedroom.

She turned and stopped right in front of his bed, waiting for him to draw closer until they were toe-to-toe.

And then she leaned into him, her forehead to his chest, and inhaled deeply. "Your room smells so good. It's like…pine or something. I can't describe it. It smells fresh. It smells like a dewy morning in springtime. It smells so much like you."

"You know me better than you think."

She let her fingernails glide up the hard plane of his stomach. "I guess I never believed I'd ever meet someone who'd put up with my shit. But you…Mr. Serious. Parker. You're a downright glutton for punishment." She looked up to him and smiled.

"It's one of my dominant personality traits." He gently but firmly pushed her to the mattress.

She landed on her ass and rested on her elbows, looking up at him, her eyes glimmering. "Bossy now, are we?"

But she yelped when his hands roughly yanked her pants from her hips and threw them on the ground. Then he grabbed her by the hips. "Is this what you like?" he murmured in her ear.

"Mmhmm…Mmhmm…" she practically whimpered.

He flipped her onto her stomach the curve of her hips and ass and legs and shoulder a tantalizing creamy display before him. He grunted as he yanked off his own jeans and boxer briefs, kicking them from his legs and feet, sending them sliding across the floor. He hovered over her back, her ribcage heaving, and brought his hand to her pussy. He could barely see the slit from behind, but still it was bare, pink, and shining. She was already wet for him. It made sense since he was always making her wait. Incidental edging. In that way, he must have been torturing *her*. Which one was really the glutton for punishment? Maybe both of them.

He rubbed two fingers against the seam of the soft silky skin. She moaned when he rubbed them all the way parallel to the slit and then dipped a finger inside her, slow and easy, pushing in and out for only a few fleeting seconds before pulling out to spread the moisture, unable to resist the urge to circle her clit with his slick fingers. She rocked her hips at the touch. "Fuck, Parker. Just fuck me already."

One more circle of her clit and he took his hand away, closing his fingers around his hard cock, rubbing the head against Elliot's wetness until he was slick too. Then he stood at the end of the bed and kicked her legs apart with his own, and knelt down on his knees so he could align his cock with her entrance. He rocked his hips so that the head of his cock pushed in slightly but then out again.

His hand slid up the curve of her ass, dipped over her back, up to her neck, where he again grasped onto her hair, pulling her head back so that she had to look at him. Her chest heaved, eyes drooped, but nevertheless gazed straight into his soul. With a snap, he pushed all the way into her, both groaning in tandem. Then he began to thrust earnestly, guttural noises expelled deep from his diaphragm with every snap of his hips. Elliot's back arched, his grip tough on her hair.

He fucked her hard then, almost without mercy, barking orders at her. *Say my name. Pinch your nipples. Rub your clit. Lick yourself off your fingers. Come around my cock like you'll die if you don't.*

And it was the one time Elliot listened without any complaint. Did as she was told.

Afterwards, he wrapped his arms around her and drew her close to his chest. Her head resting against his heavily thudding heart. She wasn't perfect, and neither was he. But together…together, they were two halves of a locket now joined together, swinging from a pendulum on the wing of an airplane.

He patted her shoulder. "Want some tea?"

She lifted her head, eyes heavy and satisfied. "Tea?"

"Yeah. A hot cup of tea. It's nice to share tea with the person you love."

A lazy smile curled on her lips. "I could go for some tea."

He folded over his duvet and they both slid out of the bed barefoot, Parker in nothing but his boxer briefs and Elliot in one of Parker's T-shirts. As they padded over to the kitchen, Elliot slapped his ass, a mischievous glint in her eye.

As the stove top clicked and the kettle heated and the tea bags soaked, soothing aromas permeated the kitchen. Parker waited for the tea to steep, then tossed the bags into the trash.

He handed a mug to Elliot. Blew on his own and took a sip. The two of them stared out into his empty living room, barren now that Avery was gone, along with all the accoutrements that came with a baby.

Elliot tilted her head, sipping from her tea. "You know, I have a couch that'd look great in here."

Chapter 25

The string quartet played a soft and melodic "Bittersweet Symphony" cover as Parker passed by, lowball of scotch fisted in his hand, the collar of his tuxedo shirt strangling him softly.

He'd owned a tuxedo for years now at Rebecca's insistence, but his sister's wedding was the first time he'd ever brought it out. He'd shed a single tear as he sat in the front row watching Jen marry a man he barely even knew. But he trusted Jen's judgment. Maybe he should've always been trusting her to take care of herself. She was making moves now. Had been making moves. Career. Marriage. Cohabitating. A row of bridesmaids in lavender ball gowns trailed in a line besides her.

Ceremonies made Parker itchy around the cufflinks. He hadn't experienced too many before his parents died, and then after that, he avoided them entirely except for Jen's graduations. But now, here he was again. His sister, all grown up.

Just like him.

Parker and Elliot had kept in touch since the moment between them in his living room. Softly, sweetly almost. The pitch that reverberated between them had capitulated to a different key entirely. And Parker was happily grappling with the implications of this brand new tune.

He wanted her to move in right away, but also, they both knew they couldn't rush things. For better or for worse, Elliot had exhausted herself over the last few years: emotionally, physically. Traveling alone and always shouldering every burden. Parker could relate. Sometimes the razor blade of life sliced away so precisely and steadily that one didn't even notice there was too much lost to easily glue back together.

So, Parker would visit Elliot at Bruno's apartment. Make her tea. Video chat with Olivia and August. Smoke a joint with Allie. Or simply sit in silence, his fingers gliding down Elliot's back, absorbing the rattling traffic outside the window four stories below. He traveled with Elliot to her therapy appointments (Bruno's mother had indeed given a good therapist referral). And picked up her medications from the pharmacy. He washed her dishes and made her bed. Did the laundry, carefully separating the reds and blacks and whites. The colors she wore most often. Her darkness, her lightness, her love. The simple, inconsequential domestic chores that bore unique and everyday closeness. The kind that could only come with...

Family. Elliot could be his family. With Elliot he could make a family.

Even though things at the wedding were a little weird. For instance, as Parker sat in the first row of wedding chairs after walking Jen down the aisle, Kate, one of her bridesmaids, had caught his eye and winked at him. That wasn't a good sign.

There were tons of guests though. So many it was possible to get swallowed up into the sea of the party.

Although he did keep his eye on one person: the raven-haired photographer with the short haircut and the sea-blue eyes. Elliot maneuvered through the crowd expertly and invisibly, snapping pictures. Well, invisible to everyone but him of course. He watched her the whole time. She didn't watch him back, not this time. She was working. Creating.

Now he was seeing her behind the smoke screen of social media. The artist doing the art. And his perspective shifted entirely.

They'd been playing a game before and all he could see was what stood in front of the camera. Now he was seeing who was behind it. The inner workings of a whole person. Everything had changed.

Elliot no longer existed behind a veil. She was all one piece and right in front of him.

"Chicken and waffle?" A server strolled by with a silver platter of bite-sized chicken and waffles with a sliver of a pickle piled on top.

Parker inclined his head, taking the stacked toothpick and popping the hors d'oeuvre in his mouth. *Mmm. Carbs.*

A hand tucked into his arm and he almost choked on his waffle. "Parker, darling. I didn't know you'd be at this wedding. Just kidding, of course I knew!"

Parker's palms went cold at the familiar voice. "Cameron?" What the fuck was Cameron doing there? "You know Jen?"

Cameron flipped her beachy blond waves over her shoulder. She'd wore a shell-pink gown with matching heels, and diamonds glittered at all junctures of her form: ears, throat, wrists. She was beautiful, but more like a cubic zirconia than a diamond to him now. "Jen, who's Jen?"

"My sister."

Cameron threw back her head in a laugh, then sipped at her champagne. "Of course. I'm here with Charles. Don't worry, he's out back smoking cigars with the other attorneys. He knows Benjamin. Benjamin Wu?"

Oh right. Benny was an attorney in New York, and Cameron's husband was a big-shot attorney as well. Parker shook his head. "Small fucking world."

Cameron's pink lips curled into a sly smile. "I see your girl is the help."

His blood ran cold. "She's a photographer. She's an artist."

Cameron twirled the straw in her drink. "Well, you know you can do better."

Before Parker could respond, *another* familiar voice interrupted. "Parker *baby!* I've been trying to find you all

339

night. You wouldn't run away from an old friend again, would you? Oh—who's this?"

Parker pursed his lips together squeezing his eyes. *Shit.* His voice came out stiff. "Kate. Hello."

"Kate, who's Kate?" Cameron asked, her gaze dipping unapologetically over Kate's lavender gown.

"I'm Kate. Who're you? An extra from *Southern Charm*?"

Oh shit. Were they about to fight? It wasn't good, and Jen would absolutely murder him if he let that happen.

"Cameron, Kate is an old friend. Kate, Cameron is…ah…also an old friend."

"Yeah, an old friend who you fuck?"

"We don't fu—"

Kate's drink sloshed dangerously close to the lip of the glass as her hands moved with her voice. "You're fucking this woman?"

"Used to…wait, no…not that it matters. That's nobody's business." Parker's eyes flitted around nervously to see if Elliot could see him, but she was nowhere in sight. Previously, he wouldn't feel bad if she witnessed this display. He might even relish her jealousy. But now things had changed. Delicately changed. And he didn't want to risk *anything.* Plus, women fighting over him? Ugh, the most embarrassing cliché.

Kate's words slurred as she talked. "Well, I fucked him when he was in college. If you think he looks good now, you have no idea. The *stamina*. He could really go all night long like a goddamn jackhammer just bang bang ba—"

Parker put his hand on Kate's shoulder. "Okay, I think we get the point, now if you'd excuse me..."

But then, his blood ran cold again when he heard a familiar voice.

"Parker, why have you been ignoring me?"

No, it couldn't be. He turned around slowly. "Tessa? What are you—what are you *doing* here?"

Tessa wore a sparkling yellow gown. Her curly hair was piled atop her head. Her skin glowed beautiful and golden. Her eyes darted around. "Doing here? Are you kidding? You ghosted me. Where the hell have you been?"

"I didn't ghost you, I ended things. I sent you a goddamn letter for Christ sake. I was very clear."

Tessa planted her hands on her hip, a defiant. "I had to do something. You didn't even give me a chance to respond! And look, I have your attention now, don't I? I received an invitation to this wedding fair and square, by the way. One was mailed to me months ago. I hid in the back at the ceremony. Saw a few too many familiar faces."

"Parker, are you cheating on me with this woman too?" That was Cameron's unwelcomed voice.

"What? No! I'm not cheating on you. Wait, I can't cheat on you, we aren't together."

"Parker would've *never* cheated on me in college. He would've done practically anything for us to be together." That was Kate.

"Kate, you're not helping. Can you shut up?"

"Who are *these* women?" That was Tessa.

Shit. "Tessa..." He ran his hand through his hair. "You really can't be here."

"You can't run away from us, you asshole!" Cameron again. Oh fuck.

"Cameron, I don't owe you anything." He kept his voice low and calm but internally he wanted to scream.

"That's right." Kate's drink sloshed onto the ground. "He doesn't like you, Barbie. He and I have history. What do you have?"

"I really thought you'd fall in love with me." Tessa wiped at her waterline with her neatly manicured fingertips. "I thought you were going to make the smart choice. That a grand gesture would show you that I can be brave enough for us both."

Parker's eyes darted between the women. *Fuck.* Elliot better not show up right now. "Tessa, you had to have known that would never work. This isn't a movie or some kind of romance novel. This is real life. I was shitty to you, and for that I'm sorry, but I can't do this with you anymore. I love someone else."

"You actually love her?" Tessa hiccupped. He had never seen her this way, but also she was clearly drunk and emotional.

"I knew it!" Kate interrupted.

"Kate, *shut up.*" Parker squeezed his fist.

"You shut up, Parker! It's me." Kate tilted her head towards Cameron. "He's always been in love with me." She swayed a bit.

Cameron narrowed her eyes. "You wish. But I know who he's in love with." She crossed her arms over her chest. "And it's none of us."

Tessa sniffed loudly too, throwing back what appeared to be some kind of clear bubbly liquid. She swallowed thickly. "I know who it is, too. It's that woman over there." She pointed to Elliot who was kneeling in a corner, camera out in front of her, focused on the beautiful lights and buzzing crowd. "He's in love with that woman."

Cameron looked over. "Yep, that's the one. That's the trashy whore."

Tessa's sniffles grew louder. Cameron scoffed in disgust. "Oh grow a fucking spine. You think Parker is interested in some kind of blubber face like you? He needs a real woman."

"Oh you think you're a real woman? You don't even weigh ninety pounds soaking wet. Fake tits. Trust me, I know all about those cheap boob jobs." There went Kate again.

"Parker, are you going to let her talk to me like this?"

"Parker, I thought you just needed some time!"

"Tessa, Kate, Cameron...I can't talk to you when you're all interrupting—"

"Where's the bitch you're in love with?" Kate slipped her drink into the crook of her elbow, unsteadily pulling off her rings and letting them clatter to the ground. "I'll fucking kill her. I'll fucking punch her eyes out."

"You're drunk, Kate."

"I'm not drunk I'm doing just fiiine..." But before she even finished her sentence the glass between her bent arm slipped to the ground, shattering loudly between them.

Heads turned in their direction.

"You are an embarrassment," Cameron sniped.

"Parker, we need to talk," said a sniffling Tessa.

"Tessa, I don't know what's left to say. Coming here was a terrible idea!" Parker's eyes scanned the room now. Heads were all turned towards them, and a server had shuffled over to clean up the mess. Another drink was promptly delivered to Kate. Likely the last thing she needed. "I'm sorry, I'm sorry..." Parker muttered, helpless.

Because now he knew. Elliot had seen. He locked eyes with her from across the room. All the women surrounding him. She knew who they all were. She knew everything.

He shook his head weakly as she made her way over. Oh no. Oh no.

She was going to skewer him alive. She was going to leave him. She was going to blow his shit up spectacularly. And he realized. He wanted it. He wanted her to. He wanted her regardless, no matter what she did.

She was there so quickly he didn't even have a moment to think. Her black cotton jumpsuit and black flats contrasted deeply with the other glittering women. She was matte, stark, high contrast in comparison to their pastel and glitz. She was herself, all the time. But even when she was underdressed, even when she was *the help*, she was a raw cut onyx in a sea of glitter.

Elliot smiled a blood red smile. "That damned *je ne sais quoi* again, huh, Parker?" Then she turned her attention to the group of women. "Hey all, everyone looks so gorgeous tonight. How about we all line up for a picture, what do you say? Don't argue, I'm in charge, now move. Move." She hustled them along.

"Fierce hag in the pink, you on the outside. Tessa in the yellow—hi, so great to see you again although I must say I'm surprised but I shouldn't be—you look beautiful, truly beautiful. A fucking angel. And ahhh, you in the lavender. Bridesmaid. That's right, we haven't met, but I know allll about you. You get on the very end. Turn your body in just so, that's right you got it. What a natural."

Then she grabbed Parker by the lapels and pushed him dead center of the lineup. "Everyone put your hands on this guy and smile pretty!"

To Parker's surprise, everyone complied, frozen in their poses, frozen with awkward smiles. The power of the camera compelled them.

Elliot lifted her camera as if to shoot the photo but then suddenly lowered it instead. "Okay, sorry, I just need to fix a few more little things so you all look your best. Fierce hag, I think you need to divorce your husband. You don't love him and you don't love Parker, so it's time to move on. You'll be happier that way. And you, Kate. Look. I know we all want to be who we were at twenty-two, but you're not twenty-two anymore, you're like…forty?" Kate huffed at that, mouth agape. "It's okay to be forty. And to find men who like you for who you are now and not who you were then. Believe me, we all have growing up to do. I should know.

"And Tessa. Beautiful, confident Tessa. Honey, baby, sweetie. *Girl.* Parker doesn't love you. And look at you. Making a whole damn joke out of yourself at a near stranger's wedding and for what? You know better than this! Why are you wasting so much time chasing after him? There are four billion men in this world, baby girl. What are you even doing here? What do you even get from him? Nothing, right? A wish, a hope, a dream? I mean, it's not that I don't admire a bold gesture—I do—but you can save your bold gestures for someone who actually gives a shit. He so clearly doesn't give a shit for you. For any of you. Not anymore. Maybe he once did. And I'm sure that mattered a great deal at the time. But now? You can do so, so, so much better. So, I'm going to take this picture. And you're all going to take a good, hard look at yourselves. And who you are with this man. And then you're all going to move on. Got it? Got it. Good. Now smile!"

Jen dabbed at the huge splatter of drinks doused all down the front of Parker's crisp white tuxedo with a white catering napkin. "Well, looks like they really got you good. Seems like you deserved it though."

They were hiding in the hallway away from the crowd. Jen hadn't seen what had gone down with Elliot and the women, but right after Elliot snapped her picture, they'd all turned and thrown their drinks on him, then stomped away. Elliot's words had been effective, apparently.

Once they were gone, Elliot had raised up on her toes and snapped a photo of him. "I know you couldn't do that on your own. So I did it for you. I get the feeling you could use some help every now and then."

Heat had rushed over his chest, his heartbeat like a bass drum. She always made his slow heart gallop crazy fast. "Say it, Elliot. Say it. I know you want to say it."

Elliot's eyes had glimmered and she'd waved her camera towards him. "Gotta go do my job, Mr. Serious. Some of us have storage units to pay for." And she'd sauntered away. That's when Jen had found him.

Jen snatched a cloth napkin from the table and handed it to him. "Here. At least attempt to dry yourself. You doing okay? You kinda seem okay, despite whatever the hell is going on."

Parker nodded, his gaze drifting past Jen back to the crowd beyond the doors. Elliot. "Don't worry about me. This is your day, I shouldn't be taking up your time anyway."

Jen slapped him on the arm. "Shut up, Parker. Are you kidding me? It's been you and me against the world for so long. I know how much you gave up so that I could fuck around and live a normal life. You became such a serious person after Mom and Dad died. Just like dad, but worse, because it's not even you, is it? Look, I know you didn't feel like you had a choice. It certainly wasn't your fault. But like...it's gonna be okay, you know? We aren't struggling kids anymore. I want you to be happy too. Actually, I got you a gift but I wasn't sure when to give it to you. Hold on."

Jen jogged towards the end of the hallway and rummaged in a stack of items on a table. She hustled back and handed Parker a box.

"What's this?"

She rolled her eyes. "It's a gift, so the point is you have to open it to find out."

Parker shook the heavy but small box and then ripped off the edge of the light blue wrapping. He glanced up at Jen. "It's weird that you got me a gift on your own wedding day."

"Just open it."

Parker chuckled, slipping the box from its wrapping and propping the top open. He removed the contents, heavy and smooth in his hand. A blue Swiss army knife. "It's nice." He flicked open a blade, closed it and flicked open a small screwdriver. Like his other one, but new. "But I already have one."

Jen snorted. "That pink one. I really thought you'd never use it. But you didn't even think twice."

"I use it all the time. Did then too. Pink's a good color."

"You're right it is. I don't know what I was thinking." She patted his hand. "Well, maybe you can find a way to re-gift this one. Find someone else who really needs it."

The bar in the hotel was quiet in the late hours. People were still partying in the ballroom at the wedding, but Parker and Elliot sat on barstools, sipping iced water.

"How'd you think that went?" Parker asked, his gaze wandering over her. Even after the long night, her skin was flushed, luminescent, and glowing.

"I think you get yourself into a lot more trouble than I've ever given you credit for, Mr. Serious. How'd you get all those women to fall in love with you? Kidding, I already know all your tricks."

He sipped his water. "I'm still waiting."

"On what?"

"You know what."

Elliot's eyelashes fluttered. "I've got edibles in my camera case if that's what you mean."

He chuckled. "You told all those women off for me tonight. You want to take care of me."

Her cheeks flushed. "*Shut up.* I didn't say it like that."

"You basically did."

"I said it more like *here I had to do this thing for you because you're a coward and you couldn't do it for yourself.*" Then she scowled at him. "Oh whatever. Maybe I did want to take care of you a little. Maybe I do."

"I know you do."

"Why do you keep bringing it up?"

"Because I need to hear you say the words, Elliot."

"What words?"

"All of them. All of the words."

Elliot rolled her eyes, but then she snatched up the bag at her feet, digging inside. "Lemme take your picture. You look so handsome right now, like you could model for Burberry or something. How do you look in plaid? Or a kilt? Oh my god, we should get you a ki—fuck. Shit. Fuck."

Parker's brow went up. "What's wrong?"

Elliot held up her camera. "It fucking broke again. The card slot. *Ugh*, this always fucking happens." She groaned, her head falling back. "This is the kinda shit that drives me to the storage unit. The little shit, you know? It's what gets ya. It adds up."

Parker put his hand on her back, rubbing gently. "Luckily, we can fix it."

She lifted an eyebrow and handed him the camera. "*You're* going to fix it, you mean."

Parker shook his head and dug in his pocket, procuring the knife Jen had gifted him earlier that night. He handed it over to Elliot. "No, *we* are gonna fix it together."

She glanced down and then looked at him. "Your knife was pink before."

"Yep, and this blue knife is your knife now. You can use it whenever you have problems with your camera."

"I can't bring a knife on a plane!"

He shook his head and chuckled. "You can check it, of course. Now, flip out the smallest little screwdriver tucked into the pocket—yep, that's it."

As Parker helped Elliot fiddle with the miniscule screws of her camera, the scent of her hair wafted into his nostrils. He closed his eyes for a moment to take it all in when her head popped up.

"I did it! I fixed it! Holy shit."

He smiled. "Well done."

"This calls for a picture." Elliot attached the lens to the camera body and lifted it up. "Say cheese Parker Lance-Loves-Laurie Donne because I fucking love you."

And a flash exploded in his eyes. He squeezed them shut, the bright spot temporarily blinding him. "Tell me again," he said, his voice strained.

"You want it? You got it. But I'm not taking it back after I say it. Parker Donne. You fucking self-serious, self-important, sometimes spineless son of a bitch, I love you. I love you."

He rubbed his eyes and then opened them, the vision of her appearing like a dark angel as the light faded away. He leaned forward to kiss her, but she held up a hand, pushing him away with the flat of her palm. Parker chuckled at her supposed anger about it but she wasn't done talking.

"I love you and now you're stuck with me. Sorry, it's your curse, it's your burden, but hey, you called for me, so you can't complain now that I've come. Now you've got me. Here I am. Problems and all. Scars and everything."

"You think I'm scared of problems, Elliot?"

She smiled, letting her hand slide on his knee. "Nope, I don't. In fact, I think you *are* the problem. No, we're both the problem. We're two huge problems. And I hope to fucking god we make tiny little problems together and make a silly little problem family."

Parker grabbed her hand, squeezing it tightly in his. "And what about your freedom?"

She picked up his hand and kissed the back of it. "I'm keeping that of course. But I'm keeping you too. And I see that look in your eye so you better slow your roll. It's not like I'm looking to get knocked up tomorrow, so relax. And I expect that you understand that my life belongs to me. And you have to take me for who I am, *the problem* that I am. But...you know...maybe... maybe after my little week in the storage unit, I realized I'm getting a little too old to be..."

"Living like a vagrant?"

She smiled in a regretful way. "Pushing people away. It's not like I want to be alone. I just don't know what else to do, old habits...they die hard. Besides, the storage unit's a little creepy even for me. So quiet. Gun to my head, I might even admit I was glad you found me."

"It really shouldn't be that hard to admit, actually."

She looked at him long and hard. "Well, then, what's next, Mr. Serious? Maybe it's time we get a little serious together."

Epilogue

"Don't forget to wear sunscreen, it's hot in Sicily!" Pamela called from the kitchen as Elliot and Parker made their way through the foyer.

"Oh honey, don't worry. I wear SPF in the trillions. Parker, can you get my bags?"

Parker lifted his arms to show Elliot the black bags hanging from his. Elliot's spinner was behind him, the ET emblem peeling off but still holding strong. "Already got 'em."

Elliot spun around and smiled, her sea-blue eyes incomprehensibly bright against the daytime sun bursting through the glass front door. "That's right. It's so nice to have a man-servant 24/7. Promise me you'll never ever go back to work."

"Why would he?" Rebecca called from the hall. She appeared, her pregnant belly large and round. "He's promised to babysit for us for at least the next year."

Elliot rolled her eyes. "Good, maybe that can stave off his baby fever a little bit longer. Momma's gotta make her mark in this world before she slows down, you know what I mean?"

It was true. Parker did indeed have baby fever, and he wanted to put a baby inside Elliot as soon as he possibly could. The very idea had him a little itchy. But also, like with everything in life, good things came to those who waited. And Parker could wait for Elliot for whenever she was ready. Besides, he was enjoying the time they were spending together, just the two of them.

"See you Friday!" Parker called out as they shut the door to Pamela and Rebecca's. They'd stopped by to drop off some dresses Rebecca had asked Elliot to model and post on her Instagram and some macarons Parker had been perfecting the recipe on. Elliot and Rebecca had come to something of a symbiotic professional arrangement as well as a friendship.

After all, Elliot had moved in with Parker. She'd brought her couch with her. And now that he was retired at the ripe old age of thirty-eight, he was finally able to get serious about those baking lessons. His teacher said he had a real natural talent for it, which he'd suspected for a while now. He was good with his hands.

They got in the car, each door shutting, the click of the seat belt, the turn of the engine. Elliot cranked the wheel this way and that in short partial rotations, manipulating the gear shifter of her six-speed 718 Porsche Cayman (a gift from Parker) until they were out of the tight parking spot on the side of the road and off to the airport. Elliot was an excellent and efficient driver. Maybe it was sexist of Parker to have been surprised, but given her general demeanor he thought she'd drive like a maniac. But no. She surprised him in lots of ways, all the time.

When they arrived at the airport, bags in tow, Elliot squealed a little. "This shoot is going to be so fucking great, Park. OMG, it almost makes me wish you still had your Instagram so you could post about."

Parker chuckled, shaking his head. *No way.* His Instagram days were over. Besides, who would he message? Who would he post for? He had done it all for her.

He was happy acting as Elliot's assistant now, traveling from location to location…baking his French cookies and babysitting for Rebecca and Pamela. "Let's head to the lounge." Parker gestured towards the sign, after they'd passed through security.

They sat in a quiet corner booth, cappuccinos and sugared doughnuts (for Elliot, although Parker also ate *one*, just one.)

"You know I'm not used to doing these trips with another person." Elliot licked milky foam from her top lip.

Parker sipped from his cup. "Come to think of it, neither am I. I mostly traveled alone."

"Me too."

Her phone lit up on the table, and she slugged down her drink. "That's our flight boarding. Hurry up, it's time to go."

Parker climbed out of the booth, picking up the bags.

"You know, you don't have to carry all those," Elliot said, while dabbing on some lip balm. "I actually can handle my own baggage."

"And I can take the weight every now and then too."

She scrunched her face at him and strode smoothly ahead, the crowded moving walkway a blur to their left. "I suppose that's okay with me. There's our gate over there."

They made their way through the crowd and to the ticket line where their first class zone had already been called. They waited in the clump of people, the two of them, side by side, until their tickets were scanned.

They settled into their seats and the flight attendant glided by with a tray of champagne. "Two please." Parker winked at Elliot.

After the flight attendant set them on their tables, Elliot picked up her flute. "You finally agreed to that drink with me."

Parker smiled, picking up his own flute. He had learned that he really liked bubbles. "What do you mean? We get drinks together all the time."

"It's different when we're flying." She tipped her glass to him. "To airplane games."

He clinked his glass back. "To these very strange airplane games."

After she took a sip, her gaze wandered over to him. "Do you still feel like you lost everything?"

He gave her a questioning look. "I never said that."

"You said I'd take all of you and you'd get nothing in return."

He made a joking face like *eek*. "You did take all of me. But maybe giving your whole self to someone is never a loss."

"Maybe you're right." She smiled, her eyes glimmered. "And maybe we aren't done playing yet."

THE END

About Author

Cat Wynn lives in a cozy house in Charleston, SC with her long-time partner and two geriatric rescue dogs. She writes late at night on an old couch that should've probably been thrown out five years ago. She's a shockingly good time at parties provided the snacks are good. You can test this theory by inviting her to your wedding. Although, she probably won't show because she stopped wearing bras three years ago.

Newsletter: https://catwynnauthor.substack.com/

Instagram: https://instagram.com/catwynnauthor

Tall, Dark & Fictional Podcast

Also By

Partner Track

Perdie Stone needs just three things in life: Her forever best friend, Lucille. Their adorable rescue pug, Bananas. And last but not least, a coveted partnership at her Charleston law firm.

A partnership she more than deserves when she goes head-to head with hotshot Ivy League attorney Carter Leplan on a big case and comes out on top. She didn't think anything would feel better than beating the annoyingly gorgeous lawyer at his own game, but that's before a freak storm leaves them both stranded.

Together.

In the last hotel room.

With only one bed.

It's a one-night stand Perdie isn't soon to forget...especially after Carter turns up at her firm and slides right into the job that should have been hers. And right back into her life—a life she thought she had all figured out.

Holiday Games

After the worst year ever, August Pointe can't wait to spend Friendsmas with her besties at her uncle's mountain house. She could really use the comfort of a few familiar faces. But when a blizzard hits, August ends up stuck at the house with a mutual acquaintance she's never met instead.

But Jack Harris is a hot, TikTok famous chef. And something about his easy going nature and excellent drink making skills are thawing out August's icy exterior. Plus, he's brought a kitten with him!

August is reluctant to get involved, but some Christmas presents are too tempting to keep wrapped up. And her friends think she deserves a little holiday cheer. Still, August isn't sure if it's worth playing bedroom games with a stranger or if she'll just end up doubly heart broken by New Years.

Hotel Games

Hair stylist Olivia Couper can't wait to celebrate Friendsmas with her besties in a secluded mountain house. So, when Olivia asks Henry, her best friend's grumpy surgeon brother, to carpool, she swears it's a matter of convenience and not a bid for Henry's attention.

Sure, they've been hooking up for years, but they always followed one unspoken rule: Never talk about the hook ups.

Unfortunately, a blizzard hits while Olivia and Henry are on the road, stranding them in the last hotel room available. And suddenly, Henry wants to break all the rules. Olivia's left with a choice: confront her real feelings for Henry or flee to the mountain house with all her walls intact. It's a game she isn't sure she's ready to play and a hotel stay she isn't soon   to   forget

Acknowledgments

As always, there are tons of people to thank for the completion of this book, so, let's go.

1. My friend and Tall, Dark & Fictional podcast cohost SJ Tilly for always being there for me, even when I'm confusing and acting like a fool.
2. Gabby Marie, also my friend and fellow writer who read a beta version of Airplane Games and said, "You know what this book reminds me of? Breakfast at Tiffany's."
3. Beatrix Sawad from Cover Apothecary who ensured that I had two covers (!) and walked me through every little step to make this book real.
4. Deborah Nemeth for her editing prowess which I will greatly miss.
5. Autumn Gantz, for all the everyhing, lol. Thanks for the phone calls.
6. Love Mikayla Eve for always responding to my voice memos at 2am AEST.
7. The Kitchen and Jorn Show on Youtube for making me feel less sad late into the night. And boy, do I get sad late into the night.
8. My husband for being a real life Mark Darcy (the Colin Firth type).

9. My dogs, Griff and Elfie, for hanging out with me in my new office every second of the day even though they absolutely hate it here. (Guys, you can leave! You're allowed to sit anywhere you want! The door is open!)

10. You, for reading this book that many a person has described as "polarizing" and "not quite what they're used to."

11. And me, for publishing it anyway because in the inevitability that we will all one day die, you should surely and firstly do whatever the fuck you want.

xoxo

Printed in Great Britain
by Amazon

22201876R00205